FLATLAND

FLATLAND

A Novel

R. Scott Yarbrough

iUniverse, Inc.
New York Lincoln Shanghai

Flatland

iUniverse books may be ordered through booksellers or by contacting:

iUniverse
2021 Pine Lake Road, Suite 100
Lincoln, NE 68512
www.iuniverse.com
1-800-Authors (1-800-288-4677)

Because of the dynamic nature of the Internet, any Web addresses or links contained in this book may have changed since publication and may no longer be valid.

ISBN: 978-0-595-47612-1 (pbk)
ISBN: 978-0-595-91878-2 (ebk)

Printed in the United States of America

Chapter One previously published as:
"Lilith and Little Boy." Just a Moment: A Literary Anthology. Pine Grove Press. III (1992): 57-62.

Chapter Three previously published as:
"The Modern Barbershop." New Texas. (1991): 196-207. The University of North Texas and The Institute of Texas Culture.

For Sandi, York, and Jenni (Chicken)

CHAPTER 1

▼

LILITH AND LITTLE BOY

In West Texas, the towns do not crawl on each other's backs like babbling cities. Instead, they spread and lounge about under the hot yellow eye of a focused sun. Flatland sat squarely in the center of a simple maze; two highways—one running north to south and the other east to west beside the railroad tracks—cut Flatland into a cultural pie.

Lilith was big and round, but her skin was tight and dark as a shaved black horse. Her only reserve was the fat, up under her upper-arms that draped in a smiling half-moon like the underbellies of two fat black puppies curled and clinging. Her eyes were white round saucers of brown coffee, lightly chocolated. And she sat on her wooden porch on the north side of the tracks in Flatland each day during the summer in her rocking chair, shelling black-eyed peas or splitting peaches for brown sugar cobbler.

During the summer, Lilith always ate homemade red sugar-water Popsicle, colored with the juice of a beet: her forearms streamed red with dye; her fat lips stained red; her teeth like those of a lioness pulling her face from a carcass, content and smiling full-bellied.

Bip had seen Lilith on his way to the Piggly Wiggly store, but his mother told him never to speak to her. Mary, Bip's mother, told him to walk with his eyes straight-ahead, arms at his side like a soldier when he passed. Despite Mary's discouragement, Bip felt an obligation, almost encouraged by Mary's insistence to seek out Lilith's mystery.

He planned the day for months. He stole a nickel a week from his stepfather's dresser and another from Mary's pocketbook. On June 1st, the money stolen, Bip ran to the Piggly Wiggly barefooted over the bubbling tar street and back to the hot sand of Lilith's dirt road and stood in front of her house with the Popsicles behind his back.

She stopped rocking.

Bip looked very small, standing alone in the dirt road: his glasses sat high on his long Roman nose; his forehead was shiny; his shiny-brown hair was parted by a cowlick; his deep brown eyes were almost black. He tried to look straight at Lilith, but his eyes fell to his feet.

A fly walking across Bip's forehead stopped just above his left eyebrow to rub his front legs together. Lilith shifted in her chair. Startled, the fly starting up its wiry legs in a panic and rushed to Bip's ear and vaulted off of his cartilage into the belly of the fat blue sky.

Bip wanted to swipe at the fly with his free hand, but he stood rigid.

Lilith stopped rocking on the porch.

"Go on and gets outa here. Go on. 'Go on,' I said." Lilith "shooed" him away with her hand.

Bip wiped his nose but stood rigid.

"Go on!" She spoke louder.

He was scared, but he raised his face to her. Her face softened some.

"What you got there behind yo' back? Show Lilly yo' hands, Little Boy."

He stood firm.

She tried softer, "Show Lilly yo' hands, Little Boy."

She said "Little Boy" in one rush, sounding like an Indian name, like "Running Horse" or "Sky Star."

"Got some Popsicles. Some red. Store bought." He tried to talk clearly and loudly enough for her to hear his voice from the dirt road. The hot sun wrestled Bip's voice to the grass before it could reach Lilith.

"I eats little boys, you know?" She rocked forward in her chair, crouched like she might spring up.

"I know. Mama told me."

"She did?" Her lips curled back into her mouth. "She tells you I eats little boys?"

"She said you was a 'Witch.'"

"I is a Witch," Lilith said proudly scooting back into the rocker. The wooden floor beneath her chair creaked and moaned.

"That's what she said."

"Them's Popsicles gonna melt out there under the sky, child."

He stood still.

"Come here, Little Boy," she said like coaxing a kitten.

He moved a bit.

"Come on here!" she barked from her stomach.

In just a matter of minutes, he was sitting at her feet listening to the creak of her rocker as he started on his second Popsicle.

"My Mama says you read palms?" He cocked his head up at her as he asked.

"Yo' Mama, she talk too much 'bout things ain't none of her business," Lilith said as her hands worked busily shelling the black-eyes.

She threw a handful of unshucked peas into Bip's lap and handed him an empty cigar box. He started shelling mindlessly. After a minute he felt his hands getting sticky from the peas.

"Could you read my palm?"

"No Sir! No Siree. Go on and get on outa here if'n you gonna talk like that. Don't no child need to know nothing 'bout the future."

Her fingers split the jacket of a pea pod. Then, she added under her breath, "Mercy sakes. Sakes alive, child."

He moved to try to get his legs out from under his weight. Lilith stopped the rocker and held her hand stiffly on his head.

"Stay sit, Little Boy."

He stayed under the weight of her hand.

"Stay sat down. I gots to relieve myself," she said as she lifted herself onto her heavy legs. She cradled the shelled peas in her white cotton apron and dumped his cigar box in with her peas and popped another handful of unshelled peas in his lap, and Lilith, in her red slippers, shuffled into the house.

He wasn't sure whether she was going into the house to empty her apron, or for a drink, or to the bathroom, but she eventually returned, taking her time getting the peas back in her lap ready to shell.

After a long silence she finally spoke. She was far-eyed and distant, separate.

"Jesus drowned last night," she said. Her voice sounded deeper.

"Pardon?" He wasn't sure he heard right.

"They was a flood last night. It left all the fairies tangled in the trees."

"After the flood?" he asked. It had not rained.

"Does you fly?" she asked him.

"No, Ma'am."

"Well, they's a boy gonna done get himself thumped out of the sky."

"By whom?" he asked politely.

She started to answer. Her mouth opened but there was no voice, just a gurgle deep in her throat.

"That what happen to me when I eat red Popsicle or banana fudge from the store. Give me gas and make me a prophet," she laughed to herself. Her body bounced up and down like Jello gently touched with a curious finger.

"Mama …" he hesitated, "Mama, also, says you drink liquor."

"I does."

Bip had never seen much hard liquor growing up and was very interested in something so taboo. Lilith produced a bottle from inside her dress and unscrewed the lid and took a drink; then she handed the bottle to Bip. He politely pushed it back away. She insisted. He took the bottle and stuck his finger in until it touched the brown liquid. He licked his finger and he cringed at the bitter-sweetness. She laughed.

"They was mermaids that curl they babies to their bellies, turning they heads, gasping for water." She took a more serious drink, a long, slow drink from the bottle. He pictured the brown liquid flowing like hot molasses down her dark throat.

Bip wanted another taste, but she didn't offer.

She went quiet again, so he watched a bee buzzing in and out of the white and yellow daisies in front of the porch.

"Little Boy?" she started again.

It had been several minutes.

"Yes, Ma'am."

"Just flash me your palm. Just a little. But don't show it all to me."

He scratched his palm and rubbed it against his pants; then, he turned his polished hand to her eyes dropping it quickly in his lap, a smile on his thin red lips.

"Longer than that, Little Boy. Lilly's eyes is bad." Lilith rolled her eyes back in her head.

He held it up longer, stretching his fingers backward, so she could see every crack and fault.

Her face shifted and her body shook like something was inside of her.

"He's drunk in some heavenly cafe," she said, almost as if she were talking to someone else.

"I'm not drunk, Lilly."

She jumped. "Don't take Big Lilly out no trance, Little Boy! I's in a trance! Don't you talk! You hear me?" Her voice was harsh.

"Yes, Ma'am," Bip apologized.

"You just listen and tell me what I say!"

"Yes, Ma'am." He paused then struggled forward. "He's drunk in some heavenly bar ..." He coaxed her forward.

"... because he thought we's all asleep." She finished her thought.

"But we ain't. I'm eating a red Popsicle with you." He gently touched just the toe of her slipper.

"And the grass is wet and green and the daisies is just spreadin' out. And the moon changes every night ... the changing moon, the changing moon." Then she added, very distant, "Rains is coming. They's gonna be another flood, Little Boy."

"My mama says to welcome the rain and to curse drought."

"Oh, but honey, this rain's gonna drown a child in his bed."

He sat in silence.

"His bed gonna be his grave."

He thought of drowning, of being underwater needing to breathe, then of taking the water into his lungs.

She didn't speak. He took a deep breath.

Tears began to gather in his eyes like stars crowded in the sky just as her black hand flowed through his hair.

"Rest easy, Little Boy," she said and laughed deep and drank from the bottle three gulps.

"Are you really a witch?" he finally asked the simple question.

She just smiled and picked up the bowl of black-eyed peas and started snapping while the last two red Popsicles melted across the cedar wood, red and syrupy, turning the surface dark with stain and black shadows, and the smell of the red cedar rose.

"Gives me them Popsicle sticks at your leg."

He handed her the four sticks. They disappeared in her hands and cracked like little bones. After a few minutes, she produced a little stick boy.

"This you, Little Boy."

She held up the figure. It was very disproportioned. She took a 'twisty' and tied the sticks. She took the toothpick from behind her ear, licked it, and dipped the end into the Garrett snuff beside her chair. She dotted two ghostly eyes and curled a mouth smiling.

"I'll keeps you in the house, close to the window, Little Boy."

She held up the figure.

"You ...?" he started, but hesitated.

"I's a good witch."

He turned and looked up into her black eyes.

"You won't die no child. You die a man, Little Boy. I promise. Lilly promise you." She paused. Then, she said to herself, "I'll swear, I got to quit protecting you boys or we gonna done get a world full of fine young men."

Mary's front tires locked, digging a row into the dirt road. Mary sat for a second, relieved to find Bip.

She took a deep breath, fumbled to unlock the door, and finding the handle without letting her eyes off of Bip, she popped the door, hesitated. Then, her long body grew out of the car.

Mary was a striking woman, coal hair that hugged her cheeks, which were always blushed; her tanned skin was like caramel ice cream. Her white cotton dress was pushed against her body by the breeze; she should have been wearing a slip, but she wasn't. Her thighs were long and reached for her hips; her hips sat firm and tight under her thin stomach which seemed even thinner under her two grand breasts, which because of the excitement were all but pointing straight at Lilith and Bip.

"You gonna melt out there under the sky, girl. Come up and sit with the child and me," Lilith said beginning to rock again.

"Thank you kindly, but the 'Child and I' must be somewhere." Mary ran her red nails dramatically through her hair and looked to Bip and changed her tone. She pulled her lips tight against each other. "Bip, get in the car, you hear?"

Bip could tell that his mother was not comfortable, so he attempted an introduction to smooth things over.

"Mother this is Miss Lilly, and Miss Lilly this is my Mama." He had wanted to say his mother's name, but "Mary" sounded so formal.

"I know who Miss Lilith is, Bip. Please, come and get in the car."

"You knows me? You never come to talk to me," Lilith started sarcastically. "You gots a fine young boy here, Miss Mama. He a good thinker and leader of men some day."

"Thank you," Mary said to Lilith, out of courtesy. Then, she addressed Bip again, "Bip, I'm not telling you again. Get in the car." Her voice was very stern this time.

Bip rose and began to leave. He turned to look at Lilith and she shooed him off of the porch.

"Go on and get on outa here likes I told you first." Her foot even gently kicked his behind as he jumped over the daisies.

Bip landed a bit off balance, then scuttled to the car a little confused. Lilith's mood seemed to flip-flop so much. Bip remembered that his friend Carl had once told him alcoholics had a lot of mood swings and he was sure witches had very moody days, too. With Lilith being an alcoholic and a witch, Bip decided she probably was doing just about the best she could.

"Miss Mama, you take care of Little Boy," Lilith said to Mary who was now standing in front of the porch with her back to Bip.

Lilith held up the stick man she had made. Bip felt a shock go through his body. His mother didn't know that the sticks cradled in Lilith's hand were Bip.

Mary merely said, "Good Day!" and turned back to the car.

Mary sat with a sigh as stiff as the vinyl seat. She blew the dark strands of hair from her eyes and pulled back the strays that clung to her crowsfeet. She hated being thirty-five. She also hated chasing Bip all over town.

She looked back from the front seat through the mirror to Bip in the back seat.

"What on God's green earth possessed you to stop and talk to that crazy woman?" She held her face postured: eyebrows up in a question, bottom lip down.

Bip didn't answer. He had learned, even at the young age of ten, that he was never to answer any question from a woman to which she already knew the answer.

CHAPTER 2

▼

VENUS AND THE DOG STAR

Rabbit Hill was just north of the city and not even tall enough to be called a hill. It was more of a roll of soil, swollen like the bare, pregnant belly of a woman in repose on her back or the pooch of dirt left over a new grave. It made a lazy effort to reach the sky. The valley before Rabbit Hill held Flatland like a prize in its palm.

Billie and Dawn were soon out of the station wagon, standing embraced under the sky.

Even though no one had seen them leave Flatland, Billie continued to throw suspicious looks around, but he was settling. He stared into the glow of the setting sun that fell behind the city. He sensed the black night rising against his back.

Dawn looked across the distance to the city. The streetlights and the neon signs started to blink on. After a fanfare, Flatland finally sat like a tiny Christmas tree against the flat pink horizon.

The air was warm and calm and dry.

Tonight Billie could hear the voices rise from the town, sounding like voices trapped under a low sky.

"The voice tunnel is working tonight. Sounds like a bunch of talking ants been captured under a plastic cup," he said. He held up his black hand to cup his ear.

"What? Is the radio still on?" Dawn asked in a big red 'O'. She had just put lipstick on and was blotting her lips on a Kleenex.

The sky was endless.

Dawn was not so preoccupied as Billie was. Her eyes vaulted upward to the spinning figures in the western sky. The setting sun sat like stained glass, red on clear wet black. After the sun dropped completely, she saw the Big Dipper pouring onto the North Star. In the east, Orion was just climbing over the horizon. She could just see his studded belt as he hoisted the twins behind him, and Sirius, the Dog Star, as if on a chain, was pulled like an obedient pup from the darkness.

Venus was the brightest body in the sky, resting like a shiny steel marble on the eastern horizon comfortably next to Sirius, and they were the two brightest objects in the sky nestled together.

There were no trees. There was no water. There was just the cotton, and the smell of clay and settling dew.

Dawn liked the stars.

"I found a new constellation out here last time we were making love," she said. Billie was thinking about something else, so she sat and found her new dot-to-dot in the sky and thought about how pretty she was with her long blonde hair, her red lips that bunched together under her model nose and her shaped, but purposely unruly, eyebrows. She looked back at Billie. He didn't look at her.

Dawn threw a clod at Billie's thigh as she started to speak.

"Does your father know?"

"You mean my grandfather?" He still didn't look at her. She was sitting on the hood. He was propped up against the door with his hands stuffed in his pockets.

"I'm sorry. Your 'grandfather,'" she said with a bit of sarcasm as if *who knew* didn't really matter, just as long as someone *knew*.

"He really doesn't care." Billie said as he pulled his hands out of his pockets and stood up straight. He walked to Dawn.

Dawn touched Billie's arm and he held her. His fingernails were whiter than her skin, but his skin was dark, like kilned black pottery, as if he had been carved and sculpted from the soil by the wind.

"I like the smell of this land." He grabbed a handful of soil and held the fistful to his nose, "Especially just plowed."

"Did you touch your mouth to that!?"

"I sniffed it."

"You licked it!"

"Well—I touched my tongue to it."

"Well! My Lord. Don't lick it. Sometimes you're the end. You know that? Licking dirt. It'll make you sneeze. You know that? Make you sick?"

"Dirt don't make people sick. People make people sick," he said as he spit a brown puddle on the sand.

"Well, it'll stop up your nose," she said.

She was concerned that if he couldn't breathe correctly that they might not be able to kiss as long as she'd like.

She smiled at him, and he smiled back slowly. She was still trying to control his passion, training him to kiss and caress, rather than demanding her and over-powering her, although ironically that's what attracted her to him in the first place.

"I'm not wearing a bra," she teased him.

She knew he liked her body. She even tanned topless so that she would feel more natural naked. But he seemed pensive, more content to look at the stars than at her.

"White people always talk about underclothing," he finally responded. Then, he added, as if his slave roots were asking a question across time, "Cain't you smell the cotton?" His grandfather had actually handpicked cotton, just as his father and his father had. Now, the grandfather shined shoes at the Modern Barbershop.

He pulled an open boll and picked the seeds from the cotton and began to twist the cotton into handmade thread without thinking.

He liked the land.

"You know Daddy hates you, Billie?"

"Let's just not talk." He wadded the cotton into a small ball.

"Come on and hold me," she said pouty. "We don't have much time." She had promised to be home on time.

He let his eyes fall from the stars down to her face as she was crouched in front of him, kneeling; her head was up eagerly.

He threw the ball of cotton from his hand and cupped her chin in the palm of his hand and looked down into her face.

She really was not as pretty as he had once thought she was. She had been prettier before he had gotten to know her. The more she talked, the less attractive she became. Silent and mysterious, her lines in her face were interesting and intriguing. Now they were garrulous and selfish, snide and judgmental.

"Let's just not talk," he said again to himself, to the dirt, and to the stars as he pulled her body close to his.

There was no moon to set their bodies off under the darkness. Their skin seemed the same as they pulled their clothes off of each other like socks off of feet.

Under the stars they were only shade and motion. They gyrated and curved and slid, bare-bodied, up and down the hood of the red station wagon. She finally rose up on top of Billie as he lifted her in one motion to the sky and Dawn screamed inside her mouth. He remained silent, but the breath from his flat nose whistled across the cotton field in the falling rhythm of the echo.

They were sitting in the station wagon when Len's car raced to a stop and shined on them. Len was Dawn's father. The reflection from his lights circled each wide-eyed face with a luminary halo, and they appeared as a star and a planet fallen precariously, sitting uncomfortably on the red vinyl seat of Billie's grandfather's station wagon.

CHAPTER 3

▼

THE MODERN BARBERSHOP

The Modern Barbershop was just off the courthouse square in Flatland; still, it was close enough to other square shops to get a cut at lunch or even on break. There was another barbershop over two blocks on Crockett Street, Garcia's, but it wasn't convenient, and really it was for the Mexicans. Garcia didn't cut a good *Regular Man's* haircut. Besides, Garcia's only had one chair. The Modern Barbershop had three chairs: Selmer's, Paul's, and Clifford's, and the men entered in suits and overalls, businessmen and farmers, and waited for their chairs.

Just as you walked in, the three chairs faced the door and were equal distance apart and were clean with shined chrome and worn-slick leather seats with leather sharpening strops on the side. Selmer owned the shop and his chair was in the middle; he used an extension, swivel chair connected to his chair to swing around to cut hair. He cut and talked more than any of the three. Clifford, in the far chair, seldom talked, but he once told his friend Oden, the mailman, that Selmer had hemorrhoids but still refused to stand up, because that's the way he "learned to cut hair."

Paul was the most popular barber, but he was also the slowest. He rented the first chair from Selmer. Most of the businessmen—and the farmers who didn't care to talk—used Paul because Paul was deaf.

Deafness in a barber can be a blessing; Paul just cut and didn't discuss the weather, or your home, or your job. He just got in front of you and slurred, "Reguulaar maan's haaircuut?" New customers often had to ask, "Beg your pardon?" However, the regulars would go through their "little off the sides. Leave some sideburns. Watch the cowlick in the back." Paul always responded in a deaf slur, "'Boout meedieum?"

All of he cuts were "About medium?"—a "Regular Man's" haircut.

"Walter. You ready?" Selmer snipped his scissors in the air and swung around in his sit-down chair. Walter was the president of the Flatland Freedom Bank and was sitting next to Jim in front of the big pane window.

"You know Paul cuts me. Besides, Jim's in front of me." Jim patted Walter as he rose and headed to Selmer's chair.

It was a pecking order of sorts; each man waited for the barber he chose. It was usually based on one's entering before another, an unwritten waiting list, but at times a farmer who had more time in between rows gave way to a businessman who had all his work during cutting hours, and vice-versa during cotton ginning season. Some had even been known to be in such a rush that they took an empty chair regardless of the cutter, but not often.

"I'd come at six if they's still open," Walter said to Jim who was now settling into Selmer's chair.

Walter Daniel was a big man, jovial like Santa Claus. And because of his position at the bank, no one had ever seen him pull up to a corner without eyeballing everyone who was passing to see if he needed to wave or not. He was afraid he'd miss someone, so he'd wave almost two-handed, left at the cars and right at pedestrians, down any street. In that way he was like Santa Claus, the ever-pleaser, afraid he'd dissatisfy someone and lose a loan to the State Bank. But, he wore a black suit always, as a businessman should, with a red tie, and he looked much like Red Baker, the funeral director. The point is that any man who reminds you of Santa Claus and the funeral director is in the least unsettling.

Paul finished and swung Oden around in his chair to see himself in the mirror. "Thaaat gooood?" Paul checked Oden's ears. Oden had big ears, so Paul rolled them down to check for stray hair.

"Goooooood," Paul confirmed his work as Oden pulled a five out of his top shirt pocket and gave it to Paul and buttoned his collar. Then, Paul patted Oden's ears back stiff and straight up against Oden's head. Everyone said "Bye" to Oden as he pulled his tie to his collar and snugged it to his throat. He stepped out into the summer heat.

"Close the damn door," Horace Crenshaw said as he fanned himself. "Sonofa-bitch always stands there to put on his tie. Stupid idiot," he added.

Crenshaw's comments were seldom favorable to anyone. Crenshaw was a small man with a Chihuahuan philosophy, lots of bark with little bite. His face was plowed by the sun; everyone simply accepted him and passed off his gruff-ness.

"Don't sit so close to the door if you don't like the heat," Walter said to Cren-shaw as he took off his tie and unbuttoned his shirt and stood at Paul's chair.

"'Bout medium, Paul. O.K.? I'm in a hurry." Walter made little running feet with his fingers. "Meeting at two," Walter finished in big-mouthed words.

Paul understood and skipped the traditional run-through, "Block in the back, etc."

Walter put his bifocals on Paul's sink and pulled the waist of his Dacron suit pants down under his belly as he sat down in Paul's chair. Paul popped the white cotton apron and fixed it under Walter's collar and slid a tissue between the apron and the collar.

"Leave what you can on top," Walter said, loud enough for everyone to hear. He was mostly bald. It was a joke and everyone laughed too loudly and took in cigarettes and coffee to stifle the obvious overreaction—most of them had bal-loon loans at his bank.

"Shave my neck, though. I'm not in that big of a hurry," Walter said as he drew a line across the back of his neck for Paul to know that he wanted a block cut with a shave.

Walter liked the shave, the hot lather when it touched his neck and the cool-ing as the blade was being flipped back and forth against the leather strop. Then, Paul would cock his head forward and he could hear the cut, and he could feel the strong push of the blade and the firm control of Paul's hand. Paul could cut his throat, but Walter trusted Paul to slide the blade against the skin. "Paul cleaned the skin better than baptism," Reverend Stephenson once said.

"Cain't shave no more," Selmer told Walter and bumped Paul as a reminder and made a "No" in his mouth and a line with his finger across his lip. Paul Nod-ded.

"What?" Walter shifted in his chair.

"Cain't shave no more," Selmer said again.

"I'll pay extra, Selmer," Walter said.

"It ain't the money. We cain't. It's not that we don't want to."

"Cain't? Who says?"

"Government."

"Now they're into barbering!" Walter was a bit angry. The papers dropped to listen. Most men cherished the end of the cut when the shave came. Only a man knows the feeling of a straight razor on his neck and the hot cloth and the brush of powder after.

"It's tradition, for Christ's sake," Crenshaw joined the conversation from the corner.

Paul read Crenshaw's lips and thought the conversation had turned to Christ.

"The government? Why do they care whether the hell you shave or not? Someone slit some congressman's neck in Washington?" Jim asked as Selmer drew the hot peppermint lather from the whirring dispenser, then remembered he couldn't shave. It was such a common thing that it had become mindless action for him.

"'Cain't' I said. See, you got me pulling the lather out just talking about it," Selmer said as he washed the hot lather down the deep porcelain basin. The smell of menthol filled the shop.

He wanted someone to ask him, "Why?"

Barbers never want to be accused of offering information without due process. That would put them in the league of hairdressers.

"Why, Selmer?" Walter asked the question.

There was a silence.

"Fags."

There was a silence.

"What?"

"Fag Disease."

Walter laughed because he figured it was a joke. Paul turned Walter's head down to his chest and snipped close to his ears.

"'Aids transmits by bleeds from cuts,' the Mormon says."

"The Mormon. Who the hell is the Mormon?" Crenshaw asked.

"That Evert Koop man, says no blades in a barbershop or you can be sued."

"Evert Koop ain't no Mormon," Dick Johnson spoke up in Selmer's chair. Dick ran for a public office once, so he was considered the town authority on political information.

"Well, he ought to be. He looks like one," Selmer conceded.

"That's right," Tabot finally spoke up from the shine stand. He was the town lawyer. "Got the notice last week."

"And we ain't doing it," Selmer pulled back almost as if he were being accused.

"Hell, Selmer. I'm not the police. Do what you want," Tabot said.

"Not in this shop. We're not catering to no fag disease."

"Fag's is ruinin' this country...." Walter started and trailed off on an under-the-breath condemnation of homosexuals. Paul watched his lips and thought Walter was asking him to shave his neck.

"Caan't cuut. Nooo raaazoor," Paul said authoritatively.

"Where's the shine boy?" Tabot was still sitting in the high shine chair.

The "*shine boy*" was not a boy at all; he was an old black man, Washington, Billie's grandfather. Washington had worked at the Modern Barbershop even before Selmer bought it from Hector Lewis. He had seen most of the men in the shop as children when they had to sit on a board across the armrests to raise them high enough for Hector to cut their hair. He had seen all of them bargain for extra pieces of Bazooka bubble gum after the cut, and watched them scuffle out smelling of hair tonic and gum, their stubborn cowlicks popping up and trading their waxed cartoons as soon as they hit the wind.

"He left last week for a funeral. He said his mother died," Selmer said.

"Siit foorwaard. I'll triiim," Paul pushed Walter's head forward.

"Sorry." Walter leaned forward. "Don't get the hair down my collar. I got a meeting at two. Don't have time to run home."

"Ben was telling me that Garcia has a new contraption that sucks the hair up a tube right as he cuts it," Jim said.

"Stupid Meskin hooked a damn Hoover to his clippers is what he did. That what you want? Want me to vacuum your head? All these new ideas. I still say a comb, scissors, and a blade's all a good barber needs." Selmer hated even the mention of Garcia's shop.

The door shook open and stayed open and the summer heat swept the shop as Len Johnson yelled back to Mary, his wife, "Go to the store and get your mother's hairnets." Her voice whined back, over the engine. No one could hear her except Len. He felt his back pocket and started to pull his wallet.

"Shut the damn door," Crenshaw said. The heat was seeping in.

"Just write a check," Len yelled back out, ignoring Crenshaw. Crenshaw was Len's father-in-law and there was little love lost between the two.

Again, Mary said something that no one but Len could hear.

"I'll cover it, for God's sake. Go and come right back and we'll go check on her."

Another whine.

"I'm worried, too."

He came in and the door closed. He pulled his shirt away from his sweating skin.

"'Bout damn time you closed the door. You ought to take care of money problems at home 'stead of in the doorway," Crenshaw said.

Clifford finished in his chair. Len looked around.

"Who's next?" Len asked. It was obvious that he was in a hurry.

"Go on," Tabot gave up his turn. "Not in no hurry to get back to a stack of papers."

"You sure you don't mind?"

"Just get in the chair before I do," Crenshaw said and feigned a move toward the chair. His son-in-law all but ignored Crenshaw.

"Thanks. Really. I'm in a hurry."

"What the hell is with you. You're hissin' and bitchin'?" Tabot asked from up in the shine box. He was not being forward. Everything among men is usually open.

"Don't need to air out my problems here."

"Things not good, Len?" Selmer asserted his position on Len.

"Don't want to talk about it," he said hard and definite.

Tabot lifted his paper and the air conditioner kicked on and whirred and lurched forward, then clicked to a full start. The air was warm at first and then started to cool as it blew over the men, now all silent in the shop. The only noise was the snip of the scissors and Paul's loud breathing.

"Tabot," Len started, "that black boy was with my daughter again last night." They had obviously talked about it before in Tabot's law office. Crenshaw raised an eyebrow but stayed silent.

"She was?" Tabot begged the question.

"That halfback boy. The one I told you about. Billie Washington."

"She was?" Tabot teased him forward.

"Hell, yes, she was. And I want him arrested like I said."

Tabot shifted in his chair. "Police do arrests, Len. Not me. I prosecute. You get him arrested and I'll bring charges, just like I told you."

"She left the house and I follered 'em. Caught 'em at Rabbit Hill. There was liquor in the car."

"From Lilith's?"

"Well, they wouldn't go to the Meskin bootlegger."

"I thought you shut that place down?" Selmer asked.

"I did too," Tabot responded a little concerned.

"I don't want him arrested for being drunk. He's with my daughter, for cryin' out loud!"

Crenshaw worked to bite his lip.

Paul pushed Walter's head back down and mouthed, "Juuuust a seecoond, Waaalt—ter."

"What do you want, Len?" Tabot asked straightforward.

"I want someone to keep that nigger away from my daughter!"

"Could be she wants to be with him." Crenshaw could no longer keep his silence.

"What're you saying, Horace? That your granddaughter's in love with some nigger?"

"Didn't say nothing about love. Dawn is just like Mary. Don't have a bit of sense of what we want, just what she's found to be right. And her looks ...," Crenshaw added, realizing Dawn was a cookie cut of Mary. "Thank God she at least has her looks."

"Not love, I bet," Selmer cut in. "Just that he's a star and maybe she takes a shine to him, that's all. It'll pass."

No one responded. The tissue paper behind Len's neck crackled and turned and hair went down his collar.

"I seen 'em kissin' for God's sake!" Len burst before he really thought.

"Kissing?!" Selmer almost dropped his scissors. That was a whole different question.

"Was he feeling on her?" Walter asked.

"Are you sick, Walter?"

"That's not good," Tabot added.

"Why the hell do you think I'm upset?"

"Takes two to tango," Crenshaw said without really moving his lips.

"What do you mean by that?" Len bit his lip.

"Takes two to kiss, is all I'm saying."

"Not if he's forcing himself on her."

"You mean he's raping her," Selmer hopped to the conclusion.

"Oh, come on!" Tabot said.

"Sounds like you got a problem to me," Walter added.

"I caught 'em in the car kissing and I hit the window and opened the door and pulled her out."

"What'd she say?" Walter asked.

"What do you mean what'd she say? She cried and ran to the car. Didn't say nothing. Just whined."

"What'd he say?"

"He said 'I's sorry.' Over and over again."

"You didn't hit him, did you?" Tabot asked.

"Hell, no. I's too goddern mad to hit him, but I yelled him up one side and down the other. Told him to stay away from Dawn."

"I would've knocked the fire out of him," Crenshaw said. He didn't want Dawn being "taken advantage of."

"Sure you would have. You'd of taken him back to his house and right in the middle of niggertown you'd beat up the star football player and called 'em all niggers to their faces," Len cut back at Crenshaw.

"I think you done the right thing. You got to be a good father in bad situations," Selmer tried to wrap it up in a single comment.

There was a long silence.

"Where's the shine boy?" Tabot tried to change the subject. He was still sitting in the shine stand.

"Up for a funeral. For his mother, I believe," Selmer said.

"He's that boy's something," Walter said.

"What?" Len asked.

"He's related to that boy."

"They're all related," Crenshaw said. "At least they all live in the same house."

"How the hell you know that, Crenshaw?!"

"They's on my route. Niggers drink milk, too."

"You seen 'em in the same house?" Len started thinking.

"Got the same name, Washington. They all live on Franklin Drive. Last house at the end. It's a dead end street."

Suddenly the door broke open and the heat swept in behind Mary. The air swirled like a little tornado and stirred the cut hair under Paul's feet. Paul looked up and smiled at Mary and waved his scissors, absolutely out of the conversation.

"Leave the car runnin', Mary. Let's go and finish it."

Mary looked concerned at Crenshaw. Crenshaw shrugged his shoulders.

Len didn't even wait for Clifford to finish his cut. He stood and started taking off the apron himself and ran his fingers through his hair to get it to smack down right. He pulled a five out of his pocket and pushed it into Clifford's fist as he dropped the apron to the floor. Len put his arm around Mary's shoulder and led her out of the door. She started to cry noticeably before the door even closed.

There was a long silence and no one moved—not even Selmer.

"What're they gonna do?" Walter finally asked.

"Selmer, you better call Watts," Tabot said.

"You think so really. The police?"

"I think so. I've talked to him in private. And Walter, you ain't helping none with your 'I'd whoop his ass.'"

Selmer let go of Jim's head and started dialing the number.

"Don't believe I'd let my temper control me quite that much," Selmer said.

"Headstrong wife causes a weak man, and a weak man raises a promiscuous daughter," Walter added.

"Dawn's always been a strong girl. I wasn't sure her mother was right for Len, but then, I said that even when they's datin'," Crenshaw was evaluating his raising of his daughter.

"What'd you expect?" Clifford asked as he picked up the apron off the floor.

"What if it was your daughter?" Tabot asked.

"Wouldn't have happened in the first place. And if it did, I wouldn't have it," Walter said.

"Well, it is my granddaughter and I ain't heared her version yet," Crenshaw was not ready to concede.

Down toward the highway at the railroad tracks, Len's car turned and honked at a truck that cut him off. The black man who was driving the truck said "Stupid white-ass" at the same time Len said, "Damn nigger." Len then repeated the words and mouthed them more noticeably at the pickup as it puttered down the road, and finally said, "Damn nigger," again for Mary's benefit. The truck wrenched through its gears slowly speeding up, going to the Modern Barbershop.

"He ain't marrying no white woman," Washington, the old shine man on the passenger-side said. Then he added, "White people can't drive worth a shit." Washington was Billie's grandfather. James, who was driving the truck, was Billie's cousin. James had graduated two years earlier and now worked at the wrecking yard.

"You tell him to leave her be?" James leaned over the steering wheel. "This seat make my butt hurt."

"I told him."

"Did he hear you? Does your butt hurt on this seat?"

"They's a stop sign." Washington pointed to the corner.

"I know they's a stop sign. No stop sign in town 'cept here. I don't know why they don't take that sign down. Nobody stops. No traffic."

"'Cause it's always been here's why."

"You's going back to work then?"

"If I still gots a job," Washington said, half laughing.

"What'd you tell them?"

"I told 'em Molly died."

They both laughed and wiggled in their seats. Molly had died several times before; Selmer simply never listened to Washington. Actually they had gotten drunk at L.M.'s.

"I cried and acted real nigger to Selmer Jackass, cryin' and wailin'."

"Hell. White man talk to a black man like they talk to a blind boy."

Then Washington pointed to the front and to the left. "Right there."

"Don't you think I know where the shop is? You think I just moved here?" He slowed down.

The truck stopped.

Suddenly, Len Johnson's car reeled around the corner. Len finally recognized soon after he had driven past the truck that the shine man was in it.

Len's car screeched to a stop just past the truck and Len yelled at Mr. Washington even before he had his car in park. Washington got out of the truck slowly and shuffled toward the door of the Modern Barbershop. Len jumped out of his car and grabbed Washington's arm just before Washington entered the shop.

"Wait, just a damn minute!" Len said, jerking Washington around. James, still in the truck, shifted uneasily in his seat. Then he reached his arm around the back of his seat, fumbling behind the vinyl.

In a second, Len and Washington were standing face-to-face against each other. Len was a good two heads taller than the thin shine man. The blinds opened in the Modern Barbershop window and all the faces turned to the scene outside.

Crenshaw and Tabot stepped outside.

"You keep that boy's hands off my Dawn. Do you hear me?" Len yelled.

"I've talked to the boy. He's got a mind of his own," he said. "And she do too," he added, half under his breath.

"She don't love him. You hear me? She don't love him."

Suddenly the door of Len's car swung open and Mary rushed Washington and she threw herself on Washington, tearing at his clothes and hitting him with small closed fists. His face remained unchanged and he defended himself by lifting his arms over his eyes, but he didn't strike back. Washington looked deep into Mary's eyes; she cowered back just as Len's big fist crashed across the rigid, cheek of Washington. Even those still in the shop heard the crack of his jaw. Paul even looked up at the ceiling as if he'd heard something for the first time in his life.

Len repeated the word "Nigger!" again as he brought his foot back to kick Washington. Washington was on the ground with his mouth moving wordlessly like a fish out of water. The kick brought blood from the stomach of the "shine man" to the corners of his mouth. Len's foot went back again and against the head of the Washington. His foot went back again.

James found the barrel behind the seat and leaned forward and took a twenty-gauge shell from the glove box, hung the barrel out of the window and aimed at the glass in the shop window. Len was just under thirty feet away.

"HEY!!!" James yelled to keep Len from kicking Washington again. Crenshaw was just moving toward Len when Len turned full front, framed by the big pane glass window of THE MODERN BARBERSHOP in big blocked, traditional letters.

James pulled the trigger.

The shot rolled through the air like a thunderstorm and thumped into Len's chest, taking him backward through the window, half into the Modern Barbershop. The glass fell in a shower over Mary, who also had been hit by a few stray pellets. As the glass hit the ground, it spread in a wave, bouncing into and off of Washington's back.

The shot echoed into the corners of the town, against the walls of the shops and trees, against the courthouse. James thought the shot would be silent for some reason, higher and make a statement by blowing out the window, but it exploded and flowed like spilled blood running over the skin of the city.

Tabot and Crenshaw scrambled to the curb and crouched behind Len's car in case James decided to shoot again.

"Get up! Come on! Get up!" James yelled at Washington. He was banging his closed fist against the red enamel of the pickup with his head jutted out the window. His lips were pulled back from his clenched teeth.

Washington got up wounded; glass was in his back and pellets had riddled his face. He stumbled to the truck to the driver's side. James reached out his arm and put it around Washington and snugged him against the outside of the truck and backed out. His barrel was still awkwardly out of the window. A block down, he stopped and pulled Washington through the open window and the truck spit and sputtered away toward the tracks.

Tabot and Crenshaw got up slowly from behind the car. They waited to make sure the truck was not coming back by.

"What should we do?" Tabot finally said, still shaking.

"Which way did he go? We can go and kill his ass," Jim said as he stepped out of the shop.

The siren two blocks away started up and started to the barbershop then turned off, heading for the railroad tracks.

"I called," Selmer stepped out. Paul stepped out; his eyes were wide open. Paul looked at Selmer's mouth waiting for him to explain.

"He called him a 'nigger,'" Selmer said matter-of-factly.

"Let's go after 'em," Jim tried to stir everyone up again.

Crenshaw looked over at Len in the puddle of blood.

Mary was thrown over his body, shaking from the fright and the heat and the mystery of it all.

CHAPTER 4

▼

LEN'S BOX

When Mary stopped in the parking lot of the funeral home, she noticed she had on one dark-blue pump and one black pump. She was spent and empty. Dawn expected her to say "Allrighty" or "Well, here we are." But Mary didn't say a word. Mary had, of course, seen Len at the scene of the accident, but she had not acknowledged him dead at that time. She deeply wished he were still alive and that he were sitting in the car complaining about the hot weather or her panty-hose or laughing at her mismatched shoes. But now his death was real. She wanted, needed—but hated—to see Len in his coffin. She hoped he looked like himself.

She poofed her hair as she entered the home and even put on lipstick, knowing she was doing it for herself instead of him. It had become habit to rub the red stick against her lips anytime she stepped from the car. She knew she was vain, but she didn't care at that moment, nor did she feel like making any habitual "no-no" speech to herself at the time.

She remembered her mother's funeral.

When they had viewed the body, she could see the stitches of thread holding her mother's lips together like a secret. She had even put blush on her mother's pallid cheeks. Humans, she figured, didn't have to avoid each other in death—only in life.

So, she gave her attention to Len.

Mary and Dawn entered the casket room. Bip had decided not to see Len in his casket even though the preacher said that it might help him to realize Len's death totally. As complicated as it may be to understand, Mary was married to Len for four years just out of high school. Dawn was a result of that union. Len and Mary then divorced. Mary then married Robert, a painter and poet, who was killed by a train during a jog. Bip was Robert and Mary's son, a result of that union. Mary remained single for several years after swearing never to love again until she and Len danced together at the class reunion and rediscovered each other. They had remarried just a year ago. Bip never thought of Len as his father, so it was just Mary and Dawn and Len and the box that held him.

Len lay very postured with his hands neatly to the side and his glasses set uncomfortably on his nose. Mary fixed the glasses on his nose almost immediately, and then began to weep. Her eyes had the same look she had seen when she and Len were making love just the night before. She had looked in the mirror in front of her just before her moment and the look was the same: empty and desperate. Dawn, in her innocence, however, simply stood and awkwardly hoped that no one saw her mother babble-crying.

Dawn continued to shift on her feet back and forth.

"Are you not even going to hug your daddy?" Mary raised her eyebrows.

Dawn didn't answer. She knew that the question was loaded and heavy. She did feel guilty that Len was dead, even though it was his temper, not her action, that had caused his death. But she also missed her daddy. She wasn't thinking at all and about everything.

Dawn walked to Len's body and held his hand.

After almost ten minutes she started, "They didn't even part his hair on the right side. Mama, give me your comb. It's like dressin' up for a Christmas morning picture; it's unnatural."

Dawn started combing her father's hair, and combed it, and continued to comb it until she and Mary fell into each other's arms and cried and sat on the floor in their starched dresses and spoke in "remembers" followed by a long complicated silence. Dawn apologized and Mary said there was no reason to and they hugged again.

"You really loved him, didn't you, Mama?" Dawn wanted to hear her mother say it, to confirm love.

"Yes, I did. Your daddy was one of a kind."

Dawn smiled to hear her mother say that. She looked at Len and his hands not moving, his eyes not open, and it hit her like a bucket of water again. Stunned and suddenly full of love, she went to Len and combed his hair one more time to leave it just right, to cover his bald spot. Mary covered Dawn's hand with her hand on Len's head like a baptism. Dawn noticed his chest caved in and squeezed Mary's hand hoping only she noticed.

They left the funeral home hand-in-hand for the first time since Mary had to walk Dawn to school when Len had taken the car keys with him when he left town to go to Amarillo. For that week, Dawn and her mother survived without the car. In retrospect, that was a good week for them. When Len had returned, he had felt true remorse, but Mary had felt a new sense of independence and loved it. For a week he had thought about her, instead of her about him. He had thought of how many miles of road were between them.

"You 'member when daddy took the keys when he went to Amarillo, Mama?"

Mary laughed and knew what Dawn was inferring. When Dawn wasn't looking, Mary looked at the picture of Len in the obituary on the seat and thought of him wrapped around her in their bed turned to the side behind her and how she had fought him off at first the night before. She almost felt an obligation to tell the town's women to have sex faithfully because of the event, but instead just considered it a mistake, and instead of making it a life's calling, she just forgave herself and kissed the obituary's picture.

"I'm glad Bip didn't come to see daddy. I think it would have scared him. He would have dreamed about it for weeks. You know how his goofy mind works," Dawn said.

"Did he sleep with you again last night?" Mary asked Dawn.

"Yes, but that's OK. I don't mind." She reached over and held her mother's hand for a second, then let it go and hummed part of a song which Bip had made up at breakfast about the advantages of oatmeal over Captain Crunch.

CHAPTER 5

▼

THE PARADE

"I bring this meeting of the Flatland city council to order," Walter's hand slapped the table. They used to have a gavel, but Crenshaw had lost it a few weeks before when he had used it during the meeting to crack some pecans.

"That hurts my hand to do that. I want you to know that, Crenshaw."

"I put the hammer back by the globe. Tabot seen me. Didn't you, Tabot?"

"That's between you and Walter, Crenshaw."

Walter changed moods and became very professional and postured.

"All of you know of the tragedy that occurred Wednesday and of Len's death. We're all deeply moved that Len met his untimely death in a barbarian manner. Watts is still trying to get a bead on the murderer. All we can do is wait." He paused. "Did you get that?" Walter motioned with his head to Zelda Merriott who was a court reporter. Walter had talked her into recording the town meetings just in case he said something so profound that humanity be forever slighted without it.

"All of you also know that tomorrow marks the beginning of the Harvest Festival. While still mourning the untimely death of Len...."

"Already said 'untimely.' We know 'untimely,'" Crenshaw cut in.

"This council is charged with the grave responsibility of deciding whether the parade and circus following should be canceled."

Not even a moment of silence passed before Crenshaw spoke.

"Hell, no! Cancel the parade?! That parade is just what my family needs to get over this mess. Time didn't stop when Clem Brown bought it in the big one!"

Clem was the most decorated WWI hero of Flatland. He had died near the end of the war.

Not even Len's absurd death could stop the Harvest Festival parade and circus in Flatland. Even though the city knew Len's death was untimely, the city council voted unanimously to go on with the parade. The only greater decision made by the council in Flatland's history concerned the heated, split argument between the adoption of squirrels or prairie dogs for the courthouse lawn. After much argument, the caucus had elected to house three squirrels in the branches of the courthouse trees. Walter shipped in three squirrels from East Texas and Crenshaw had made some little tree houses.

They had had a big "to do" one Saturday and Walter pointed each squirrel to its new home and promptly opened the cage to free them to take over the courthouse lawn. Instead, all three squirrels headed directly southeast at a full gallop; they never hesitated, stopped, barked—nothing. Someone has since reported a sighting of one near Abilene, by its earmark, but who can be sure? After that humiliation, the council decided to stay local with their city mascot. They erected a prairie dog town, complete with little prairie dog town square and little prairie dog houses. One special hole even had a little prairie dog condominium on top, and over the years, the little doggies had become tame and obedient and very much a part of all the celebrations in town.

So, the town gathered in the summer heat and lined up along Travis Avenue around the square. The twisted, sun-dried farmers with callused hands held their grandchildren's pink palms. The children sweated in anticipation of the candy that was to be thrown from the floats. They lined the west side of the square. On the south side of the square, the blacks gathered in a shadowy mass. The Mexicans sprinkled the northern side, dressed in fiesta celebration garb, and some of the children in Catholic school uniforms.

Around the inside of the square on the courthouse lawn were endless booths of civic organizations—Kiwanis, Lions, Rotarians, Lady Lions, Descendants of the Buffalo Soldiers, Welcome New Business, Daughters of Zion, Veterans of Foreign War, and all the Methodist and Baptist Men's and Women's groups, the Bible thumpers from the Assembly of God, and all the Catholic factions. The square smelled of burritos, fried jalapenos, corn dogs fried in deep pits of lard, corn popped off the husk, barbecue rich and red, sizzling fajitas, fried catfish covered with lemon and parsley tartar sauce.

The conversations all revolved around Len's death and where "one was" and what "one was doing" when he was murdered. The voices rose and fell and the story was told by eyewitnesses with different perspectives. Paul's version drew the most attention, a slurred version performed as a mime show. He shook his fists and kicked his feet, held the gun and staggered back as if shot holding his chest and finally fell exhausted in the green grass wiping his brow with the sleeve of his shirt. When he looked up, he was startled to see Scott Camel, who was perched above the square on top of the Rose Theatre, the only three-story building in town. Scott had his camera focused on the crowd below. He always photographed the town's events.

The town sat in blacks and whites and browns in gathered lumps under the green globes of the weeping willow trees and elms on the courthouse lawn. The stone of the courthouse was bleached white with ancient streaks from rains that had flowed down its scarred face into the beds of daisies that outlined the base. There was no wind, but the air was cool under the sun. The weather was perfect for a parade.

The parade always started on North Avenue, just this side of the tracks in the industrial section. The industrial section was actually a group of major farm implement and corrugated steel feed stores that had gone belly up. So the road was not very well traveled. However, it was sprinkled with a few surviving businesses, but most of the buildings were sheet metal and wood and leaned and sagged under the weight of time, looking gray and dark and spent, like houses made of glue and set in the sun. Like a blessing, the colors of the parade seemed to lift up the buildings each year, temporarily inflating their bellies like balloons.

Dub Butler, the mayor, had the job of starting the parade. No one ever knew whether to pronounce both "B's," when saying Dub's first and last name, so everyone said his name "Dub Utler." No one liked Dub at all because he had refused to call a play in the favor of the PRAIRIE DOGS in a State playoff game in 1962, so everyone got together and elected him mayor every year since.

He brought his whistle to his mouth. He had a slight harelip so he bit it between his teeth. Officer Watts, the police chief, looked at his watch and gave the signal. Dub inhaled deeply and blew into the whistle full force. The whistle, because of the overblowing and the tremendous pressure from the mayor's mouth, shot from his harelip, bounced across the asphalt and settled under the hoof of Brockman's lead horse who stomped the whistle, dropped dung, and lurched forward.

The parade had begun.

Flora Hatchet and the fantastic four led the parade. Flora was a widowed oil queen who had more years on her than an ancient turtle. She and Oleda Price and Oleda's two sisters, Bula Fae and Ginger, drove four Cadillacs with golden grills. Flora had also insisted that Len's body be driven in the Hearse behind her car, and after some cajoling, Mary had agreed. Flora had convinced Mary at the florist's that the spirited move would be equivalent to J.F.K.'s funeral march with Mary the broken Jackie O.

"They started her all right. I heard the whistle," Oden said across town as he leaned back against the brick of the Modern Barbershop, relaxing, knowing it'd be several minutes before the parade actually got to the square.

Many people were packed in front of the Modern Barbershop. The window was now plywood, and the stray glass that had avoided Paul's broom was cracking, grinding into the chalk-outline legs of Len left by the police. Only Len's chalk legs were outside the shop. The rest of his body had fallen inside the shop. Now he lay cut in half like a magician's helper: half behind the board and half smeared by the soles of shoes across the pavement like a child's hopscotch.

The people started to look down the road as the obnoxious sound of the siren grew nearer like a herd of screaming children all yelling at the tops of their lungs. This brought the actual squeals of the children along the curbs who slowly emerged into the street cautiously like the Munchkins in the "Wizard of the Oz." They were dressed in a rainbow of colors: patriotic red, white, and blues; white and red and black plaid skirts and shirts; leftover Easter dresses and cowboy boots and bandannas. All the children, whites and blacks and browns, all gathered like sheep on the curb holding colorless, sexless hands, waiting to wrestle for the candy.

Flora and the fantastic four followed by the solemn black Hearse were the first to pass. Flora drove by at a quickened pace to save the crowd undue suffering. Respects were paid as hats fell off of heads into hands, mumbling was heard, crosses were outlined across chests; still, Flora kept the speed up.

Dub, who was now on horseback, was followed by Walter in his midget go-cart with a placard sign that made it appear as a child's model-T. It said 'Remember The Depression—Save at Flatland Freedom Bank.' Walter's big body was stuffed into the cart and his painted clown face was so white that his teeth looked marred and yellow. His cart was the meandering head of the snake of the parade that followed.

Following Walter and Dub were the Shriners in their great rising fezzes on hot-rod mini-carts doing figure eight's and hexagons over horse dung and Walter's spilled candy.

"I was going to join the Shriners and drive one of them buggies, but Crenshaw told me that you had to be asked to join," Selmer whispered to Oden, who had stood up now.

"Here comes the Baptist float. Looks like they got new tires on the trailer this year. What size you figure them are—fourteens?" Oden asked Selmer. They had seen many parades.

The Baptist church float did all but float by. Even though the tires were new, the axle was still very bent from when Crenshaw had become irate over the noise of "Buffalo's" big Harley bike, and after asking politely for Buffalo to "kindly turn the sonofabitch off," Crenshaw had *accidentally* pulled the trailer over the Harley after a football halftime show. The float now bumped up and down like a Tonka toy.

The Baptists had won the toss between churches as to who got to be the first Christian float in the parade. The Church of Christ's minister was still upset that the decision had to be made by flipping a coin, which he considered gambling and wanted no part of. The Baptist's float was an attempt at "A Rainbow for Jesus" with a horrendous number of children packed into slotted places in a great arch in the appropriately colored shirt: red, yellow, green, indigo, and violet. They all waved methodically as they robotically told the curbside audience to, "Love Jesus and accept him as your personal savior," and tacked on "Remember Noah's flood!" as a sort of scare tactic. The plea was reminiscent of "Remember the Alamo." It was very moving and received generous applause from most of the audience.

Behind the Baptist float was the Methodist Hospital's float which was terribly out of place; it was professionally made and shipped over from Grandville with immaculate decorations and nurses giving IV's to a man in cardiac arrest; it was very dramatic; the slogan across the bottom of the float read: "Do you know CPR?" It was a very scary float and they failed to throw candy, and any seasoned parade professional knows that any float that emulated any form of reality and failed to throw candy was a flop.

"I learned CPR in my milkman's class," Crenshaw leaned over and told Lee Stephenson, the preacher, who had been standing by himself up to this point and was still very concerned with the gum that stretched and rebounded his shoe on and off the pavement.

Next was the Kiwanian's float. It was extremely long, being made of two flat-bed trailers hooked together. Near the back they had a constructed a big K of cardboard boxes contributed by R & B's Supermarket; below the K it read "Show Me You're a K: Men in Service Skilled," except the S in Skilled had fallen off.

Their queen in the center was dressed in a rollerskater-drive-in motif with a very short cheerleader's skirt. The boxes kept falling or blowing back against the Kiwanian's queen until she finally gave up her prissy pose for a crucifix, standing and blocking the boxes from movement. So the crowd misinterpreted the float from one of blatant sex appeal as one making a social statement and discussed how many Kiwanians had been killed in the line of service and saluted the dramatic position of the queen. The only comment heard from a Kiwanian was from Buddy Montgomery who said under his breath, "Who told her to stand like that? She looks like porno queen. Did Mike say to stand like that?" Mike was the president of the club.

After several more groups and decorated bicycles and the long snake of wagons pulled behind a pickup truck, a minute of nothing was seen.

The crowd knew what was coming.

All of the booths quit selling for a moment and the crowd squeezed against the street waiting for the sound of the big engines. There was the presence of something deep and strong and slow moving as water. It was time for the tractors with fertility and reverence on their plows. The soil dropped from their blades, bringing a cheer from the crowd. Their powerful bodies seemed ill spent on the asphalt in a parade, almost as if they were gods taking a break to come into the town.

After their passing, the squeak of broken reeds and the blats of trombones steadily grew. The dogs ran. Crenshaw said he even saw one cover its ears with its front paws. For this one event all the bands were combined. The parade band was made up of the high school band, which reluctantly allowed the junior high school band to join. They both reluctantly allowed any ex-band member to join on the playing of Sousa's "Stars and Stripes," a tradition that took place on their march around the courthouse square. The song never sounded as strict and meticulous as it should, being a military march; instead, it slid chromatically up and down, ambled and sped, blasted and moaned its way through the bodies of the crowd. Still, it always was played with vigor.

Of course the band was protected in the front by flag girls and junior cheerleaders.

It always seemed an injustice to pair cheerleaders against the flag girls. The cheerleaders led, as their name suggested, the imperfect mob behind them. They lifted and strutted their long legs and perfect thighs, big breasts, cotton candy hair, and miserable futures ahead of the flag girls who were thunder-thighed, peanut-breasted, hook-nosed and brainy: potential intellects, queens, and savior's mothers. Selmer had assured Watts in the donut shop that "Jesus' mother was not a cheerleader, nor did she have large breasts or lean thighs." Watts had been convinced that Jesus' mother had had to be a fairly good-looking cheerleader type to be Jesus' mom. So the argument remained in a deadlock.

The flag girls, instead of fluffy pom-poms of no substance held rods of steel over staunch, heavy thighs, which waved the Flatland flag, a prairie dog with a squirrel in its mouth.

Following them in thigh high skirts were the Junior High School cheerleaders leading the Class of 47's State winning football team; Flatland had not even advanced to state since the 47 team—thanks again to Dub Butler. So the team was god to their public. The stories emerged as they passed: how Jimmy Klien had come in after Billy Jones had his bell rung and thrown two touchdown passes; how Palmero, fresh across the Rio Grande, had kicked the winning field goal from forty-two-and-a-half yards out. But to the eyes of the youth of the city, they appeared as broken old men who now were senile and a bit foolish; the antique members of the team even confirmed this youthful vision by straying once in a while and "accidentally" rubbing against the behind, or the thigh, of a cheerleader. But the girls were too young to know that old men had desire and they passed it off as playfulness.

The traditional butchering of Sousa complete, the crowd further packed themselves against the curb. The greatest event of the parade was to come.

They all wanted to see the circus tease.

The city council always scheduled a circus during the Old Settler's Harvest Festival. The teaser sent by the circus owner was a clown car full of midgets and stilted clowns who burst out of a Volkswagen like a human bouquet of summer flowers. The crowd separated as if a magnet of opposing force moved through them. The clowns juggled and fell and broke bottles over each other's heads, pulled each other's pants down, pied each other's faces until the crowd rolled with laughter. Then the crowd fell silent.

Zorbinetta, a large elephant, appeared almost from nowhere pulling three cages. The elephant seemed like a walking stone. Her skin was tough and tight. Her feet sank into the hot asphalt. Some of the children, who were less afraid than their peers or parents, ran out to touch the creature as it came to a stop. The parents were throwing themselves in heroic postures at their children to fold them back to safety. Atop the elephant was the ringmaster, who only after full silence was achieved, lifted the megaphone to his mouth.

The cages behind him were covered with elaborate painted canvases with pictures of previous star acts of the circus, all dead and now replaced: Donna the Dog Lady, Tartuffe the Tattooed Boy, Talley the Turtle Man, Helga the Fat

Lady, and Ron and Don the Siamese twins. The painting was of grand nature and appeared as old and aged as a classic oil masterpiece.

The ringmaster began with an eloquent speech that revealed the mysteries of Zorbinetta the Great, the elephant. He talked about Zorbinetta and said that she would be seven hundred and sixteen years old in August on the twenty-seventh.

The crowd "ooohhed" and "aaaahhed."

The ringmaster, finally feeling the audience had been teased properly, made some sort of secret motion that brought clowns like thread through the crowd stitching together all curiosity. They grandiosely removed the cover on the first cage.

The Minotaur rushed the bars.

He looked ridiculous in the cage. He was part bull, no doubt, with strong horns and muzzle, eyes black and taut skin. But below the head of the bull was a human torso, strong and a bit dwarfed by the large head, but nevertheless not a body to scoff at. His privates, Sandra Stephenson the preacher's wife noted, were covered with a make-do loincloth. She added a "Thank the Lord" to her observation. The Minotaur seemed more human than animal, but still a bit detached. He would have looked even more strange reversed: a human head on the wild body of a bull. Still his appearance was the difference between the tame muscles of a domesticated dog and those of a coyote caught in bright lights drinking water at midnight from a playa lake: stark, harsh, powerful, wild and mysterious.

He rushed the bars and shook them. Several of the children up front growled back at him.

"You can see where they sewed the head on," Juan Ramon pointed out to his wife. She squinted her eyes and looked closely. "But the guy's doing a good job," he added in a heavy Spanish accent.

After a few more "args" and "snarls" the clowns moved in rhythm and covered the cage, feigned relief, and moved to the next cage. The ringmaster warned the people, "Please do not look directly at the next oddity, else you might turn to stone."

The clowns drug off the cover, averting their eyes at the necessary moment.

The woman was beautiful: ice green eyes, high cheekbones, dark eyebrows, and full red lips and long throat. She was dressed in sequins that barely covered her full breasts. A G-string disappeared in the back leaving her buttocks totally exposed. Her hair, however, was snakes. How the circus had done it was a great subject of debate. Crenshaw had come the closest. They had modified a swim cap, he figured, that had holes, which allowed a series of live bull snakes and garter snakes to lay and writhe in great disorder over her face and shoulders. Most of the women were amazed that the lady could hold her composure. One man in the audience, a circus plant, had already complained of becoming rigid. So to save his life, the clowns rushed the cage and covered it and the lady screamed like having her head separated from her body.

The clowns reluctantly moved to the final cage. A true roar of a mad beast was coming from under the cover. The clowns, obviously apprehensive, uncovered the cage.

It was an albino gorilla. It was real, perhaps dyed, but real and it was violent and very agitated at being caged. He threw himself against the cage bars with tremendous force. He was truly frightening. Instead of covering his cage back up though, the ringmaster coaxed Zorbinetta forward. As the stone steps of the elephant increased in speed, the ring master threw out his arms from under his satin black cape; miraculously the flyers spread and separated and fell like paper leaves falling from a cardboard tree turning in the sun.

As the flyers fell, the face of the albino gorilla flashed on one side and the circus tent on the other. Crenshaw moved in closer to Tabot.

"That's that animal that killed the little girl," Tabot said matter-of-factly.

"I thought that's all made up."

Bip, in an attempt to get closer to the cage, tried to move in between Tabot and Crenshaw. Crenshaw squeezed Bip between the two men until Bip let out a little whine.

"Go back. That's a bad gorilla."

Bip turned and went back over by Mary into the crowd.

"Nope. It's verified," Tabot continued. "She coerced it, no doubt. Said the girl threw some corndog at it and couple of pieces of ice. And they said it pretty well grabbed her through the bars and rang her head against the metal," Tabot reported.

"It killed her?"

"Well, hell, goodness yes, it killed her. Broke her glasses into and bent her nose up." Tabot pushed up the end of his nose.

"Was she killed all out or later at the hospital?"

"Crenshaw. She died," Tabot said emphatically. "What more do you need to know. I'm tellin' you, this is one mean gorilla."

"The Kiwanias ought to make a killing off the circus."

"I know it. They always have the best money makers," Tabot whined. He was a Rotarian.

Flatland watched as the cage moved forward in jerks. The gorilla seemed to settle as long as the cage was in motion forward, but anytime it stopped, the gorilla raged against the bars; however, once the elephant even moved a bit backwards, the gorilla seemed to crouch under the heavy weight of gravity as if Newton's law had fallen on his shoulders and forced the gorilla into some Darwinian reversal; the crowd sat in awe and reverence of the animal.

The bargaining of the parents with the children had already begun: "When would they go?," "How much cotton candy could they have?," "Could they have chili on their hot dogs, and could they have one of those funnel cake things made of bread and cinnamon and red sugar?"

With the oddities gone, the crowd went home to get ready for the circus.

It had been a good parade, Bip decided. He was excited about the circus. He left Mary and went and squeezed Crenshaw's hand. Crenshaw had offered to take Bip to the circus while Mary tended to the funeral arrangements.

"Bip, Len's brother …," Crenshaw started.

"Hank?" Bip offered.

"Yes. Hank can't come in from Alaska for four more days. They're going to have to hold off on the funeral." Crenshaw didn't know how else or when else to break the news to Bip. He knew Mary wouldn't tell him, either.

"That's all right, Pawpaw. I'm sorry about Len." Bip really had tried to feel compassion, but in reality he knew Len very little and had always seemed to understand death in a prophetic sense, seeing it actually as rather inconsequential, except, of course, to the person who was actually doing the dying.

Crenshaw knew Bip was different, so he simply squeezed his hand, feeling better that he had at least told Bip about the arrangements.

"Do you know Miss Lilith, Pawpaw," Bip asked, hoping his grandfather would understand.

"Yes." Crenshaw wanted to say much more than just 'yes' but he held his tongue.

"I met her the other day." Bip held his grandfather's hand and stood with his feet in the dirt like small roots growing into the West Texas soil. "Is Dawn coming with us to the Circus?" Bip hoped she would. "Is Miss Lilith a witch?"

"I doubt it." Crenshaw spoke truthfully.

Bip wasn't sure which question Crenshaw was answering.

CHAPTER 6

▼

BILLIE AND DAWN

When the phone rang, Billie put down his yearbook. He had been looking through it to see his pictures and what his friends had written about him. He really didn't like summer that much.

"Hello." Billie didn't put much into his 'hello.'

"Hi, baby." It was Dawn.

At first Billie was not excited. He hated to talk on the phone.

"Hi, baby. What's happenin'?"

"Well, just get right to business, then. Don't you even want to talk to me."

"I want to talk to you," he lied. "I just don't like talking on the phone." That was the truth.

"What're you doing?"

"Right now? Or do you mean, 'Do I have anything planned?'"

"Yes."

"Yes, both?" He didn't feel like playing her games.

"Bip and my PawPaw are going to that stupid Circus Vargas, and mom's going into Grandville to be taking care of some 'business.'" She paused, "Why don't you come over for a while," she said the last with a sexy voice.

"I don't have a ride over. My Grandpa has the Buick." He wasn't hedging. Nothing would be better than to go over and to hold her and to touch her.

"Start walking now. They're not leaving for thirty minutes."

There was silence.

"You sure your mama is gonna be gone?"
"I'm sure. I can already taste you."
He got excited.
"You sure she's gone."
"MMMMMMMMM," she mouthed over the phone.
There was another pause.
"I'll start walking."

Billie played a game as he walked to Dawn's house. He had walked there several times and always loved the excitement and expectation that accompanied the walk. The game he played was to find a can. Then, while he was walking, he kicked the can over any concrete, across the front yards to Dawn's house. Driveways and sidewalks, anything the can hit, or skimmed off of the concrete was a failure. This game was not a point of off or on; it was a win lose: if he hit the concrete with the can, any concrete, he was out. But if he kicked the can to his destination, over the last concrete and into that flowerbed or the green lawn, then Billie won. It helped pass the time and made him concentrate on the walk. He was excited, and he needed to walk slowly as not to get there too soon. He really was patient for his age, he thought. He wondered why no one had written that in his yearbook: 'patient and methodical.' He smiled to himself and thought of Dawn's red lips pressed against his and open.
Dawn was changing into a dress. Bip walked in just as she let the dress drop to conceal her body.
"Sis, are you going to wear that to the circus? That's kind of dressy."
"I'm not going to the circus, Bip."
Bip's feelings were hurt. He wanted her to be with him. He felt kind of empty now. She felt empty, too.
"I'm going to stay here, Bip."
He knew she'd made up her mind.
"What're you gonna do all alone. Mama's going to town. Maybe even in to Grandville, she says."
"She is going into Grandville. She already told me. I'm just gonna hang out and maybe do some things for myself." She smiled at Bip and he smiled back. He went over and hugged her. They didn't hug much. A tear was flowing down her cheek and they both began to cry quietly but deep and exhaustive until Bip heard the honk of Crenshaw's horn.
"I love you, Sis." He looked her in the eye. She rubbed his head and reached in her purse and got out a five-dollar bill.

"Bring me back some cotton candy and use the rest for you something."

Bip took the five-dollar bill and ran out the door wiping his nose on his sleeve. As he was getting in Crenshaw's car, she heard Crenshaw say, "Who the hell gave you money. We ain't buying a bunch of junk …" and the door closed and the car clicked into gear, rolled out of the driveway and started toward the Circus.

"Honey, you OK." Mary was standing at the door looking at Dawn.

"It's just hard, mama." She didn't know what to say.

"I don't think it's really hit me yet, honey. I don't think it will until later. Or at night." She smiled a 'I'm trying to be happy in spite of all the confusion' smile at Dawn. "You sure you don't want to go? You don't want to be alone?"

"I'm sure mama." She feigned a smile back.

Mary left the house in a Sunday dress and with her black purse and black mid-heeled shoes. She 'goodbyed' from the back door and was gone. Seconds after, Dawn heard a tiny tapping on the back screen door.

She sighed and stood up and straightened her dress and went to the back door. She considered whether she wished she wouldn't have called now, but Billie was standing there wide-eyed with a twig of bush pushed into his hair. Dawn smiled but didn't laugh.

"Were you hiding in the bushes?"

Billie shook his head, "Yes."

Dawn was glad he didn't talk.

She crossed her lips with her finger, which told him not to talk, and she slowly lifted the dress up and off of her body. Instead of smiling or hooting, Billie simply dropped his jaw and drank her in. There was a desperate calmness in their glances as if they knew something that words would only confuse. He opened the door and she turned slowly and led him to her bed where she laid down and pulled him on top of her. He had undressed shoe by shoe by sock by sock by pants by shirt on his way through the house.

If they could have held each other any closer, he would have been behind her.

CHAPTER 7

▼

OUTLAW THE SHEPHERD

The circus grew from the West Texas soil like Adam's ribs, a cage curved against the sky then covered with stretch canvas over the dirt parking lot of the co-op cotton gin. The banner arched over the highway that ran into Flatland: "The World's Greatest Big Top." The ambiguity lay in "Greatest;" it was not greatest; it was comprised mostly of illegal aliens with fraudulent work visas. With the coupons from the parade in hand, the people of Flatland began to mill back and forth on the highway like ants on a path between an Oreo and the mound to try to catch glimpses of the Albino Gorilla.

The coupon resembled a dollar bill with the face of the Albino Gorilla in a mug shot on the front. On the back of the coupon was the gruesome story of how the Albino Gorilla had pulled the young girl against the bars and killed her in some far away town. The description of the murder was poetic, saying, "He pulled her against the bars with a ring, and the limp body fell to the ground twisted like fresh green roots." So all day, all that the town could think about was the circus. The Albino Gorilla was a true monster capable of most anything.

The carnies pulled out the cage using Zorbinetta, the elephant. They stopped just by the banner next to the highway and uncovered the gorilla. He was shackled to the bars making him look very Frankenstein-like: a passionate idiot who now was as calm as water, chained and caged and misunderstood; some even expected a scarlet M, for murder, to be braided on his white chest. But he seemed to accept his lot in the cage and played his part by sporadically making deep jungle sounds from the inside of his chest.

The vehicles began to stop and the families poured out of their vans and station wagons, and from the backs of pickup trucks, and they walked carefully to the gorilla cage. It was there that the carnies started their work, raising their voices through megaphoned mouths. And by secretive controls, they started the lights on the rides; the smell of the corndogs and cotton candy seeped from the windows of food trailers that now had happy clowns peering out, hawking their goods as the "Best On the Circus Midway."

Past the gorilla cage, the carnies had their ticket stand where they sold tickets to the circus and also for all the rides that circled the tent. To enter any of the fantasyland at all you had to purchase an entry ticket, after which you had to walk beneath the thirty foot balloon figure: OUTLAW THE SHEPHERD. Several of the less fortunate children were destined to watch the entire event from outside the temporary wire fence, only dreaming of what lay inside.

Outlaw the Shepherd's balloon figure was thin and wobbly, under-inflated, a strange, almost bowing balloon man; he had canes in both hands, however, that seemed to just hold him up.

Outlaw was the main attraction—a circus prophet. His balloon body swayed and sagged in the sky like a deflated god, and it was a bit unnerving to cross under his figure into fantasyland, especially since the only way in was to walk between his legs. Very few patrons could resist the urge to look up into his balloon crotch as they passed under.

Once through the gate inside the circus yard, anything familiar disappeared. The lights chased each other across the rides reflecting lemon and cherry across the faces of mothers and fathers and children. Young children even reached for their mothers' throats to try to touch the changing colors. And the Oompa music from the carrousel carried and mixed and mingled with the aroma of coconut-oil popcorn, pizza with hand-squeezed tomatoes, and the sweet red webs of cotton candy. In dark corners, the smell of whiskey and Coke sat on the air like a heavily drowned decision.

Stirred up dust under the feet of the patrons was the only familiar smell; thus, the carnival was exotic and more mysterious than even Len's death and the mystery mangling of the child by the Albino Gorilla.

After the men had provided their families with the obligatory ride or two, and stocked each member's hands with Cokes in sweating wax cups and hot dogs loaded with chili wrapped in white tissue, they gathered their families together like loose change and worked their way to the funnel that popped each family, one-by-one into the tent.

Inside the tent was even more mysterious.

Inside, the heavens were hung in a spider web of rope and wires crawling with bodies swinging, catching, some merely sitting like dressed up monkeys on tall poles and grappling lines. The floor, hours before just a cotton field, was strewn with cedar chips and had now mixed with the dung and urine of the exotic animals. Pandora's cedar box had been spilled across the west Texas sand.

Most of the men, their primitive instincts aroused, began to alertly race their eyes around to search for danger to protect their brood. Several of the circus women sitting the patrons down were very beautiful and had very little on, so the conversation then turned to twisted pictures of great circus orgies which lasted into the night after each show, and the men pictured every combination: the roasted peanut girls with the sad-faced clowns, contortionists with the trapeze artists making love in mid-air between catches, the stilted man with the tightrope walkers, the ticket girls with the lion tamer, and finally the midgets and the dog lady with anyone who would have them.

The crowd sensed the beginning was near and engaged in frantic purchasing. Others began rounding up children as the band began to reel as the lights dropped. One teenage couple, unable—or unwilling—to control their passion with the lowering of the lights, chose to slither under the bleachers and out of a seam in the tent to grope in the darkness under the big flat sky. They explored each other's bodies with passion and caring while their parents sat staunchly in the anxious circus tent stiffly holding hands.

Crenshaw was just beginning to sit down as the ring announcer entered the center ring; Crenshaw was obviously overloaded with the purchases of Bip.

"Goddernit, Bip, sit down! And quit grabbin' on my leg. Don't do that." He squeezed Bip's leg. "Like that, dammit."

"Ow! Pawpaw!!" Bip responded.

"Does that feel good?"

"No, sir."

"All right, then, Goddernit, don't do it."

Bip was used to Crenshaw's temper when he was in tight situations and Crenshaw had really not squeezed Bip that hard anyway.

Crenshaw turned to make sure the bleachers were still under him before he sat down just as Bip dropped his chili dog. Bip did manage to catch most of it as it bounced off his lap.

"Here! Here. I'll take care of that," Crenshaw hated a mess or to get his hands dirty. Still, he wiped the chili off of Bip's lap while under his breath he cussed the chili vender. "Goddern circus shit." Then, he looked at Bip. There were small tears in Bip eyes. Bip felt he was doing the best he could; he was just excited was all. Crenshaw reminded himself to Bip, he said, "We're here to get your mind off your daddy." He looked at Bip with puppy-dog eyes, sorry for being so abrupt with Bip.

"It's all right, Paw Paw." Bip smiled up at Crenshaw and took a bite of his chili dog that immediately squeezed a blop of chili out that plopped on Bip's leg. He smiled a chili and mustard mustache up at Crenshaw.

Just as Crenshaw looked back to the center ring, the ring announcer mouthed the microphone and the last of the work lights fell black except for the one bright spotlight on each ring.

"Ladies and Gentlemen, Circus Vargas is proud to present for your entertainment," and Crenshaw pulled the greasy white sheet that had held the chili dog and wadded it up and threw it under the bleachers. The ring announcer continued in the center ring.

The rings featured twisting, new, young entertainers—daughters and sons of the circus veterans. They were dressed in tightly fit tumbling outfits and were well-rehearsed but lacked entertainer's meat. In ring one were the Junior Jugglers. The girls were actually better jugglers than the young boys were. The boys struggled and missed beats; however they never dropped anything, which made them more interesting than the smooth agility of the young ladies. Selmer, sitting just behind Crenshaw, leaned over to his sons and told them what losers they were since they were merely watching the event rather than being at home practicing some art so that they might earn money with their talents. Neither of Selmer's sons heard him; they merely nodded as they concentrated on the budding breasts of the young girls. Bip even asked Crenshaw how old he thought the girls were and Crenshaw told Bip that Mexican girls develop early and would just eat too many tortillas and explode like a bucket of lard when they reached Quinceañera.

In the ring to Crenshaw's left was a group of trampoline artists. Although they were very new to their craft and missed most of the hard passes, they did not lack passion. One even straddled the springs by accident. He waved with his left hand while holding himself with his right as he was being carried off.

Center ring was a just-below-advanced juggler who was very good, but he was so interested in the difficulty of his passes that he ignored showmanship and expected too much applause for his sawing of the air, catching his planets and universes. He made it look too easy.

Paul entered the tent during the parade that followed the jugglers and trampo-line artists led by two of the pregnant clowns who held hands and looked like Tweedle Dee and Tweedle Dum. Paul looked around confused. Seeing the rest-ing elephants in the corner, Paul ventured further into the belly of the tent, walk-ing without intent. Just off sweeping the shop and with the lights flashing and the smells confusing him, Paul wandered recklessly around the tent like a pinball bouncing back and forth from section to section; he finally settled without thought in the all black section.

They didn't mind and neither did Paul.

Paul, the one white, was perched in the hills and valleys of blackness, he seemed singled out in a sea of floating white smiles.

Suddenly, the tent went black—totally black just as big fat Betsy Fancher was sitting down with her three chili dogs.

"God, that woman is fat," Selmer said as if he had forgotten just how big Betsy was.

"Shhhh. You want her to hear you? She's got feelings, you know," Tabot reminded Selmer.

"Well, if she does, she's got 'em hidden pretty well. Hell, they'll probably offer her a job after the show and the town will be left to raise her little Jimmy Todd." Selmer shifted in his chair and pulled at his pant's waist. He didn't like being rep-rimanded. 'She really is fat,' he thought again to himself.

Her legs were so large that they rubbed together like a millstone grinding corn to meal, and her femininity was lost somewhere beneath her rolls of fat since she had given birth to little Jimmy Todd in November. With the lights off, she could not see where she was sitting, and off balance, she sat down full on Jimmy Todd who was now, if he survived, six months old.

The muffled shriek broke the darkness and everyone frantically eyeballed the darkness. The parents were uncomfortable, wondering where the murder was taking place, but the children marveled, holding their hands in front of their faces, blowing streams of air to see if they could feel the pressure. The tenseness grew: the patrons were rigid on their wooden seats; the teens outside the tent froze in twisted embraces; the peanut ladies fell silent in their hawking.

In the midst of the hush, "Outlaw the Shepherd" was brought up in tall glit-tery letters lit by one burning white eye of light.

With the light finally on, Betsy stood up, frantically knowing full well that Jimmy Todd was almost wedged between her buttocks. Selmer started to grab the child but thought better of himself and reluctantly, wanting to look away but unable to, watched as Betsy fished the child to safety and readjusted her skirt. Jimmy Todd was fine—a bit winded—but fine. Everyone knew the event was over as she lifted the little body up with one arm like a sacrifice while lifting a chili dog with the other.

The people's attention rolled back down to the ring. Miraculously, the actual Outlaw the Shepherd had replaced the sign.

The white eye of the spotlight bleached Outlaw's thin body. Outlaw rubbed his eyes like a grandfather chipmunk pulled from a decaying hollow oak. The children rejoiced to find their lost eyesight, now moving their fingers and mouths in each other's faces in confirmation of the light.

Outlaw the Shepherd was an old circus prophet. Half of his face was tattooed black, and the other side white. He was an ex-clown who had given up the facade of the tragi-comdedian. He stood as a raw human paradox committed to the inner battle between darkness and light: a strange marriage of "Sun and Moon," just as the program had described—had anyone bought one. His hair stuck out in gray wires. His features were as stark as an iron sculpture; he possessed an exaggerated heaviness aged by the rust of time, of sun, and of burdensome knowledge. He face was an apple left in the sun, once full and red, now had deflated; his skin like bark merely draped over his bones; he was feeble, frail, and broken. But he stood as proud as any prophet in his condition might, as well as say Tiresias might stand, knowing what horrible secrets he knew.

Lilith shivered. She knew the Outlaw. Bip sensed something too, although he simply thought in his innocence that it was the chili from the hot dog or even the last ride on the Tilt-O-Whirl. He belched inside his mouth and it burned his nose.

The Outlaw carried two canes to direct his crippled feet. He carried "The Devil's Cane" in his right hand—a red glitter cane made of mesquite which was topped with a rattlesnake's head. "God's rod" was in his left hand, a white cane with white dove feathers glued top-to-bottom with one all-seeing diamond eye on the handle.

He stood in the spotlight, white as a single star surrounded by the darkness.

The crowd sat in an electric silence waiting for him to do something, but for the longest time he merely stood and looked accusingly at the audience. Some began to fidget. He didn't agitate the children. In fact, they were quite content to just marvel in his mystery and to watch their parents squirm.

Finally there was movement. Outlaw the Shepherd lifted his canes and balanced on his crippled legs; he spread the canes as far apart as his arms could reach across time, and slowly he brought the canes closed together. He shook and strained. When they touched, Bip felt a shock run through his body, just like the shock he felt when Lilith had made the stick man. He thought he might even throw up. Ice blue and hot red sparks shot out and showered over the unmoving Outlaw the Shepherd. Bip's eyes burned.

"That's gonna set his ass on fire," Tabot said out of the side of his mouth to Crenshaw who was now practically sitting like a mother hen on his grandbaby boy, Bip.

"The crazy idiot's gonna set the tent on fire is what's gonna happen. And then what's he gonna do?" Crenshaw said.

"Shhhhh. He's fixin' to say something," a voice from above in the bleachers quietened everyone.

Outlaw's mouth contorted and lifted at the corners and finally became a big wide "O". Then, he abruptly started to spew out words as if he were speaking in tongues; none made a complete sentence. He stood as a spewing fragment of a man trying to pass universal truths through code and fire and sparks and blinding spotlights posed dramatically against pitch blackness: he was a single man against the darkness who was determined and would, even if his legs folded beneath him, remain committed to his craft of prophecy.

"He's snagdoodleing," Bip said in amazement.

"What in the hell is 'snagdoodleing?'" Crenshaw asked his grandson.

"What Miss Ester does at the Assembly of God."

"What does this crazy circus idiot *do*?" Crenshaw was now asking Tabot and the others behind him what significance the Prophet pretended, and if they should pack up and leave before the crazy jackass killed himself there in front of God and everybody.

"Evidently he stands around," Tabot said. He was a bit put out with the "Outlaw" himself. Tabot considered himself a decent judge of quality entertainment.

The "O's" stopped. The "snagdoodleing" stopped. And Outlaw stood firm and proud—just before he fell face down to the ground in a monumental conniption.

He lay on his face with his nose in the exact center of the center ring. As the conniption grew, he traveled around the ring on his belly as an oxymoronic, stiff-but-loose, epileptic snake. Once in a while he would flip over on his back and spit red and roll his eyes back in his head, then he would flip back to his belly to rub his face in the dirt. Then, once again, he would continue to snake forward around the ring.

As suddenly as he began, he stopped.

He was exhausted.

Only after several minutes did his body grow erect as slowly as the balloon fig-ure representation of him that stood recklessly in the sky outside. Once he was as tall as he could lift himself, his head rolled back as sad as a full moon, and his mouth opened, and his eyes were full of tears.

He had had the vision.

He said quietly and soberly, "Love one another."

Three words. And his face fell stiffly forward, not even bothering to catch his fall, again face into the dirt, his nostrils blowing miniature whirlwinds out that breezed against his clothes and finally settled, caught in the palms of his deter-mined fists.

"What'd he say?" Crenshaw asked Tabot, "Glub a pucker? What the hell does that mean? Crazy jackass clown."

"No. Not Glub, 'Love,' I think" Selmer said from behind as he took a wad of popcorn and stuffed it in his mouth. "This is good corn."

"Love a pucker? Well, what the hell is that? Is that some more of that 'snag-doodleing,' Bip?" Crenshaw turned on Bip. Bip was sweating. He looked at Lilith. She seemed to see Bip but did not necessarily acknowledge him.

From behind Crenshaw, Walter rose his voice to Crenshaw, "Love one another, stupid."

"Well, hell. That's from the Bible. That ain't nothing new," Crenshaw said terribly disappointed. "You'd at least expect new news from a prophet," he said to Bip.

The allusive haunting of the moment was completely broken as the carnival band broke into a twisting, chromatic upheaval of notes in a traditional circus fanfare completely erasing Outlaw the Shepherd's appearance.

CHAPTER 8

▼

KEESHA'S NOSE

As suddenly as Outlaw the Shepherd's performance had begun, it was over. He immediately seemed a dream. The children and parents wondered if they had indeed seen the prophet, or if he had somehow appeared to all of them in one mass hallucination.

Still, at least now everything seemed back to normal, and replacing the prophet center stage were three young ladies who were dressed in bathing suits which the costume designer, Velma Luis Felix Hernandez, had drowned in sequins and sparklies. The ladies bedazzled and posed and pointed around behind fake smiles like prima donnas. The ropes lowered from the sky of the tent.

The Flying Angelinas were three Mexican sisters—it was even rumored at one time that they were fallen nuns—who swung around on ropes hooked only by their teeth. The children in the audience, if they didn't see their parents looking, made snarling, biting faces unconsciously as they watched the sisters stuff the ends of the ropes into their mouths, and the three ladies lifted off the soil. The ropes stretched, finally pulled firm. The Angelinas' legs shot out in dramatic poses. Crenshaw worked very hard not to look straight into the crotches of the women but didn't do very well. Still, he checked once in a while to make sure Bip was not watching him watch the ladies.

Just as the three Angelinas were spinning off into the heavens, arms thrown out in a triple crucifix, their legs spread, and their teeth firmly in their heads, a loud scream, a true scream of a child, was heard over the kaleidoscopic band.

A little back girl, Kheesa, was dancing as if possessed just in front of Lilith.

She rolled in the dirt, then she stood, then she rubbed her face furiously against the clothing of anyone near her and then repeated the whole order.

The whites tried to ignore the outburst at first. They had seen similar outbreaks during basketball games and community church Thanksgiving picnics. But this time it was different. Keesha was in obvious possession. After several more passes through the crowd, thrashing and rubbing, she stood staunchly in front of Paul and cocked her head back.

Aimed directly at Paul, stuck in her left nostril hole, was a tamale, not a dinner, table-type tamale, but a long, cylindrical-shaped, cinnamon-flavored, red-hot candy.

Paul saw the red end in her swollen nose and looked around pleadingly for a mother to give her consent for him to help her. All the women turned their eyes except for Lilith. She stared into Paul's eyes. Entranced, Paul looked to the little boy sitting beside Kheesa—they called him "Biscuit"—he merely popped another candy tamale into his mouth and shrugged his shoulders.

Keesha danced back over in front of Paul.

"Thay's a oven inside my nose!" Keesha screamed. "It's hurtin' like thay's matches in my nose hole!" She uncontrollably convulsed as she wiggled underneath the bleachers in her continued possession.

"Cooome heeere," Paul said authoritatively. Then, he added sternly, "Up!" Keesha looked sadly through the slats of the bleachers. She was afraid.

Across the tent Crenshaw and Tabot and Walter were already trying to figure out the connection between her conniption and that of Outlaw the Shepherd and decided that the two almost parallel acts must indeed have some cosmic significance.

Keesha gathered her strength into a tiny ball, tamed by Paul's voice, and rolled out like a little kitten, wobbly and stray and scrawny. Paul lifted her the rest of the way between the slats, knocking her knees on the wood and sat her on his leg.

"Cloooose yoouuur eyes."

"Don't you hurt her," a voice behind Paul started in, but, of course, Paul didn't hear.

"That Paul Boy. He know what he doin'," Lilith said over her shoulder. She protected Paul.

The little girl cocked her head back, her eyes closed, crying silently except for an occasional starting-all-over cry. With the air passing roughly through her open nostril, Keesha pointed the tamale over Paul's shoulder, across the crowd, and the swinging Angelinas and their strong teeth.

Paul pulled his barber scissors from his shirt pocket case and positioned himself in front of her.

"You gonna cut her nose hole?" Demetria Jones stood with one firm hand on her hip and her head gyrating. "Oh, Lordy. He gonna cut up her nose hole. Lord forbid. Get a doctor, girl." She poked Lilith who was taking a drink from her bottle. "That deaf white man done gone crazy thinking he a doctor now." She gyrated her head on "doctor" and "now."

Paul grabbed the end of the tamale with the points of the scissors.

"Thaaaaat huuuurrt?"

"Oh, Lordy! God, Lord, baby Jesus, yes! Yes, sir!" Kheesha squirmed just with her body and held her head erect and unmoving. Paul jerked away with the scissors and the tamale came out, stuck on the points of the scissors.

"O.K." Paul made a big O.K. sign by meeting his fingers in a circle.

Keesha hugged Paul and kissed his head.

"How you know he *not* gonna cut her nose hole, girl?" Mrs. Jones asked Lilith. Lilith didn't answer.

Keesha was just leaving to go snort some water up her nose to get rid of the burn when she heard the tamale ding against the metal frame of the bleachers.

"Can I keeps it?" She ran back to Paul who was cleaning the points of his scissors. She dug in the sawdust. She retrieved it and put it in her pocket.

She started up the bleachers, but stopped part way up and turned and looked as if she might say, "Thank You."

Instead, she affirmed, "I won't eats it."

But Paul, not expecting any more than the kiss, had already turned back around to see the finale of the spinning angels who now appeared drunk and tired and worn out as they were lowered to the earth which rose to meet them.

With the crisis solved, Flatland wiggled down into the wooden bench seats as if they were in bean bag chairs and watched the artists finish their work.

The circus became relaxed, and now the audience, even after an artist missed a trick on the trapeze, cheered and insisted that the performer try again. The boy, the Amazing Antonio, attempted a triple somersault six times and was on the verge of giving up until the audience cheered him on through to a seventh attempt. Fatigued and now possessed with succeeding, he attempted the feat one last time and was caught by one arm. It dislocated his shoulder. His courage brought the audience to their feet. He stood heroically balanced on the wire next to his high box and waved his good hand, but he never made reference to his limp right side.

The parade of elephants was the last ritual, and the clowns, who should have been tired, were somewhat revived and even peppy. Their physical affectations seemed to lift from their bodies as they followed the elephants. They meandered in and out of the dung in skips and hops and playful jumps, following as the empty Coke cups and wadded-up popcorn sacks compacted under the heavy feet of the elephants. Finally Zorbinetta, who was now sporting a fine pink bow to accentuate her femininity, towered above the other two elephants and the zebras. She was pulling the Albino Gorilla's cage through the exotic smells and sounds of applause. Still shackled, the gorilla was not peaceful. In fact, he was shaking the bars and roaring a voice that made all who watched him pass whisper into each other's cupped ears. Many merely sat in awe and pointed.

Finally the gorilla passed Paul.

Paul didn't recognize it as a Gorilla at first, so he waved. Then, he drew back his hand.

He laughed at himself.

Paul was always honest, even in his mistakes.

Across the tent Bip watched Paul sit down. He had helped the girl and simply been Paul.

"PawPaw, what do you know about Paul?"

"I know he'll cut your hair too damn short if you don't tell him medium." Crenshaw was past conversation.

"He was in a dream I had last night. He's eating peanuts now, PawPaw."

"Hush. Watch the elephants." Crenshaw hushed Bip in a stern but thoughtful way and patted his leg. "Paul is a good person, Bip." He knew that was what Bip was asking, or at least he thought that was what Bip was asking. Anymore, he never knew.

CHAPTER 9

▼

THE DRAG

Dawn made Billie turn into the Burger Barn and stop by all the other cars. The cars lined the front of the parking lot and faced the street and watch "the drag." They turned on their lights as a show of some linear power, and the lights caught the group across the street. Across the street, forearms rose to cover eyes and they glared back; they were the science club and student Government type. They parked across from the Burger Barn in the Flatland Florist's drive.

The Burger Barn lot had the best lighting, so that's where the cheerleaders and athletes stopped and anyone else who elevated to visual coolness.

"Is this the only car your grandfather has?"

Dawn hated driving up in the Buick station wagon. She wished Billie would work at the grocery store more hours so he could make payments on a car.

Billie worked at the store because his father was dead; his mother had left him and his five sisters with his grandfather. Billie and his grandfather, who was the shine-man, raised the four little girls; however, Billie always managed to keep out enough money to get Dawn some perfume, or money for a date, or a shirt or something. He wanted her to have nice things.

"I'll get a good car after we graduate and I can work full-time."

"What about your scholarship offers," she always threw out his leash and jerked him back just as he was about to feel freedom.

"After graduation … during next summer … You know what I mean. You always do that."

Raegene ran up and knocked on the passenger-side window. She was wearing her cheerleader outfit.

Raegene had Firestix candy color hair and fingernails to match. She had extremely long legs and was traffic-stop beautiful.

"Coach Lucy said, 'feel comfortable with our outfits before cheer practice even started.' So, I'm wearing it once a week just to get used to it." She stepped back far enough and curtsied and the two boys behind her whistled at her. She turned around quickly so the skirt would rush around to catch her waist, and then having gone too far, back up, show her panties, then drop like a quick quarter peep show.

"She is such a slut," Dawn said half under her breath and Billie almost heard it.

Raegene was thinking the same phrase about Dawn.

"Dawn?" Billie asked.

"Huh," I'm sorry. I was thinking.

She had been in her own mind on a gyre downwards. She had gone from thinking Raegene was a slut to what Raegene had to do to concoct her story so she could wear her cheerleading skirt and rub in the fact that Dawn wasn't a cheerleader even though she had tried out after Raegene convinced her to when they were eating at Taco City and Raegene asking her why her Mom and Dad had not put Dawn in gymnastics, because they were divorced at the time and money was short, but then Len came back at the reunion to Mary and Len …

Her daddy was dead.

She tried so hard to hold back the tears.

"What's wrong, Baby," Billie saw her shaking. "Don't worry 'bout Raegene."

"Daddy."

"I know, Baby." Billie didn't know what to say. "You want to go?"

"Do you mind taking me home?"

"I don't mind," Billie hesitated, "It's not me, is it?"

"No." She said. She grabbed his hand and lifted it and kissed the back.

"No. What?" He wondered if he had thought out loud.

"It's not you."

"OK." Billie knew when to let something drop.

The car squeaked and rattled out of the lot. Billie accidentally caught the back tire on the curb by mistake.

"Goddamit! I hate this!" Dawn exploded. She hit her fists against her legs over and over and screamed. "I'm tired of losing people! Goddamit! Goddamit!"

"Do you want me to stop," Billie asked. Everything had been chaos.

"Billie, honk the horn!"

Dawn always honked the horn of Billie's Buick to vent her frustration. The horn was an incredibly loud minor-thirteenth chord. The dissonance resonated against walls and bounced dead, back in the grass, and Dawn reached over and honked the horn over and over on the way home and said "Goddamit" between honks. She didn't usually use the Lord's name in any fashion, much less in vain, but tonight she felt God had turned his head and walked far away and left her world in darkness. Like a newborn wailing in an empty dark church, her honks and curses rang and fell on nothingness. Billie drank his chocolate Oak Farms milk and sat still and drove and watched Dawn honk and "Goddamit" her way past the park by Hicks street where her house was fourth down on the left.

Billie stayed silent and silent and silent.

They arrived at the house. Dawn kissed him quickly, honked one last honk, super "Goddamitted" one last time, and said, "Life's just peachy, ain't it." Billie just smiled a gratuitous smile at her sarcasm. Billie was winding up to go to work the night shift as Dawn was winding down to dream.

CHAPTER 10

▼

THE SEARCH

"If Paul drives, then Tabot can ride shotgun," Walter said.

The argument had been going on for some time. The four men pulled and pushed the conversation back and forth like taffy. They failed to notice the clouds above them turn from white clay globs, to pink, to burning orange, and finally to a red, eaten by shadows.

"C'mon, it's getting dark. We don't want to be down there too late," Crenshaw said. He was standing behind Paul. He looked at the back of Paul's head. He added, "Paul can't hear. He shouldn't drive."

"We're doing the right thing. Len would want his killer in jail before he's laid to rest," Tabot said. He was actually still trying to justify going into the Black community after dark. James had been hidden just well enough so that the police had been absolutely ineffective in finding him.

"Why's the funeral so dang far away, Crenshaw? Still got three days until—" Walter just realized that Len was a bit like a Greek hero, dead but unburied and roaming the earth waiting for his final rites. Then, he thought of Hamlet in a sort of stream of consciousness … "Hamlet's daddy roamed around 'till his death was avenged by his son. That's kinda what you're doing, Crenshaw, ain't it?"

"We're waiting on Len's brother in Alaska. He works pipeline and it takes time to get him the message and then for him to get to the airport and get here. It just takes time is all," Crenshaw answered Walter's original question.

"Paul, let's go," Tabot said loudly behind Paul who was standing with his back to Crenshaw waiting for some decision to be made.

All Paul knew was that he was driving, which was fine with him.

"I'll ride up front with Paul," Crenshaw finally said across the roof of Paul's green Mercury Marquis. "You two ride in the back," Crenshaw added, which was stupid unless three were going to ride shoulder-to-shoulder in the front while one rode alone in the back.

"Crenshaw. Tell Paul 'let's go,'" Tabot said as he got in the back seat.

Walter tapped Paul's shoulder.

Paul got in and lowered his tilt steering just to touch his pants and adjusted his mirror.

"Think this car's long enough? The blacks are going to want to buy it right out from under us," Crenshaw said as he continued to fumble with his seatbelt.

"You expecting a fast ride, Crenshaw?" Tabot said from the back seat as he lit a cigarette and held the end up by the crack in the window.

All of the men were uneasy, except for Paul. He was driving slowly pretending to whistle. He had see a man whistle in a movie once and decided that that was suave. So, now when he wanted to be suave and cool-headed, he would poke out his lips in a whistle. However, Paul didn't know that to whistle one had to blow, that there was also sound involved with the protrusion of the lips. No one knew, then, what Paul was doing pushing and pulling his lips in and out except Paul.

"Paul's making that goofy face again," Crenshaw reported to the back seat.

"We're all nervous, Crenshaw," Tabot responded.

Crenshaw had been in the Black community daily for some ten years delivering milk. He was the type to simply deliver and collect and did not converse to any extent, except to say "Is this your dog I'm fixin' to kill?"

It was Crenshaw who knew where to look for the murderer. Walter was along out of civic duty as a member of the city council. He felt it was his moral obligation and a plus for reelection.

Paul stopped at the stop sign.

"Turn on his lights," Tabot said from the back seat.

Instead of trying to tell Paul, Crenshaw just reached over and turned them on himself. The covered lights folded up like two eyelids.

The long green car stretched through the town toward the tracks.

Walter, in spite of no one recognizing him in the back seat of Paul's car and it being dusk, was still waving at every car and pedestrian they passed.

"Turn here, Paul," Crenshaw bumped Paul and pointed left. "And back to the right here," he poked him again.

Paul turned off of the highway and the car shook and bounced onto the unpaved road and then back to the left between a row of shacks.

George Washington Carver Blvd., which was not a boulevard at all, was lined with houses built of scrap wood and old asbestos siding. Being dark now, only movement could be seen around the houses; and the figures being dark, it was hard for the four in the car to discern if anyone was looking at them. Some of the figures seemed to disappear in and out of holes in the walls, and once in a while, Paul's lights would catch a pair of eyes and the figure would freeze like a cat or a Jack Rabbit caught in the light.

When their eyes would shine, Walter, out of unchecked habit, would wave.

"Would you cut it out, Walter?" Tabot finally said. "They can't even see in," he added.

"This is it, Paul," Crenshaw started but remembered Paul couldn't hear so he touched his arm and mouthed, "Stop."

"I wish you'd stop being deaf," Crenshaw added.

"He lives here?" Walter asked. There were at least twenty cars outside the shack. Cadillacs with furry dashboards and veneer gold-plated hubcaps. Three black men and one young black girl were standing outside drinking Schlitz Malt Liquor from a quart, passing the bottle. The girl was dressed in just a muscle shirt and short Levi's. Her full lips reached out and caught the opening of the bottle and the men listened to the gurgle of the fizzy beer burn down her throat.

"This is where I think he is," Crenshaw corrected Walter.

"This is L.M.'s," Tabot knew where he was. They had raided the illegal bar only two weeks before. "I'm not very popular in there."

"How do you know this is L.M.'s?" Walter asked surprised.

Crenshaw, not knowing to whom the question was directed, answered, "Alcoholics drink a lot of milk in the morning."

They all sat like weighted mannequins in the Mercury.

L.M.'s was the social gathering house for the blacks who wanted to drink. Most of the time the club was rather lively and sometimes rough. The actual shack moved every few months after raids by the county police. After the raids, the bar was closed, and L.M. was arrested, fined, and soon released on bond. By arresting her every so often, the city did its duty to uphold morality but also gathered a part of L.M.'s revenue. Actually the law left the establishment alone most of the time because it did function as a sort a churchless fellowship hall for the Black community, a place to gather and to laugh.

The smoke carried out of the cracks between the walls, and the building seemed to be a living, breathing thing itself with its mouth opening once in a while to spit a patron out or swallow one in. When the mouth of the shack opened, the sound of voices would rise from its belly and then muffle as the spring would bring the screen door back with a smack. The two windows that sat on each side wall appeared as ears pushed tightly against a head. They had glass in only part of the panes. Inside the room it was bright, but smoky and hot, and the odor was of spilled liquor and sweat. But the cardboard smell of the card tables and the chalk from the cue sticks surfaced once in a while, and those smells were pleasant. There was one pool table and it was red felt and it was faded but clean and well maintained. The coin box was broken so when someone played a game they clinked a quarter in the Surefine coffee can that hung on the wall. Many men would change dollar bills for quarters in the can to make laundry money.

Crenshaw and Tabot and Walter were still sitting rigidly in Paul's parked car as Paul was cleaning his fingernails with his pocketknife.

"What? Are you blind, too? Turn off the lights," Crenshaw reached over Paul's arm and turned off the headlights. Paul had bumped a trashcan a bit stopping, put the car in reverse, backed up a bit, and then killed the engine.

"You think it's safe here?" Walter asked.

"Walter. It's not safe anywhere here," Crenshaw said.

"It'll be OK," Tabot tried to clam them down.

They all got out and stood with their bodies pressed to the green of the car like caramel on a candied apple. The three boys and the girl looked at them suspiciously but resumed their conversation about Tanika's cousin who was a chef on a cruise ship.

"Now, what's your plan, Crenshaw," Tabot whispered.

"The man's got to be here. It's the only refuse he has," Crenshaw explained.

"Refuge," Tabot corrected.

"OK. Where the hell would you go if you'd killed a man?"

"To jail," Walter answered.

"Hell no, you wouldn't! You'd go to this sleazy goddern place."

"Shoooould I Lo-Loock the Doooors?" Paul asked in full voice.

"Shhhh," Tabot shhhhed.

"You can't just 'shhhh.' You got to show him 'shhhh,'" Crenshaw crossed his lip with his finger. Paul reacted as usual. He feigned cowering like a beat dog then continued to talk in full voice and make the same amount of noise as he had been.

"No reason to lock the doors. They'll just break out the windows." Tabot explained to Paul making like a little spelunker hammering on a precious rock.

"What are we going to do? Knock on the door and say, 'Come out killer man?'" Walter started to realize the actual danger of the situation.

"That's why we brung Tabot," Crenshaw explained. Then, he turned around to tell Paul to lock the doors anyway, but Paul wasn't there. "Where's Paul?" Crenshaw asked calmly.

"He's…. Maybe he's on the other side of the car bending over," Tabot offered. They looked on the other side of the car.

"Paul. Paul!" Walter spotted Paul who was opening the door to LM's. "Paul!!" Tabot tried to call Paul back.

"He can't hear you, stupid." Crenshaw said, but actually was worried about Paul who opened the door and was swallowed in.

There was a large guffaw that bloated the building then fell to whispers and speculation. Tabot and Walter and Crenshaw only heard the barrage of words, making out a few: "I didn't now you's a drinker, deaf man" and, "Hey, they's the barber man that cain't talk" and, "What's wrong? You blind, too, Mr. Haircut."

Their ridicule fell in a rush, but all of it was delivered in a domesticated tone, indicating the basic acceptance of Paul's presence. Buffalo handed Paul his quart of malt liquor.

"Takes a drink," Buffalo said in a deep voice. Buffalo's belly was as big as two feather pillows stuffed under a white T-shirt covered with black-sock hose. Buffalo was smiling.

Paul knew Buffalo's generous offer was a test, so he drank a long drink.

Tabot and Crenshaw and Walter had, by this time made their way to the window outside and were peeking in.

"Move over," Crenshaw pushed Walter.

"'Shhhh,' Tabot 'shhhhh.'"

"Don't tell me, 'shhhh.' You, 'shhhh.'"

Inside they saw Paul lifting his arms above his head.

"I haaaave an aaan-aaanouncemeent," Paul slurred as authoritatively as he could.

The room was already relatively quiet, but to humor Paul they all sat very still and some even pretended to stop talking even though they weren't talking in the first place. In all reality, all that was going on was that a bunch of men, who happened to be black, had gathered with several cases of quarts and some cards and a pool table to help pass the summer heat for a few minutes.

"Get's up on the table," Cheetah said.

Most of the men in the black community went by the nickname of an animal; they felt it connected them back to their African roots. Cheetah was said to be the fastest man born. He had long lean legs with strong sinewy thighs.

Fox and Barracuda moved the snooker balls away to clear Paul room to stand on red felt of the pool table to make his announcement.

Buffalo made Paul take another drink of his quart before Paul moved toward the table. Buffalo had just gotten the bottle out of the huge metal cooler, which was a cow tank Hippo had welded and filled with ice-picked slabs of blocked ice. Buffalo twisted the cap just in front of Paul and offered Paul the first drink, so the beer was ice cold and fizzed in Paul's nose. Paul offered it back, but Buffalo made him take one more drink for good measure.

Paul nuzzled a few stripped balls with his toes as Black Widow and Possum directed Paul down on the table and scooted back for his testimony.

"Theeere's a m-m-m-maaaan's who K-k-Kiiilled Mr. Leeen Strip-Stiiip-laaaand. Heee"'s waaanted by the P-P-poooolice. Is Heee heeere?"

Paul's request was simple. He stood as a brave monument frozen in a dramatic pose surrounded by wide eyes. L.M. entered the room from the back. The room hushed and all the heads unconsciously bowed in reverence for the mother of vision.

Lilith could be a bitch when she wanted to be. She could muster power over the room because she owned it. And she could multiply that power by each bat of her eye.

"Go on and get outa here! 'Go on!' I said." She flailed her arms like a flag shredded in the wind.

Paul stood firm.

"'Go on!' And get your prissy ass white feets offa my pool table," she said. She was defending the sacred ground.

Lilith's power in the black community was revered; she was never questioned and never met any disobedience to her desire.

She moved toward Paul. Her skin was shiny from sweat and oil. Her fat body hung by the neck as the dapper of an overgrown bell dapper underneath the triangular, oversized dress she wore.

"What's the problem in here? Why's this mans on my table?" Lilith was defending the pack.

"A-a-a-a maaaan kiiilled Leeen," Paul said dramatically pointing his finger like an evangelist; he stood his ground. He wasn't totally sure what had been said up to this point, but he did feel the syrupy-thickness of the air.

"You's the deaf barber, ain't you?" Lilith calmed, sensing no immediate danger. She mouthed the words to Paul, not in jest but with conviction.

"Y-y-yeees Ma'aam," Paul said.

Paul had just developed a stutter now with this slur.

"Well, heaven sakes. Get on down offa that table." Lilith bunched her lips together like a wadded up rubber band. She held out her hand to Paul, and he, rather gingerly, hopped from the table to the slatted floor, careful not to hit the wood too hard else he might go clean through it and wake up in China. He partially knocked off one of his loafers and quickly stepped back into it and dusted himself, not out of necessity but out of courtesy as if to tidy himself.

Outside, Crenshaw and Tabot and Walter were crowded around the window. They could see the action, but they could not hear the conversation.

"She's fixin' to zap him," Walter said.

"Hell no. He's just a barber. Why would she zap a barber?" Crenshaw said.

"Some people just kill for pleasure, I'm telling you. That's Lilith in there. You remember that boy who disappeared last year?"

"The one who ran away," Tabot said and rolled his eyes.

"Well, I figure he wandered over 'cross the tracks and she pretty well took care of him."

Tabot had to switch the weight of his body. His foot was going to sleep.

"Switch places with me, Walter."

"I cain't see good out of my left eye. You know that," Walter said.

"Crenshaw?" Tabot asked Crenshaw.

"OK. But hurry. Come." Crenshaw ran like a awkward puppy crossing Tabot to his new position.

"Are you trying to say she killed that boy, Walter?" Tabot asked just as Crenshaw stopped and looked back into the window. "We investigated that, Walter. The real father took the child and ran away with him. That's very common."

"You mean to tell me Butch wasn't even Kelton's boy?" Walter almost stood up.

"Hush!!! Now, don't go spreadin' that around. Dana's had a hard enough time as it is."

"And she's a pretty girl. I didn't know she took to messin' around. Just goes to show you can never tell. You just can never tell, can you?" Walter said.

"Who's was it?" Crenshaw asked.

"Fob Johnson's." He said rather silently.

"Sonofabitch. Sonofabitch! Tell me you're kiddin'. Well, my Lord! He's got a pot belly twice mine."

"Weren't nothing in the paper about it," Crenshaw said.

"Well, that's 'cause the paper's got some class as to what needs to be public and what don't."

Suddenly Lilith grabbed Paul's head between her hands and her head fell back and her eyes rolled in her head like ice black marbles on a white plate rolling dangerously around the edges.

"She's cursing him to hell," Walter said.

"Cursing him?" Tabot questioned. "Well, good Lord."

"He'll never survive that," Walter added.

"She's fixin' to Voodoo Paul," Crenshaw added matter-of-factly.

"A Voodoo woman? Cursing him, like 'to hell' you say, or like hexing his family?" Tabot was taken in.

The bar was quiet now, except for Lilith's garbled gibberish, idiomatic language resembling speaking in tongues, but much more personal. Then, she cocked back her arm. The half moon of black fat attached under her arm dangled and then grew tight. Lilith slapped Paul so hard that his eyes disappeared to the back of his head and that he nearly bit part of his tongue off as he fell to the floor with the blood running from the side of his mouth onto the smooth wooden floor.

The bar stayed silent.

Paul slowly lifted his head from the wood floor still gathering from the heavy blow. He shook his head.

Lilith looked into his eyes with great compassion and whispered one word.

"Cornbread," she whispered.

Paul lay unmoving.

"Well?" she added.

Paul merely stared at her, blood running from his mouth.

"Hello," she whispered.

The blood dripped from his chin.

"OK. OK!" Lilith lifted her voice again, obviously very agitated. "It didn't work." She held out her arms. "He still can't hear me."

"Nooooo, Ma'aaam." Paul read her lips, still a bit afraid of another attack.

"Well, I'll be. Could'a sworn I had the heal today." Lillith pulled at her bra.

"He ain't stuttering nan's more," Fox offered reluctantly.

"That's right. He was a stuttering," Buffalo backed up Fox. "Say something, barber man," Buffalo got in front of Paul's face. Buffalo's eyes were almost lost in the rolls of black fat.

"Can I have another drink?" Paul wanted to wash the blood from his mouth.

"You was stuttering whens you comes in, Paul boy?" Lilith's attention was rekindled.

"Yeeees."

"That's right! And Lilly done healed you, boy!"

The bar became a great hoot-and-holler for a minute and Lilith handed out some free beers and even gave Paul a quart that had actually been touching the block of ice in the cooler.

Lilith raised her hand.

There was silence.

"What you want from us, Silent Man." Lilith's mood shifted uneasily. Paul marked the difference in her attitude. "You come to stack us one by one in the earth like buttons on a shirt? Take us all to jail?"

Paul stood firm.

"No?" She paused still waiting for a response. Paul said nothing.

"Sing me a song, Paul boy," Lilith was trying to keep Paul off guard. She wanted to know that he was trustworthy. She had trusted as good of men before and been taken advantage of. She wanted to know that Paul was only after the murderer but had no intention of dragging everyone else into the matter.

"I am here for Len's murderer," Paul said slurless, flawless, and stutterless.

"Sing it, 'I said!'" Lilith yelled. Her voice rose from her belly and through her heavy open chest.

The bar sat in electric silence as Paul sang, very badly, "I am here for Len's murderer." Lilith's eyes sat unmoving on Paul. He felt as if she were sitting on his chest. Her arm lifted mechanically.

"Well, I wouldn't quit your day job. He right over there," Lilith pointed and postured as if her arm was a ballerina's leg.

"Go with Paul, honey. It's the best for all us."

Buffalo and Black Widow were holding James, not too tight, but enough for James to know that the game was over. His time was up.

"He my gift to you Paul boy, 'cause you got the heart." Paul merely smiled at Lilith. He didn't want to be any hero; he just wanted what was right.

"Now gets out of here 'fore I shoot you."

Paul wasn't sure if that was a joke or a half-truth, but the two men left the bar, Paul carrying his half cold quart in one hand and holding the wrist of James, the murderer, with the other.

Crenshaw and Tabot and Walter fell from the window like a stack of cans toppled, and they snaked half-erect back to Paul's car.

James sat between Paul and Crenshaw all the way back to the jail. Paul handed the quart back and forth to the men. Nothing was said. Paul merely drove and stuck out his lips pretending to whistle.

CHAPTER 11

▼

THE CAPTURE OF CORNDOG

"You little son-of-a-bitch. You just think you're sweaty now!"

At first, Crenshaw decided to simply finish his milk route and let the profanity that vaulted over the house and tumble roughly down the asphalt shingles fade behind his back. However as milkman of Flatland, he was required to report any suspected foul play involving children. He stopped and listened. Nothing. He started walking again. Again he heard, "You sons-of-bitches look like shit." He stopped. In spite of his own general distaste for children, he still felt that they deserved to be treated with some respect and certainly not to be abused physically or verbally. He stopped and listened to discern the exact situation.

Crenshaw knew the voice was coming from Flora Hatchet's backyard.

"I'm thirsty, Miss Hatchet," a small voice climbed meekly over the roof.

"Well, I bet Jesus was thirsty on his way to the goddammed cross, too."

Miss Hatchet had never been married and was in her late fifties. She was perhaps the ugliest woman God had ever made. She looked like a gruff troll badly stuffed into the facade of a woman: she was very hairy, having only one eyebrow; she was squatty and had no figure to speak of, like a mutated overripe garden cucumber; and her voice always crawled through her throat over rocks and cactus.

Although Flora was aging and ugly, she did have two children. The little girl, Princess, had been in prison since she was in seventh grade. The boy, however, who was no less than seven foot tall, still lived with Flora and kept her convertible Corvette running. He worked for the city as animal control; he was the dog catcher. Most people of the city still believed that the children were the only two children since Jesus to be born of immaculate conception—others less religious or gentile said they were hatched from evolution. Still, Flora was tolerated because she really had good intentions under her stone hard outlook and also she had oil money.

The voice was obviously a young man's voice, eleven years old at the most. Crenshaw stopped to listen. He heard nothing for a moment, and again was just about to step forward and finish his route when he heard the crack of wood like it was slammed against a tree. It sent a shiver down his spine.

"Now, how'd that feel!?"

Crenshaw crouched; he waddled half-squatted to the curb, looked both ways as if he were going to tell an ethnic joke, and slid between two cars and ended prone-flat behind some roses parallel to Flora's fence. Crenshaw slipped left then right with his eye squinted to find a big enough knot hole in the fence to see what was going on. Finally, he saw Flora and a small herd of boys.

There were about ten boys, shirt tails out, with gloves, bat and ball, all in Scout uniforms; Flora was helping the boys to get their sports badge.

"Now slide! You see! Now we're lookin' like a goddamn team!"

"Miss Hatchet!" Crenshaw, himself a harsh enough man, was appalled, stood and yelled over the fence.

"Who said that?" Miss Hatchet looked accusingly at the sky.

"Over here," Crenshaw crawled up on the first tier of the fence and waved his arms. She could just see his head and chest.

"Well, scared me half to damn death. I thought Jesus was calling me home." She fanned her sweating face.

He saw Bip. "Bip, come here," Crenshaw called his grandson.

"Hello, Pawpaw. Watch this," Bip threw a ball up and attempted to catch it. He missed it and it hit his chest. Then, he ran over panting, rubbing his chest, his hat was pulled too far down which curled his ears out. He was sunburned on his cheeks and nose, and his lips were red and a bit puffed.

"Has Miss Hatchet been using foul language in front of you boys."

"Some, I guess."

"What'd she say."

"You told me not to say those words."

"Bip?" Crenshaw said raising his eyebrow.

"She called Willie a 'turd.'" Bip pointed at Willie and Willie waved to Crenshaw and swung his bat to show how much he had learned. He almost hit Carl in the back of the head.

"Did you call him a "turd!'"

"Son-of-a-bitch is a turd," Miss Hatchet clapped her hands and gave some more commands to the boys.

Across town, Watts was just sitting at his desk in the jailhouse. The jailhouse had six cells that were dark and smelled of metal and dust. They were not used very often except for drunks and for Princess between crime sprees. But since the murder, Watts had cleaned the cell with bleach and Pine Sol. He looked at James in the cell. James smiled. Watts knew that James would be in the cell for a while until his trial. Watts felt comfort knowing that James was in his cell and that the murder was behind them. James had signed a full confession although his lawyer had counseled him to plead not guilty which had confused James.

"Mister officer," James spoke from the cell. His black hands held the bars like a caged animal who didn't understand why he was imprisoned. His nose stuck out sadly between the bars.

"What do you need, James?" Watts was patient with James. He'd never had a real murderer in a cell before.

"Does you has any Spearmint gum?" James smiled. His cot dropped sadly toward the floor behind him like a drunkard's belly. There were no other prisoners.

"Do I look like a candy store, James? I swear, you beat everything. This morning you ask do I serve breakfast hot. Then you ask for coffee. James, I don't cater to no murderer. I ain't gonna give no murderer a piece of gum."

"Tabot told me not to commit to no crime."

"'Admit' to the crime, James. The word's 'admit.' You done already committed it and admitted to it."

"Is you sure that's right, 'admit' not 'commit'?" James was confused.

"Admit."

Watts was not trying to make things difficult for James. He was merely trying to make his point clear.

Just as Watts was pouring himself a cup of coffee wondering if there might be an old stray stick of Spearmint in the bottom of his file drawer, the door shoved open with a pop and scared Watts enough to spill most of his coffee on the floor.

The door had a problem sticking, and it made a sound, when opened, like a giant piece of cellophane tape being pulled from an enormous roll.

"Well, hell, Tabot, you scared the coffee out of my cup," Watts cleaned the coffee from his desk by running his palm over the desk glass then against the leg of his pants.

"You need to fix that door so it's easier to open," Tabot said as he moved to the cell.

"Let me in, Watts. I've got to talk to James."

Watts let Tabot into the cell.

Crenshaw by this time was in the backyard helping Flora train the boys and soon his language got almost as rough as hers, but the boys tried very hard to do the right thing by swinging their bats at the air, and by hitting their gloves with little closed fists. But soon they were bored and became more interested in the rollie-pollie bugs on the ground than the balls in the air.

The game was finally, totally called when the chicken stumbled under the back gate.

Flora was used to stray chickens wandering into her backyard. She lived a half a mile from an egg farm and the practice was that when the chicken stopped producing, then Russell, the retarded boy, was paid a dime to wring its neck. Since Russell was slow of mind, he sometimes forgot exactly what it was that he was doing; thus, as cruel as it may sound, several of the chickens over the years had partially survived the wringing. Hence, the chicken that entered Flora's yard was less than whole, and it entered more so out of not being able to control its path. If chickens drank beer, they would walk like Russell's chickens.

"Miss Flora!" Bip noticed first. "Holy Cow! A real live chicken." Bip ran to the back gate and closed the chicken in. The chicken seemed to notice the danger and turned, googol-eyed, to leave; it noticed a hole under the gate and stooped on its little chicken knees in one last ditch effort to try to escape.

The Scout's gloves fell as if to field a grounder and the boys all assumed a catching-a-chicken stance and ran around the yard squatted and crouched and whistling as if to a dog.

"Chickens don't answer dog whistling. What kind of Scouts are you? You boys don't know nothing about wild animals," Crenshaw said.

"Help us, Pawpaw," Bip eagerly looked up at Crenshaw. Bip was in mid-whistle.

Crenshaw didn't want to catch the chicken, but he did want the children to know that he could catch the chicken, so he walked over, cornered it against the cinder block fence, and in one pass had the chicken by her neck.

The chicken looked at him as if, "Well, here we go again."

"You really ought to wring the chicken. It's in such a bad condition," Flora showed what she thought to be compassion.

Crenshaw had the chick cocked and ready to wring, arm high against the sky when the wild dog slobbered under the gate into the backyard.

It was Corndog.

Corndog was a mixed-breed weenie-type dog with wiry golden hair. Corndog had no owner, although there was some speculation that he was Russell's. Corndog was born from two dogs that were brother and sister. So, besides being wild and mean he was also a bit unpredictable.

Corndog went straight for the chicken in Crenshaw's hands. Crenshaw eyeballed an empty gallon pickle jar by his foot and considered stuffing the chicken in it but decided to offer the chicken, instead, as a sacrifice to Corndog. Being the milkman, Crenshaw knew all about Corndog.

Crenshaw was just firming his stance when Corndog's little weenie dog legs left the ground. His mouth opened for Crenshaw's hand that held the flopping chicken. Flora considered for a moment letting Corndog have a go at Crenshaw, but then decided to use the bat in her hand. She swung squarely and firmly, but not enough to kill the dog. The bat cracked against the dog's head and Corndog fell to the ground limp.

"If I've called Watts about this damn dog once, I've called ten times. Little son-of-a-bitch chewed up my garden hose last week and tried to eat my outside shoes. My own son's the dog catcher and he's too damn much of a woman to carry away a little puppy dog. I never should have payed that boy's father. Peas in a pod," Flora said as she poked Corndog to make sure he was out.

"Holy Moly!" Bip and the others were beside themselves already beginning to recount the story. "He had to be three feet off the ground."

"Mr. Crenhaw, was you scared?" Carl asked. He had his arm around Bip. They were now best friends.

"I'd of thrown up. I always throw up when I get scared," Peter added. Peter always threw up.

While the Scouts continued to talk, Flora walked uneventfully to her garage and found a burlap sack. After she found one large enough to hold Corndog, she returned to the backyard.

"I told Watts to tell my boy to get this dog," she started again. "There, grab his leg, Horace, and put him in this bag."

"He ain't dead, Flora." Crenshaw didn't want to kill the animal.

"I know. But he's gonna be plenty mad when he wakes up."

Crenshaw considered Corndog waking up and the headache he'd have and decided Flora was right. They'd be much better off if Corndog were in some prison. Rather than grabbing the dog's leg, Crenshaw grabbed Corndog's ears and stuffed him head first into the sack and tied the top. Flora loaded the animal into the back seat of her car and drove away.

At the jailhouse James was still waiting for a stick of gum. He was in such deep thought that it scared him when Tabot said, "James."

"Yes, sir."

"Let's try it again."

"Mr. Len caught Crow, my uncle, outside the barber shop and just started yelling 'nigger' in his face, and I'll be if his lady didn't get in the middle of them. Ain't a woman's place in no fight between men."

"So they were fighting."

"They wasn't fighting. Len was fighting. He was plenty angry but not even at 'Crow.'"

"'Crow' is Washington," Tabot offered his actual name.

"That's right. I ain't heared nobody calls him that in years." He laughed to himself. "Washington." He said the name out loud. "But that 'cause Billie was dating the white girl," James said.

"Not the old man, Washington. His grandson?" Tabot clarified for clarification's sake. James laughed, picturing Crow and Len's daughter together.

James started to understand, "Was that his daughter? Well, no wonder he's so upset. I wouldn't have my daughter date Billie either. He need to be concentrating on football. Billie don't need that. Still you don't call a 'nigger' one to his face."

Just as James was about to continue, Tabot stopped him and told him that Lilith had set bond for him and that basically he could leave but that he needed to stay available in town. He also gave James two hundred dollars.

"That's from Lilith, too. She says for you to get a room at the King's Inn and stay in town and to come by and see her tonight. She also says not to buy any liquor with the money, only groceries and a room at the King's Inn." The King's Inn was a low-income housing apartment that had one-room efficiencies. It was just a few car lengths down from the Modern Barbershop on the other side of the Rose Theater.

Watts was just opening the cell door to let James fill out the paper work when the front door moved a bit as if it were breathing. Then, it ripped open.

The open towsack didn't even touch the floor until it was almost halfway across the floor. It twisted and slid and stopped against the gun rack. And as soon as it stopped with a thud, Flora's middle finger slipped back out the door and pulled it tight. Her gravel laugh cackled like a witch outside.

If the floor had not just been waxed, there was a good possibility that James and Watts and Tabot would all three have been killed by Corndog. Corndog's little legs started up churning and pumping like a toy locomotive until he reached full speed just on the other side of the desk, but the three men managed to stay several steps ahead of the dog. He would catch the pant leg of James once in a while but overall didn't ever get a good bite on any man. During the third circling of the desk and the swing around the gun rack, Watts managed to pick up a shotgun.

"Get in the cell," Watts yelled to the other two.

"I's out on bail," James had no intention of returning to the cell.

"I ain't arresting you, James. I'm trying to save you!"

Tabot was the first in the cell followed by James followed by Watts followed by Corndog.

Watts raised the gun up in the air holding it by the barrel and dropped the butt on Corndog's head. As Corndog fell limp to the floor, the gun fired between Holder's arm and his side and thumped into the cinder cinder-blocked wall.

"Who's in hell's dog is this sonofabitch!" Tabot almost screamed.

"Sonofabrothersister's its problem. It's retarded is all! Am I bleeding?" He tried to explain as he looked under his arm as he sat on James' cot and sank to the floor. "This cot isn't worth a damn."

"Is all!!! Retarded is all!"

"He'll be better when he wakes up. I hit him pretty hard."

"Flora's been meaning for me to come get him."

CHAPTER 12

▼

THE ROSE THEATER

The Rose Theater towered three stories above and shared a cinder-blocked wall with the Modern Barbershop. On the other side, the King's Inn shared the north wall rising almost as high. Over the pink adobe, an airbrushed twenty-foot pink rose curled and climbed and finally clung with its thorns to the marquee. If anyone thought of going to the movie in Flatland, the large pink rose would crowd their brain in a strange association game so that no title to any movie could be referred to in town without "and the Rose" being tacked on the end: "Gone With The Wind And The Rose" or "Jaws And The Rose," or "Shaft And The Rose." The movie The Rose caused a double entendre festival for almost a year.

Jesus Sanchez, the first Mexican to settle in the area, built the Rose Theater. He was a very good carpenter and had added many decorative touches to the theater, including three elaborate wooden chandeliers in the lobby and a faux silver soda fountain spigot. The spigot was a voluptuous mermaid expertly crafted; the men of the community held it in high reverence. The men, to show their deepest appreciation of the work of art, would order a Root Beer just to see Jean Ann wrap her hand around the mermaid's bare breasts and bury her head deep in her palm, and then pull the root beer up from the head of the keg into the frosted mug. "Pure art," Tabot had once said.

The whole town was disappointed that the theater had closed just seven months before. But its time had come. It had given way to the playoffs and had been showing, in a desperate attempt to draw a crowd, Spanish X-rated movies.

The town saw it, rightfully so, as a public disgrace for their community's image. Finally, Watts had declared the building itself unsafe, especially the balcony section, and no one in town had either the desire or the money to refurbish the old theater, so Tabot bought the building as a tax write-off. It was destined to be torn down for parking access to the courthouse, the barbershop, and the King's Inn.

The stained glass windows in the rotating door were broken almost immediately after the Rose closed. It was boarded up, padlocked, dead bolted shut, and considered, even within the one short week, "an eyesore" by the Chamber. Tabot's funds were "invested,' so he was merely waiting until he could afford to tear down the theater to rid the town as a metamorphosing eyesore. Hence, the Rose became, to Flora's Scout troop, an immediate Pandora's box, full of secrets and dark memories, curiosities buried in the belly of a building, where once wishes and dreams and even wicked desire had been cast at the silver screen.

With their newly found tools of rappelling and climbing and jumping and cussing, all taught to them by their founders, the Boy Scouts were determined to enter the Rose to taste its dark secrets. The mini-troop heroically dedicated itself to rescue what memories they could from the guts and soul of the theater, without even a merit badge as an incentive. It was going to be their unselfish gift to the city.

Bip was the leader. When Bip chose to conquer something, then any means which led to that end were justifiable, the mark of any great conqueror. Thus, the rest of the Scouts served as counselors, sitting on his subconscious shoulders like tiny angels and devils mulling over all of his decisions.

When "The Sound of Music" began, they knew. That was their cue to leave. Knowing that the Dallas Cowboys had just finished, they knew all their fathers and mothers would be inseparably meshed with their armchairs and home-knitted afghans for hours. With the two programs back-to-back, they knew the streets of Flatland would be clear from three until almost nine and humming "Edelweiss" into breakfast the next morning.

Only three of the Scouts had had the determination to slip away: Bip and Willie and Carl. They left just on cue as Julie Andrews watched "The Military Man," as Carl put it, whistle down the children. Willie had forced Carl and Bip to stay until the oldest girl came down the stairs, the one sixteen going on seventeen. Then, they left and started their walk to the theater.

"That's what I was telling you, 'She's just sixteen years old,'" Willie explained again. Willie had a big nose, so he felt the only way for him to look "cool" with a woman was to find a woman with big breasts to offset the size of his nose.

"I want to marry Wendy Johnson," Bip said from out of the blue as he pulled a long strand of hair from his eyes and put it behind his ear like a pencil. He wiggled his Roman nose to lift his black-rimmed glasses. His irises were just almost as black as his frames. Mary had always worried about the color of Bip's eyes because they were so dark, thinking maybe she had oil painted too much and the fumes had affected him when she was pregnant.

Bip had thought about who he was going to marry ever since he was in Kindergarten. Now, he was in fifth grade.

Bip pulled his pants down on his hips so they wouldn't look as short as they were. Then from nowhere he said, "My step-father's funeral is Monday." Carl and Willie didn't say a thing. They knew that Bip had been thinking about it, but they hadn't known what to say.

"I'm sorry," Carl finally said.

"Me, too," Willie said. And they patted him on the back.

"Do you hate that Black guy?" Willie had been the first of the community to ask.

"Yes," Bip answered honestly. "Not because he's Black though, but because he killed Len."

"I heard your father was hurting that man bad."

"Step-father."

"I know. I don't want to talk about it. I don't know what to think." Bip had already milled the thoughts over in his mind until he had made a stone into sand.

They walked silently for quite some time.

"Dad told me I'd probably think about women a bunch for the next few years," Willie said, his mind had flipped back over to think about girls again. "I'd like to see one girl naked besides my sister," Willie added.

"Sometimes you're sick, Willie," Carl said, but secretly he wished the same thing.

The boys reached the end of the alley and could now see the Rose climbing above the other buildings a couple of blocks away.

"It's boarded up on the ground level," Bip said as he was unbuttoning the top button of his pants. They were hurting his stomach. Mary had made him eat all the chicken fry on his plate.

"There's a tree in the alley," Carl said. Carl was the type who feared only his father and would probably end up dead sooner than everyone else in the world.

"We can climb the tree up to the roof. It's strong and it's only a few feet away at the top from the roof."

The sun was just starting to set when the Scouts started climbing the tree. The sun melted over the bright red vinyl belt of the horizon and the boys got their flashlights and probed the building with groping poles of light, up and down. Finding handholds in the tree, they began their ascent with flashlights in one arm, the tree in the other.

The climb really was rather routine and uneventful except for the moment of doubt when each boy had to let go of the tree to fly two stories above the earth to the top of the building. But soon all three were on the roof catching their breaths, regrouping their thoughts and ambitions. Carl turned his flashlight to the roof to find a myriad of holes and rotting wood.

"Careful," Bip said as he planned each tiptoed step.

Carl, on the other side of the roof, however, moved forward with recklessness through the potted roof to reach the front of the theater. Carl had an obsession after conquering something to stand majestically on top of it for a second. Once during a fist fight with Joe Strum, Carl delivered a blow that buckled Joe like punching risen yeast dough, and Carl, of course, stood on Joe's back for a few seconds almost like a dog marking a corner of his territory. So, Carl stood like a marble statue for a second on the front ledge of the building, almost as if he were a petrified forefather looking over his city.

"I can see where your step-dad got killed, the chalk of his body outline," Carl said without really thinking.

"Roger said more than two quarts of blood were on the concrete," Bip said.

"What'd he do measure it?" Willie challenged Bip.

"He was at the lumberyard across the street and said he heard the shot even," Bip continued, in spite of Willie's disbelief.

"I'm sorry; that was mean."

People close to the dead sometimes need to discuss the gruesome details for some reason to cleanse their mind of such absurdity.

"Dawn saw him at the funeral home and said his chest was caved in. I didn't go. She said she didn't notice if Mama noticed his sinking chest."

As Carl was walking back toward the other two, who were still slowly moving toward the front, the roof gave way under Carl's feet, and with a rip, a verbal "Oomph," and a thud, he disappeared.

"You OK!" Bip said. He forgot his mind which was spiraling away in depressing thoughts and mindlessly ran over the danger, concerned only for Carl. He and Willie shined their lights in and saw Carl straddling a seat as the dust was clearing.

"You're on the balcony!"

"I landed between my legs," Carl said bravely.

Bip, realizing how far Carl could have fallen had he not hit the balcony, carefully checked his own footing.

"Here, I'll lower you down," Willie tied off his rope and offered the free end to Bip.

Willie lowered Bip in, while Carl steered Bip's feet to the back of a chair, and then Willie lowered himself into the dark hole.

The boys were three shades in the black room and were connected only to the light they projected. Willie snapped his fingers and the acoustical wall tile immediately ate the sound.

"Pretty tight, huh?" Willie said loudly to see if his voice would survive in the air.

His voice, too, was muffled, eaten by the wall.

The boys were on the balcony, which was as long as a cotton trailer and as deep as the T-ball infield diamond. Below were seats and seats in a sea of darkness. The air smelled of dust and aging cloth, musty carpet and rotting wood.

"My dad said that on Saturday nights it used to be packed with Mexicans. He said all night the building breathed and moved and that high pitched yelps came out of it." Carl always had a story his father had told him. "Just like KLVD does when they change over to Mexican music at five on Fridays." Carl finished his description as he produced a small bottle of vanilla extract. They always drank bits of the extract because they had heard it would make them drunk, so they would all touch the liquid to their tongues. The vanilla was like many things; it smelled delicious but tasted bitter and did not make them drunk: they could never drink enough to get drunk. It did make the boys throats burn and made them smell like an angel food cake. The only thing better they had found was aspirin in a small bottled Coke sucked through a straw, but that hurt Bip's stomach.

The flashlight poles of light split as Willie and Bip went toward the front of the balcony. Carl found some stairs and went down the dark throat leading to the main auditorium of the building. The tunnel downward had the odor of his grandmother's wet hose stockings.

Halfway down the stairs, Carl found an old cigarette that had been broken at the filter. He put it in his mouth and fished for the matches in his coat pocket. There was a hole in his pocket, so he ended up chasing the matches all over his coat. He finally caught them midway up his back. He lit the cigarette and practiced inhaling without coughing as he started down the stairs. He was bound and determined to become a successful smoker, even though he didn't like it.

He turned the corner and found the doors that opened into the theater. He pushed them and shined his light toward the screen.

"Holy Cow!!" Carl almost yelled. It scared Willie and Bip, who were still upstairs.

Carl rushed forward to the front near the screen. Willie and Bip turned their lights through the darkness and finally focused in one spotlight on Carl who had found a huge wooden chair with manacles center stage in front of the screen.

"It's an electric chair," Carl's voice crawled up.

"An electric chair?" Bip was puzzled.

"Why in the world would they have an electric chair?" Willie spilled his voice over the balcony to Carl.

"It's not real," Carl confirmed as he looked for a plug-in. "Still, it's weird," he added.

The chair, even though the boys didn't know it, had been placed in front of the screen to deter Russel, the retarded boy who killed the chickens, from dancing on stage before the movies. Russel rode his bike and attended the theater every Saturday dollar day special. He would dance on the stage before the feature began, extending his oversized tongue and making gross gyrations on stage. The manager, as much as he loved Russel, became tired of his dancing and had noticed one Saturday matinee during "Frankenstein" that Russel was horrified at the chair and equipment in the laboratory. So, he had the boy, Chester, at the lumber company across the street make the faux electric chair and put it on stage. The chair made Russel furious. He never got back on stage, but could be seen sitting in the balcony talking to himself and making throaty noises as if a peanut husk were caught in his throat.

Just as Carl was sitting down in the chair and trying a shackle on his left leg, a blinding box of light broke the darkness.

"It works!" Bip's voice squealed down from the projection booth, shot over the balcony, and pierced the screen. The projector sputtered forward and a picture came on without sound; evidently, Tabot had never turned off the electricity to the building.

"Turn that off. What'd you want to do? Get us in trouble?" Willie was concerned.

"It's OK. No one's going to hear." Bip was right.

It didn't take much coercing for Bip to talk Willie into staying and watching. The film was a Spanish X-movie, "EL CARNAL." In just a matter of minutes the three boys were in the center of the theater smoking stale cigarette butts and passing the vanilla bottle back and forth. They had their legs propped up on the chairs in front of them. A wad of gum was strung from Carl's shoe to the floor, and the smell of Juicy Fruit mixed with the smoke and dust and vanilla.

"Those seats are not footrests, boys!" Carl mimicked the voice of the attendant as he smeared the gum against the back of the seat in front of him.

"I don't get it. I thought she was his girl," Bip tried to follow the plot.

"She's everybody's girl, stupid," Willie answered.

"Well, I should say so."

"She's only been with one guy she hasn't done it with," Carl observed.

"'Cept when she had both of those guys at one time," Willie added.

"I still don't see how she works that out," Bip questioned.

"Yeah, I'd be jealous," Carl responded.

"No, stupid. I mean it's just weird math."

"Ohhhh. Look. That was kinda gross," Willie was even starting to suspect the validity of the film.

"What about two women?" Carl asked.

"You mean with guys or together alone."

"Alone. With no men."

"Lesbians," Willie offered the correct word.

"Women fags," Carl confirmed.

"I don't think there's such a thing as women fags. They might like girls but mostly it's just 'cause men aren't sensitive enough. Least that's what my sister says. She says if you want a woman to love you, then don't be too touchy-rough—except sometimes," Bip explained.

"You think there's a woman in town like her?" Carl wondered.

"Yeah, your mother," Willie said.

"No. C'mon really."

"Wow! Look how many naked people there are now," Carl was impressed that everyone in the movie had seemed to reconcile his or her differences and now be together in one great reunion.

"I wish they'd move the camera back so I could see someone's whole body."

"Let's turn it off and look around some more."

"I don't get the point of the movie. Is she going to marry the drug guy or not?"

"I think he'll get killed."

"Yeah, and like who cares?"

"What a sorry movie."

The boys tried a few more cans of film and were about to give up on humanity when Bip found the final can of "Frankenstein Meets the Wolfman" which was in Spanish but with English subtitles.

Mankind was back to normal as monsters battled each other, men were kissing women who still had their clothes on, and the good guys were easily separated from the bad, with misunderstood monsters, and makers who couldn't understand why their monsters wanted to be free.

The boys cheered at the end when Frankenstein and Wolfman were washed away when the dam broke, even though they were also sad for the monsters.

With the bottle of vanilla gone, the world saved, and their faith renewed in mankind, the boys decided to go home. Bip turned off the projector and they pulled themselves one-by-one out of the Rose Theater, having unlocked the secrets of Flatland's box.

CHAPTER 13

▼

WHEN FIRE MEETS MORNING

The Rose Theater was in full blaze by two A.M., lashing its yellow hair against the black opaque sky. Van Gogh would have studied each rise and fall of the flame, and then passionately have carved the colors into the canvas and cut off both ears. Most of Flatland missed the start of the blaze; they had already settled into their beds. The Scouts were warm in their beds dreaming as the flames violated the air. If it had not been for Crenshaw going to the bathroom "for the fourth damn time," the town might very well have slept right through it. But Crensahw immediately called Watts.

In just a matter of minutes the entire population was standing, watching the blaze while the fireman pulled the hoses as the canvas lines unfolded to the fire. Then, the word was given, and the water rushed through the canvas; the canvas pulled and held tight, harnessing the snake of water inside and the water rushed and exploded against the fire. Heavy steam floated up from the mist.

The fire in the center appeared as sunset, a polished orange, oily and firm across the faces of the citizens of Flatland.

In the front were the three Scouts: Willie and Carl and Bip. Bip was picturing the sinewy naked Mexican bodies on the film melting and twisting and catching fire, turning to dark smoke, mingling and mixing, churning in pornographic positions in the heavens with Frankenstein and the Wolfman and the electric chair and the empty bottle of vanilla extract.

Carl considered whether he had a hangover or not.

The fire trucks continued pouring water onto the fire. On the street, the red of the fire truck reflected across the black water and looked as rich as red enamel dripped and sloshed across hot black tar. The orange of the fire danced against the enamel red truck.

The orphaned mist cooled the faces of the Scouts. It moved in a steamy wall against the fire, then back in a rotation.

The smell was of antiques and of traditions, of dust-filled garages being cleaned with a green spring water hose, of pine campfires doused with water, of moist hot air in a locker room shower. The fire swallowed the sound from the air like a great vacuum; it was hot and lofted everything up and up and up.

The Modern Barbershop was burning from the roof inwards. Its cinder blocks, however, were steady against the heat and arches of water, even though the fire had turned the bricks black. In front of the barbershop, Len's chalk out-line was finally gone. Along with the bloodstain and the few pieces of glass that Paul missed with the broom, Len was all but sprayed roughly against the curb to fall into the gutters and through the pipes that ran under the town. Now, Len, for all practical purposes, lay diluted in the middle of Prairie Dog Pete Pond, half a mile wide and half a mile away.

The King's Inn, on the other side of the Rose, however, was not so fortunate.

"Did everyone get out of the King?" Sarge was holding the hose and Watts was returning to help fight the fire. Watts had been part of the search and rescue team going inside the King. He looked sick.

"Let me hold this a while. Clint needs to see you." His tone was very abrupt and serious. A shiver went down Sarge's back. Evidently everyone had not gotten out of the building.

Sarge reluctantly went over behind the barricade. He was stricken as if some-one had killed a child in front of him. Three bodies lay in front of him in awk-ward stiff poses like statues that had been surprised and immediately cast into a permanent mold. Their mouths were wide open, gasping for air and their fingers and arms were open and curled in tense posture. Their skin was charred and black and the smell was unbearable. Sarge eased up behind Clint.

"God. What a horrible death."

"Call the funeral home. The sooner the better. See what we got in county funds."

"What a way to go," Clint said one more time under his breath. He looked at the face that was stripped of skin and was all but an outline of a horrified skull. He cringed a bit knowing that in a few minutes he would have to help lift and put the bodies into bags to the taken away. For a second, life seemed so absurd and abrupt.

Everyone had escaped the low income housing in time but Benzil Jackson, an older black man who was bedridden, and Willie May, his sister who cared for him. James, the man who had killed Len, was the third dead.

Only after hours of unpredictable tongue-lapping fire, which caused screams and singed eyebrows, did the fire become tamed, not by man, but by time, dying as a fire must, with no more fuel, with no more food for its mouth. It sat, finally, as a domesticated fireplace; the flue was the sky, and the smoke rose in changing faces in the growing glow of the horizon.

The firemen sat around and pointed to different bellows of smoke, saying, "There's a snake with hands standing up holding a Twinkie, see it?" and, "No, below the Lassie dog smoking the cigar."

When the fire met morning, the power of God was apparent. The fire had been a mere firecracker sideshow, a millionth of a split second of manmade miracle in God's grand machine of time, cheap spectacle compared to the majesty of the sunrise and the hot burning eye that colored the enormous mountains of clouds hanging over the head of Flatland.

All that was left of the Rose was a ribbed carcass while its soul clouded the sky.

Later in the morning, after the sun had cleaned the sky, the blue soothed the charcoaled skeleton of the Rose and commanded it to stand rugged as the firemen rattled in and out of her blackened ribs.

"Appears to be a hobo." Clint, the fireman, reached into the pile, and from a fistful of ashes and mud lifted the evidence, a little bottle of vanilla extract. Watts agreed.

"List it as an arson, then. Damn hoboes is what it is, coming in, setting fires and cooking weenies and pork and beans and shit in those cans. Then they drink that damn vanilla extract and shaving lotion. We can hardly stand to hold 'em in the cell 'cause they always smell like they just made love to a pig that was wearing cologne, cooking a banana pie. Yeah, go ahead and list it arson," Watts said.

He looked at his watch.

"Len's funeral's tomorrow and I reckon the others. We'll have to hurry to make it. Smoke smell'll be on us for days," Watts said as he started out through the wet, black wood. He smelled like a doused campfire. He stumbled and slipped until he finally stood on the solid concrete sidewalk of the Modern Barbershop. He stomped his feet clean of the soot.

After Watts left, Clint and one other of the firemen remained behind to look for stray hot spots.

"I ain't going to no funeral," Sarge squirted a spot that was still smoking.

"If I didn't have to, I wouldn't." Clint took a bite of his sandwich. The smell was fresh. He offered a potato chip to Sarge. "I didn't even know him, really."

"Then why're you going?"

"He taught my daughter Sunday school. He told 'em Eve sinned but she didn't go to hell. I didn't like that. I didn't like that at all. But, I didn't want to teach no class, and he liked it, or least said he did."

"Well, I ain't going. I don't like funerals. They're manmade," Sarge said as he almost fell over a buried seat, but he regained his footing and sprayed the electric chair one more time.

"What the hell you mean, 'manmade'?"

"They're like weddings. Like true things that God already knows about, that man feels like he has to write down somewhere so God'll know about it. Man and woman marry out of love and law confirms it. A man dies out of natural law and then man's law confirms it."

"'Cept Len didn't die of no natural law."

"When your heart stops beating, you die. That's nature."

"Clint? That ain't natural law. Len was shot."

"What a way to go," Clint was still disturbed.

"I'm not sure there is a good way to go," Sarge said matter of fact.

"But God, burning or being shot in the chest. Being alive one second ... What a way to go."

The smell of burned wood and water lifted and settled like a meal in the belly of the clouds and rumbled and cussed and hung like a grumpy shadow over the city.

Chapter 14

▼

Len's Funeral

At two o'clock in the afternoon, a cockroach, the size of a small cigar with legs, uprooted himself from between the cracks of the sidewalk, splitting the remains of the Rose Theater and the Modern Barbershop. He was absolutely beat. He had, in just a few short weeks, been born, survived a shooting, a parade, a fire, been almost cooked and drowned, after all of which he was ultimately auctioned to the streets to find a new home.

He gathered his energy enough just to pull his head from the darkness between the cracks of concrete.

Even after the orange tongue of the blaze the night before, he felt the pure heat of the rising sun and winced under the awesome winding white purity that blared through the clouds. The clouds broke and separated, allowing the light to fill the air like opening lungs.

He lifted his front cockroach leg almost as if to shield his eyes from the sun so that he might gain some bearing. He shifted, and scratched his shoulder against the red brick of the wall behind him as he checked his whereabouts, making sure he was still near safety. He was just in front of the barbershop and smelled the faded sweet scent of Len's blood. He sniffed again. He was teased by the smell of the blood and dirt washed away by the fireman's water.

Determined to find a new home and not to be eaten by the blue jays circling above, he regrouped his legs in tight rows and marched parallel to the wall.

He stopped at the "Caw. Caw."

He waited as a blue jay streaked against the green of a globe willow.

He took time as he monitored the sky. He scolded himself for not questioning his safety of living near the barbershop since the 'loud bang.' He had run under the wooden floors of the Rose and the barbershop for weeks, most of his life, and now he was concerned only about finding a new home. He had attempted to twist out earlier, near the spilled caramel corn from the last movie shown in the theater, but he had become exhausted and simply screwed himself back between the wooden floor slats of the theater.

He decided the only thing to do now, however, after the barrage of incidents, was to look for a new home, to risk the chance of being eaten, until he could burrow back into some dark hovel close to the earth's skin. He committed himself, waiting for the blue jay to circle away from him.

He scuttled in lame spurts across the pavement. He hadn't been "up top" in days except to eat scraps off the floor of the theater. He regressed for a moment as his primitive memory craved the ancestral memories of buttered popcorn and Jr. Mints his family had once defended, standing staunchly in front of the mice on the floor of the theater.

He stood bravely like a soldier and began marching in his hungry hallucination until he bumped his head on a Bit-O-Honey stuck to the sidewalk that Crenshaw had dropped during the parade.

For a second he buried his head in the Karo congealment and sucked. There was a caw from the heavens. He reluctantly moved. Casting aside the frivolity of sweets and memories, he promised to keep his head firmly forward as he scooted past the floral shop. Stop. Across the street to Ben Franklin's variety. Stop. Past Johnny's Boot Shop, pausing in front of the window to smell the scent of the eel and ostrich leather. Run. Across the courthouse lawn, being still as he heard a prairie dog.

He started and stopped all over the square looking for a place to live. He found absolutely nothing. He tried to wedge himself into the bakery but couldn't, got into the floral shop but found nothing but fresh flowers and the smell nauseated him. He considered the music store but remembered he hated country music.

Then despondent, he walked, without pride or fear, slowly on his black wires, as hopelessly as a fly without wings, to finally find himself crawl up the tire of Benson's old Chevy truck outside the Goodwill. He had nestled on a piece of gum stuck under the fender when Benson started the truck and took off before the cockroach could drop. Benson pulled in minutes later at the front gate of the graveyard, several blocks down the highway from downtown, just in front of Spud's Donut Shop.

The roach smelled the air. He shifted excitedly. He smelled again. He rose up on his back legs. He had caught the scent of a fully-risen, fresh maple donut. He sniffed left and right. He lowered his front legs to the ground. He sniffed up and down. Ironically, the smell was rising from the graveyard itself, not from the donut shop at all, climbing the sky like a sweet sinful pole of flavor.

He had found a home.

In jubilation, he dropped hitting his back but flipped over immediately. He ran back and forth across the curb. He was elated. Then, he located the direct target with his keen sense of smell and ran like a committed wildebeest, rising and falling across the graves in a fluid motion, strong and as beautiful as a cockroach might run with total abandonment to Len's open grave. He didn't even slow or even pause as he threw himself like a lemming off the cliff, the full six feet, head back, eyes closed, his legs churning like a long jumper, onto the maple donut Flora's son had left when he dug Len's grave.

He hit the bottom of the hole in a jolt that left him breathless and stunned. He raised his two front wires in a dizzy triumph as he buried his head in his maple meal.

Just at the gate, Len's funeral procession entered.

The cars had their lights on, even though there was not evidence of even a shadow in the bright two-o-clock summer sun. The cars meandered into the graveyard, a thread, stitching and mending the course broken by the needling hearse.

Funerals are always sobering, serious and revealing, and even the cars in their seeming drunken weaving were not jesting or even cajoling their way into the yard; they merely moved behind the truth to the finish line, just as a stream meanders to the bottomless ocean.

When most of the cars had started to put their parking brakes on, although there was no real reason to do so on the flat plains of West Texas, time itself rushed up on the backs of the congregation. The cars compacted uncomfortably close, slowly like an accordion squeezed together in one final dramatic wheeze.

And the blossom of darkness emerged: the black car birthed the black casket that birthed the black suits that held the long fingers of the black dresses. It was like a black rose opening its wet petals.

Crenshaw got out of his car holding Bip's hand.

Bip was sad and tired, but glad that his grandfather, instead of his mother, was holding his hand. Mary and Dawn were putting lipstick on and holding each other in the back seat. Dawn was crying uncontrollably. Everything seemed so displaced for her. The simple order was broken and would be broken for a long, long, time. Mary tried to be a model of firmness and stoicism; she kissed Dawn and left a mark on her cheek and wiped it off then smudged the makeup to cover the lipstick smudge and then both cried because her makeup was ruined.

Bip looked away from the scene in the car. Bip needed stability now. He was looking at his grandfather when he noticed the movement across the graveyard and somewhat whispered, "Pawpaw, there's the others," but Crenshaw "shhh-hed" Bip and reached down and held Bip's tongue between his pointer finger and his thumb. Bip wiggled his body but kept his head stiff trying to retrieve his tongue.

Lilith was leading a procession who were entering the back entrance of the cemetery. Crenshaw and Bip saw Lilith.

The earth in Flatland rose to the east in the cemetery, so that the Black's funeral procession was actually higher than that of Len's. Lilith was the highest human in the graveyard.

The blacks had come to bury Willie May, her brother, and James. Their procession was disfigured and broken. The lines were scattered in places and crowded almost like a rash in others. Their dotted line stretched from the railroad tracks to the grave, like a trail of fire ants to a carcass.

The two funerals were destined to be performed at the same time, in spite of the fact that Len had died days before James and the others. Sarge insisted that the funeral home make prudent work of the fire victims, so the community could cleanse themselves of the tragedy.

There was a deep tension in the graveyard.

Lilith, had decided that for this one day she would lay aside her brown liquor to feel the total sobering impact of the passing of her brethren. The effort she had from morning to noon without the repast of liquor was almost as great a tragedy as the deaths themselves. Her suffering was tremendous. She shook and saw mysterious hallucinations which she reported to Fox and Buffalo. Buffalo remembered the visions of Pistol Bill, an octoroon evangelical alcoholic who had stirred the city in 1958. Pistol Bill had pushed the message of suffering as a way to spiritual knowledge. And Bill, himself an avid drinker, would abstain from drinking only until the tremens hit, and then in blinding insanity he would consume liquor by bottles and profess himself to be God. After, he would convince the congregation that God wanted humanity naked and commenced to try and mate with anyone stupid enough to take his irreverent bait. Lilith's DT visions were a bit more humble.

In one vision Lilith had had in the bathtub just minutes before the funeral, James, who was dead in the dream as well as in real life, was now in a tremendous hourglass of people of all colors and economic structures.

She had reported that all the people were crawling the sides of the top section of the hourglass, pressing their faces desperately against the sides, distorting their faces in twisting silent screams against the glass. The hourglass was devouring the living, one-by-one, who were captured in the top; the heaviness made the mass crowd the tip like plastic toy soldiers melting in a fire hot funnel. All those people trapped in the top triangle, she said, were systematically passing one-by-one through the tip by a gargoyle who was sitting on his haunches at the intersection of the two triangles, where the two tips of the hourglass met. His job was to smack each individual who passed through the opening into the bottom of the hourglass. Thus, he held a Neanderthal club and systematically whacked each individual as he or she dropped onto the others in the lower triangle to sit like stunned mother hens on those who had already fallen. Lilith saw all walks of life represented: blacks, whites, Mexicans, and even some movie stars like Shirley Temple Black, and Al Jolson, and wrestlers like Andre the Giant, and political figures like Martin Luther King Jr. and George Wallace who, she said, fell through in his wheelchair with a resounding clang; religious and non-religious, rich and poor, all were falling onto the dead bodies below. The bodies in the bottom triangle, she said, eventually mutated keeping only their faces, and they moved around like small hermit crabs, their dead bodies being pulled around by their souls. She said she was disturbed.

Buffalo interpreted the dream to explain something about how eclairs and oatmeal for breakfast without the assistance of a good belt of whisky could do that. Fox was a bit more philosophical. He had suggested that God cursed man with a body—he remembered that from a distant Sunday sermon of Lee Weldon, and that if people weren't good in this life, they might have to drag around the carcass. Buffalo told Fox to "shut up" and Fox had.

Still, Buffalo took the visions with great seriousness and consoled Lilith wholeheartedly.

Buffalo had told no one in the funeral procession line, but he had brought a pint of dark liquor just in case Lilith could not take the visions any longer. She always had more visions sober than drunk; in fact, being drunk was her only defense against her gift.

So the mass of darkness of the blacks was led by the lone hallucinations of one great mother who was celebrating her friends' deaths with one day of blinding sobriety.

On the other side of the yard, the funeral was a bit more traditional with the cars and lights and black suits and solemn pale faces. Crenshaw was beat; it was hot, very hot and unusually humid, and his stomach had been hurting.

The tension grew.

The groups were short-tempered and irritable, and they were greedy as the opportunity arose to fight for chairs under the small tent by the grave because of the heat.

Bip looked at the box that held Len's body; a tear started to well up and he began to cry. When Bip began to cry, Crenshaw began to cry. To think that life was reduced to this, Crenshaw thought, to placing your used body in a box and burying it under the earth; that disturbed Crenshaw, especially when it was someone close to him, someone he had watched gripe about eating spinach just a few days before. Len had done a lot for Bip and Mary and Dawn.

Crenshaw had been very hard on Len when he first came back into Mary's life, but after several revealing moments, Crenshaw had finally been convinced that Len had changed and was a better man. Crenshaw also wanted Bip to have a father role model, and, in fact, Bip was starting to settle into the idea of having someone who was going to be around a while. Crenshaw even felt a moment of deep anxiety as he imagined as few people do that one day he would have to face death; but even in that realization, it was still so far removed from him. Crenshaw squeezed Bip's hand. Bip squeezed back—hard.

Lee was just finishing the part about God's will and divine justice and the "big scheme," when the sober voice of Lilith across the yard rang out in one monumental hallucinogenic song.

She covered the pains and heights of Willie May's father's life, how he had held the hand of his mother when she took her driver's license test, how he had shooed Coco dog away from the pumpkin pies and cleaned up the pumpkin pie paw prints off the new carpet, had offered unconditional love to his mother in her death. She exalted him in a spiritual song sung as greatly as any human could ever have done.

After she finished, she recapped Len's death and James' action, and then she quickly covered Willie May's life; Lilith didn't like women very much, and, as always, Lilith apologized after her last note for being able to sing so well. She knew that her ability to sing well angered some of the other black women.

It was halfway through the funeral when Buffalo noticed Moonpie Boogie Dew just behind Crenshaw. Moonpie Boogie Dew was the cemetery she-cat and was as wild a cat as ever lived and had the reputation for hiding behind tombstones until someone came up to place flowers, then attacking them. Buffalo picked up a clod from the pile of dirt of the empty graves. He calculated the distance and calmly heaved the clod towards Moonpie Boogie Dew to scare her off. You have to say her full name every time since she's the cemetery cat and if you don't you will loose your mind like Buckus Berry did and cut your whacker off.

The clod hit Crenshaw square on the forehead.

Just as in the American Revolution, there was only speculation really as to who cast the first clod. Crenshaw just knew that it hit him, and Crenshaw was not the one to be provoked at that time in any way; he was hot and tired and mournful. Crenshaw didn't even hesitate to speak up about the injustice.

"Some nigger hit me with a clod," Crenshaw felt of his head. "Shhhhhhhh," Flora was standing just next to him and looked at his head.

"Goddernit. I'm not kiddin'. Some nigger hit me with a clod. It's right there." He even tried to accentuate the seriousness by spitting wildly as if his mouth were now diseased with dirt.

"They can't throw that far," Walter on the other side tried to quieten him. "Besides that's mostly a rock." Walter nudged the clod across the grass with his boot and it began to fall apart, leaving small stones that had been trapped inside. "See? Not a clod."

Lee tried to continue, but Crenshaw was now a bit beside himself, yelling at the dark figures across the yard.

"Wanna be clowns, huh! That what you want?!" He yelled as he pulled himself through the crowd to the pile of dirt that used to occupy the hole that Len was about to fill. Crenshaw picked up a clod and threw it, very off balance, much like one might expect a milkman to throw. The clod whirred through the air flipping and flopping like a wounded duck and landed at the foot of Bisquit, the small black boy who'd put the tamale in Keesa's nose; it landed just short of the crowd. Bisquit, thinking Crenshaw wanted to play catch to ease the tension, picked up the clod and threw it back.

In a moment the graveyard was full of flying clods.

The clods fell like brown hail stones across the yard, glancing off of the tombstones, hitting flat in the grass, splashing in puddles from the water sprinklers, and once in a while, but very seldomly, hitting a shoulder or a leg.

Those hit were immediately the wounded warriors and began to hurl the clods with less loft and the more abandonment, more of a hardball pitching style.

At the height of the battle, a second clod, mostly conglomerated stone, hit Crenshaw squarely on his forehead. His eyes rolled back in his head and his tongue, for a split second, lopped out of his mouth. He fell to his knees. No blood flowed from his forehead; instead, a monstrous knot grew straight out just above his squinted eyes like a great risen mountain. Even after only a few seconds, Crenshaw looked like a poorly made unicorn.

"Hold it!!! Goddernnit!!! Hold it just a damn minute!!!" Crenshaw waved from the ground.

Most of the throwers stopped, except for some of the more passionate and stupid ones. Both sides approached their martyrs and idiots and finally all clods stopped.

The yard was spotted with clods as if a hail storm of dirt had fallen from God to bury the event. The flowers of the yard were torn and scattered like confetti in purples and yellows and blood reds against the green carpet of the grass, and the rising fragrance was sweet but now over pollinated, so the groups were sneezing and coughing. The women fished in their handbags for tissues.

Crenshaw stepped forward and walked with his now huge forehead to the center of the graveyard and stood directly in front of the Jesus statue erected by the Rotarians. The crucified concrete Christ, like Michelangelo's David twice-sized, towered above the moving flesh beneath him. His head was lost on his chest, his arms sinewy and tight, his calves and thighs stringy and taut. The concrete robe wrapped around his waist held him rigid, while his basset-hound eyes fell earthly, yearning to turn upward to look to the sky. The inscription, "Why hast thou forsaken me?," was under his feet.

"For Christ's sake," Crenshaw muttered.

Bip, who was standing mindlessly under the crucified arm of Christ, looked to the statue for confirmation. Jesus stood solid, unmoving.

The black mob gathered inside itself for a moment as a discussion rose with increasing intensity. Finally, Lilith stepped out of the group and the black mass fell silent. She continued to walk. All of the whites kept expecting Lilith to stop, but she continued forward.

Crenshaw decided to appoint himself as spokesman.

"What are you, crazy? Are you going to talk to that witch?" Selmer said to Crenshaw. Crenshaw completely ignored Selmer.

Crenshaw took the long walk over to meet Lilith midway. Lilith was just taller than Crenshaw and three times as wide.

"What in the hell is going on!" Crenshaw was very upset.

"Excuse me ifs I breaks wind. I ain't had a drop today and my bowels is confused, Mr. Crenshaw."

"We're trying to bury a man, to pay him respect!" Crenshaw was yelling. Lilith was not nearly as moved.

"Bip-child is your grandbaby boy?"

"He says you're a witch." Crenshaw picked back at her.

"I is a witch. But I ain't worth a shit today." Lilith wasn't having a good moment. Then she relaxed. "There, it's passed." Her face relaxed. "I's a witch." She lifted her perspiring hands to the sky as a sparkling gift to the sun.

"Well, then, tell me something …"

"You's wearing two differed colored sock," Lilith broke in on Crenshaw. He hesitated, but lowered his arms to his side and lifted his pant legs. He was wearing one black sock and one blue sock.

"Well, hell, that's not witchy," he said, almost offended by her parlor games.

Lilith pulled at her dress not even in the least disturbed by his non-belief. The dress was hiked up on her buttocks.

"I hates this damn dress. I makes me look fat. Does you think it makes me look fat?"

Crenshaw shifted uneasily. There was silence. He wasn't about to touch that question. She looked into Crenshaw's ice-blue eyes.

"Why in the world did you throw a rock at me?"

"It was clod. I didn't throws it either. Lilly's arm shake plum off if'n she got her fat moving like that." She shook the fat on her arm and shook her jowls to mimic the back and forth. "It was Buffalo. He was trying to hit Moonpie Boogie Dew. That the cemetery cat. She bite Buffalo on his thigh one time when he come out to see his dead daddy. That one mean cat. Lilly don't even mess with that witch."

Crenshaw tried to get a word in, but she flowed on like a river. "That cat get her name because she look like a chocolate Moonpie cookie sandwich that done got squashed in its package while dancing morning dew glistened on the cellophane package."

Across the yard a concerned voice yelled at Crenshaw.

"What's going on? Are you fine, or what?"

Crenshaw yelled back, "Shut up."

Lilith pulled at her dress again. "I gots to get me a new Sunday meet and go to church dress. Sorry Buffalo hit you with a clod." She turned to leave.

"That's it!?" Crenshaw was not satisfied.

She walked a few feet then stopped dramatically, and without turning around, she said in a hard, sincere voice, clearly unmasked enough that it almost scared Crenshaw, "We'll quit throwing clods."

"Good," Crenshaw said loudly. He felt he had full victory.

Most of both crowds had expected a long verbose compromise, a sort of long drawn-out peace summit, but the thing was done.

As Crenshaw turned to leave, he heard Lilith's voice low, singing a phrase from a song. She stopped in mid-verse. "Crenshaw," She said very seriously without even turning around. The clarity of her intention escalated. "Stop calling us 'niggers.'"

Crenshaw felt a shock go through his body, almost as if someone had told him a secret that only he knew. He looked back over his shoulder, stern and solid. Lilith knew he was looking. She could feel his eyes. She turned and looked at him. He fell into her.

"I can only speak for myself."

"That's all any of us can be responsible for," Lilith said. "'Cept you teach that boy, too."

"You don't put no stray thoughts in my grandbaby boy's head, Lilly. You hear me?" Crenshaw added pointed an accusing finger.

Lilith stood almost as a statue for a second. She looked at Crenshaw as if a promise.

"Little Boy die a man." She turned and started her shuffle back to the black mass.

The thing was done and the compromise was apparent and Crenshaw turned contemplatively and took one step, and as his heavy foot hit the soil to tell his group their 'New Deal: Based upon the Emancipation Proclamation,' he heard a large thud behind him. He started not to look, thinking Lilith had dropped some secret boulder she had brought under her dress to whack him over the head with. But he had that 'feeling' and turned out of curiosity.

Lilith was laying face down in the grass as if she were a boulder dropped from heaven, half sunk in the ground.

Crenshaw walked to her reluctantly, expecting a ploy of some kind, and attempted to rouse her by poking her. He became more concerned and tried to turn her over, but she was too heavy. His heart raced. She was out cold. He continued trying to turn her. He groaned and grunted and struggled with the body, but she was an immovable object.

Paul, across the yard, ran to Crenshaw and all the whites gathered up clods as if they were in a western waiting to cover their hero with gunfire under the guise of some concocted chess move.

Paul crouched down beside Crenshaw and on the count of three—Crenshaw had to show Paul counting fingers—they flipped her big body over. Crenshaw, without thinking, grabbed Paul's hands and shoved them on Lilith's large breasts. Paul was a bit startled but he stayed. Crenshaw then indicated to Paul how to go up and down rhythmically on her chest.

Buffalo was now running full speed towards Lilith, pulling the bottle from under his coat as he ran. The brown liquor jostled and spewed like a small brown ocean captured in a bottle. The liquor clung to the sides and then slid slowly back, dragging its nails down the glass walls only to drown over and over again in the brown reservoir.

Then Crenshaw's head fell back as his mouth opened wide enough to inhale the entire sky. He was just about to start mouth-to-mouth when Buffalo pulled Crenshaw and Paul off of Lilith in one jerk and lowered the medicine to her lips.

She restored back to life slowly then grabbed the bottle like a starving baby and drank the liquor in gulps.

Both groups were slow to move their ground, but finally in a sort of mutual agreement, the groups moved "en masse" to the four on the ground in the center of the cemetery.

After a few long seconds of drinking, Lilith started to come around.

"Call an ambulance," Crenshaw said to nobody but everybody.

"What are you doing, Crenshaw?" Walter started.

Selmer moved in closer.

Lilith's eyes opened and Crenshaw looked into her eyes and they sunk through a dark tunnel where she embraced him in a promise that lasted no more than a falling star tearing through the black sky.

No words were said as she passed the single-most resounding passing of gas ever. She was not having a heart attack. She was having a gaseous backup due to her lack of liquor.

Lilith insisted on everything continuing. Even as she was standing, her lifted voice echoed across the yard like an opera star singing through a hollow tin can in a holy rendition of "Amazing Grace." No one, white or black, moved until the song was over. Only after the singing did the whites leave in their cars and the blacks on foot, as tradition would have it, though the front gate.

The front gate was a great arch made of chicken wire which allowed the visitors to the cemetery to place flowers in the holes. Over the days, the arch had become a rainbow of colors.

Moonpie Boogie Dew slinked along the fence line until she found the hole that let her into the town dump just behind the graveyard. She wove like an agile snake to the top of her trash heap. She timed her eerie meow, and when the silence was just perfect, she resounded a high pitched screamish meow, enough to stop the nutria by the sewer water from their rummaging just for a moment's silence. Lilith even stopped just beside a grave stone.

"What'd Lilith say, Crenshaw?" Tabot eased himself up beside Crenshaw.

"She said they's throwing at that cat."

"Well, I did see that cat just behind Walter."

"They say it's a mean cat."

"You think we need to get Flora's boy on it." Tabot wanted to ease the tension a bit, to do the right thing.

"She said for us to quit calling 'em 'niggers'."

Tabot thought Crenshaw was through talking and this took him by surprise.

"What'd you say?" Tabot was interested.

"I said, 'all right.'"

Tabot didn't say anything for a minute.

"I think that's probably a good idea," Tabot finally offered.

CHAPTER 15

▼

CRENSHAW'S CHECKUP

Crenshaw didn't like the big city. He wouldn't have gone into Grandville if Dr. Bill wouldn't have insisted. The knot was "big" Dr. Bill had said, and it wouldn't hurt to get some "other things" that had been bothering Crenshaw checked on.

In the big city there existed senselessness to Crenshaw. There, he was reminded of how many people actually existed in the world and that really each of us is ultimately rather insignificant, that we are all just some small mortal thing on some blue ball spinning through the universe. And Crenshaw, as he suspected anyone did, felt especially insignificant in a doctor's office.

"The doctor will be right with you Mr. Crenshaw." The nurse was writing something in curls and squiggles on the clipboard. "That's a nasty bump. He'll probably want to get x-rays."

"Goddern cat's what caused it," Crenshaw tried to explain as he took off his shirt. He noticed the window was open, so he drew the shades, even though he was on the seventeenth floor. "I hate the city," Crenshaw confessed to the nurse.

"A cat?" The nurse was confused. "You'll need to put the robe on, but please wait until I'm gone, Mr. Crenshaw." She paused then asked confused, "That knot is from a cat?"

"You already told me to put the robe on." Crenshaw sat in a chair to remove his shoes. "Hell yes, from a cat. Little piece of tamale was walking behind me at Len's funeral and that nigger—Crenshaw remembered his vow—that Buffalo

- 96 -

tried to hit it with a godderned clod 'cause he thought that Moonpie's fixing to bite one of Len's mourner's." Crenshaw explained the entire ordeal in one spurt and then looked at the nurse.

"And the cat bit your head?" She was still confused.

Crenshaw was still undressing.

"Mr. Crenshaw I'm not supposed to be in here when you change." She fixed her hat properly on her head.

He pulled down his pants. "My lord, if you ain't seen one, you won't know what it is, and if you have, it won't be nothing new." He put the robe on and turned so she could tie it in the back.

"Those are very smart briefs, Mr. Crenshaw." She didn't know what to say, so she complemented his undergarment and wished she wouldn't have said anything.

Crenshaw had been to the hospital enough that he had already resigned himself to the humiliation of being treated like a machine of flesh and bone that could rebuild itself with the right medicine and prodding. The human animal was one of few things that could regenerate itself and Crenshaw knew that. He knew he was old; he was past being humble or shy or even precursingly explanatory in any situation where he was the one who was going to be put under the glass and observed. His philosophy was, 'Here I am,' arms out wide, 'Poke me. Prod me. Heal me. Bill me.'

"Have you been having any head pain?" She switched into a nursing mode and started to fill out the questionnaire. She clicked the pen against her name-tag.

"Well, hell, yes! I've been having head pain. Half my goddern brain's been knocked outside my skull. I'm surprised I'm not eating left-handed and walking backwards now."

"No, Mr. Crenshaw, I mean before the accident."

"I get a headache everyday."

"Everyday?" She was different. "Everyday?"

"Since I started delivering afternoons."

Crenshaw had just been delivering milk in the mornings, except recently he was having trouble finishing his route without getting extremely tired. Now he rose at five instead of six and delivered until two-thirty instead of one. Crenshaw was starting to regret even coming in now. What were they going to do, he thought to himself, say, "Yes, Mr. Crenshaw, your skull is cracked so you need to take it easy," or, "Yes, Mr. Crenshaw, your brains are now on the outside of your skull and we'll have to stuff them back between the cracks." Doctors can't fix the human condition. They can only direct it in the proper direction. Suddenly he knew that heads, unlike shoulders and knees were about as uncomplicated as a thick glass jar; they are round and they can crack; they can break; they can shatter; however, unlike glass, they can't be glued. They simply must repair themselves. Crenshaw wondered if he had come to the doctor simply for the doctor to say, "Boy, that's one hell of a bump. I bet that hurt. How did it happen?" And then to listen empathetically to Crenshaw's long story and say, "Well, you'll be all right eventually. Just take it easy, and if you get any kind of headache, then take some of these incredible pain pills that totally blur the world into a palatable place. And, if you get dizzy, come back because there's some more stuff I can charge you for that will do absolutely nothing for your head but will make you feel better about yourself."

Crenshaw liked doctors when the problem was one that a pill could solve; Crenshaw knew how to simply suffer already.

The nurse eventually left after more questions that were obvious or that the hospital already had or that were simply not any of her damn business.

Crenshaw sat uncomfortably in the room alone and he waited and he waited and he waited.

After a bit, he began browsing in the office and turned on the ear light and looked in the trashcan with its pop-up lid and tested his reflexes with the tomahawk rubber mallet and even tried to see his tonsils by putting the Popsicle stick down his throat and looking in the mirror. He tasted the sterile wood like biting into a balsa airplane. He was just looking at some X-rays he had found in the drawer when the doctor came into the room.

"Mr. Crenshaw?" The doctor asked to make sure.

"That's me." Crenshaw turned around.

"Holy Cow. That's some knot on your head, Mr. Crenshaw." He immediately moved over and took the X-rays Crenshaw had been playing with out of Crenshaw's hands. "These are private information."

"Well, you shouldn't leave them in the room, then." Crenshaw wasn't in the mood for hand slapping. "What's wrong with my head and can you do anything for it to make it better?"

The doctor turned professional and put on his doctor's facade.

They went through the "cough" and "is this too cold?" and "breath out." Crenshaw obliged each test. The nurse simply stood behind the doctor and handed him things and smiled an empty smile.

"Mr. Crenshaw, we'd like to run some tests."

"My head's what's hurting. Here." Crenshaw pointed to his head. "Why do you keep looking at everything but my head?" Crenshaw wanted everything to be clear.

"Yes, I know your 'head.' We're going to run some tests on your 'head,'" Doctor Roy used Crenshaw's terminology. "But I'd also like to run some tests to check some other things."

"The godderned rock's what caused the knot," Crenshaw stated the obvious just in case the doctor had not read the chart. "Doctors are about as stupid as a bowling ball," Crenshaw added under his breath.

"I'm not stupid, Mr. Crenshaw. I'm very concerned." The doctor was unfazed by Crenshaw's harassment. "I'm going to give you a prescription and you take the medicine before you come in and it will clean you out." He tore the paper from the pad. "You don't eat Thursday after noon and drink only liquids, but not alcohol, and come in at seven—that's in the morning, not at night—you come to the hospital. We'll give you a sort of sedative that will put you out."

"Just to check my head?" Crenshaw was very confused. He sat down and crossed his legs. Bip always sat the same way with his legs crossed and his arms crossed in an X over his knees leaning inquisitively but comfortably forward.

"Mr. Crenshaw ..." The doctor's tone changed and he took off his stethoscope and laid it on the crinkly paper of the stirrup bed. Crenshaw looked at the stirrups and remembered how cold they were in his hands just a few minutes earlier when he was waiting for the doctor. 'Hospitals are simply cold places,' Crenshaw thought. Cold and harsh and stark and degrading. They are meat markets. Body repair stations where you are either regenerated or cast out.

"Your file from Dr. Bill says you're borderline anemic. You have complained of irritable bowel for two years. You suffer headaches daily, and you complain recently of lack of energy and motivation at times. All of these symptoms may be interrelated or not, but you're not a young man and it's time to find out some things—just to be safe."

"It might be that I have a crazy daughter and a grandson who wants to be a Voodoo Sambo when he grows up, and God knows delivering milk for twenty-seven years gets old after a while, all on top of getting hit by a boulder dropped out of the sky."

The nurse bumped the tray behind Crenshaw and he jumped and looked at her like a wild animal. He felt completely out of his environment and resented being diagnosed by a man who'd barely known him six-and-a-half minutes but had already decided to take a look under his hood.

"I've been healthy all my life. I quit smoking in ninth grade and I only drink during Christmas, the Cowboys' and Rangers' baseball season. I eat three times a day and I even get my exercise delivering my route, even though I hate it."

"Mr. Crenshaw...."

"You don't have to say my name every time you talk to me. We're the only three godderned people in the room."

"I'm not here to debate what you do and don't do. I'm here to find the cause of your problems. You had the headaches before the accident. If there's something we can do, we need to know now instead of waiting."

"Buffalo hit me on purpose," Crenshaw said slightly under his breath.

"Whatever." The doctor crossed his arms. He was through and was only waiting for Crenshaw's decision. "It's your decision."

Crenshaw looked at Doctor Roy with a long silence. The doctor's glasses were sitting down on the tip of his nose as if they might just slide off the end and drop with a clank to the antiseptic floor. Crenshaw wanted to reach over and push them back in place, maybe even a little roughly and then thump the doctor on the forehead. Instead he turned and looked at the nurse who was still smiling her empty doll-like smile. Her dress was bleach white and her teeth were bleach white, too.

He knew they would probe every hole in his body before it was all said and done, and every last bit of dignity would flow out of a tube to be analyzed like an animal at the vet, and that they would talk about him like a step-child in front of his face as he lay there. He knew that they would throw terms around like a baseball and cover their trails with pills and diagnosis and checkups until he may never know exactly what's been ailing him.

All he wanted, suddenly, was a burrito and a beer, Tony Dorsett and a pack of cigarettes, and a shotgun to shoot gallons of milk off the top of the television and a dirty movie starring the "Smiling Nurse."

"I'll be in on Thursday."

"Daddy, do you mind if I stop at Sacker's to get a cup of coffee; we're fifteen minutes early anyway?" Mary was still working on her makeup. She had woken up late.

"I'm hungry, too, Paw Paw," Bip usually ate Cream of Wheat for breakfast, but because Mary got up late, Bip didn't get to eat. "I can get some little white donuts and a Big Red," he looked at Crenshaw with hopeful eyes.

"I'm the one who's starving to death," Crenshaw whined. He was looking out the front window of the pickup calculating if they had enough time to stop.

"I haven't eaten a thing since that chicken fried steak. Mary, that was the worst gravy I've ever eaten."

Mary didn't say anything.

Mary had agreed to make him chicken fried steak as his proverbial last-meal-before-the-hospital. She had breaded the meat well and dipped it in the milk and egg and back into the peppered and salted flour and then into the hot lard, but she had also used more of the milk than she needed for breading and thus discovered she'd run out when she poured what she had left in the milk carton into the pan over the sizzling flour, and desperately trying to keep it from lumping, she had used the only milk she could find, Bip's chocolate Oak Farms from the refrigerator. Thus, she successfully created chocolate gravy.

Crenshaw had almost gotten sick when he tasted it.

They pulled into Sacker's and all went in. Bip ran from place to place because Crenshaw had over emphasized the importance of their expediency. Mary, on the other side of the store, however, was methodically fingering all the chip bags. Finally she settled on a Snickers bar, instead. She grabbed a Diet Coke just before the checkout stand. Soon, they were all back in the truck on their thirty-mile drive to the hospital.

Crenshaw pointed out the exact telephone pole where Brock's cow had fallen out of the trailer on the way to the stock show. Brock's daughter had failed to check the lock on the stock trailer and the cow had backed out of the trailer while Brock was clipping down the highway. His description of the event was always vivid.

"Said, 'It was like the cow was tied to a big rock in the highway and all at once the cow was ripped from the trailer as her hoofs caught the pavement. Flipped up into the air as her neck broke and slid on her side leaving a red line deep in the asphalt." It was tradition for Crenshaw to point out the place, even though he'd done it for the six years, ever since the accident.

"Paw Paw, why do you always say, 'That's the pole that Brock's cow ended up by?' You say that every time."

Crenshaw took Bip's Big Red and took a sip of it. "I'd kill the Pope for one of those little white donuts." Bip smiled his white little mouth up at his grandfather; Crenshaw took the half-eaten donut out of Bip's package and ate it in one bite and stole one more sip of the Big Red. Bip wiped his hands on his pant's leg.

"Bip, honey," Mary talked with her mouth wrapped around the Snicker. She kept the bottom half still in the wrapper so that the chocolate wouldn't get on her hand, "Don't get that white powder all over; it's sugar, honey. You know how I hate sticky …" Bip cut in over her.

"Paw Paw, what're they gonna do to you at the hospital."

Crenshaw didn't really know who to tell Bip. Adult stuff is always a little foreign to young ears. He decided the direct approach.

"They're gonna stick a telescope up my bottom and look at my colon."

"Holy Cow!" The little white donuts didn't sound as good suddenly. "What on earth for, Paw Paw? Do you want 'em to do that?!"

"Hell no, I don't want 'em to do that. I rather eat broken Coke bottles and see Flora Hatchett naked than that."

"Daddy!"

"I'm sorry, honey. I ain't just real excited is all."

"Are they looking for something, Paw Paw, or just doing it to hurt you?"

The sun broke over the horizon and a ray of light fell across the sky and spotlighted the three on their way to the city.

"I just want to be done with it. Let's don't talk about it anymore. My tummy hurts."

"Just relax, Daddy. I love you," Mary said and added as she looked at him long enough to go off the side of the road a bit and throw some gravel.

"Watch the road. What do want to do, kill me?"

Bip shoved the last donut in his mouth and drank the last of his Big Red and then clenched his butt cheeks together and mumbled a slightly audible "ouch" and looked up at his Paw Paw who was staunchly looking out the front window into the sunrise.

The red and yellow colored Crenshaw's face like paint.

CHAPTER 16

▼

LILITH'S VISION

Death is an end. After a person has died, only then can all the equations be squared-up and a final sum be calculated. In Len's case, his death was most certainly an ending, obviously, but his death, also, slowly became a mercurial and heated beginning for the town, a conscious black tar oozing from the summer pavement. The town, after the funeral's curious clod fight, realized finally, after years of head-turning and shopping only in the market nearest them, that the other existed. It was a tremendous revelation for all of the community. The town was like a couple caught in bed, as if a blanket had been torn back from their naked bodies and the spotlights thrust against their black and white eyes.

Also, Benzel, Willie May, James and Len's deaths grew as an infectious reminder to the community that death is always near and hungry. They had been reminded only one year earlier of death's tongue when Sire Johnson lifted his irrigation pipe to the sky to catch a rabbit who was hiding in its dark tunnel, and Sire caught the highline wire. The tragedy had spun the town together into death's whirlpool throat and drowned them for the better part of three months and would have made it into the next month if Jessie Cruz hadn't died by running his company car under that school bus trying to get that cassette tape off the passenger's side floorboard. It took the top of his car clean off. People said the accident was so hideous that even Flora wouldn't even go view the body.

Death turns life into statistics and final answers because the living chaos is gone and only certainty remains.

The town itself was quiet for very many days. The Lions club was too depressed to throw ping-pong balls or biscuits at their noon meeting. The senior citizens had lost their vigor. The Viva La Raza car club drove the speed limit for the first time since the Cuban Missile Crisis and didn't even raise and lower their vehicles at the Burger Barn, which disappointed the bright eyes of the smallest children whose lot in life was to peer out of side windows with their gums full of soft-push ice cream and delight at the men who could make their cars jump. Lilith's liquor consumption fell to an all-time low. It was even rumored that Buffalo had been broken to drinking Thunderbird instead of beer, which left his hangover heavy.

The town was broken. The feeling was as deep and empty as the hollow stone caves at Striker's Canyon, just out of town, that tunneled crookedly like veins into the round heart of the earth. The sadness seemed to generate from the blackened soil under the Rose theater, to spread like brown sugar-water against the courthouse, flowing like thick honey down the gutters until every house in Flatland was sweetly sluggish, mourning with sugary concern: wives moved from their beds to thinking couches; daughters moved into showers of sagging streams of water onto confused bodies; sons pushed the heavy pedals of their bicycles to the stores for errands; and the fathers dropped their trot-lines into the stock tanks waiting for the blood bait to sit heavily on the silted landscape under the calm of the dark water. The town was slow and broken.

They were waiting.

Across the tracks, Lilith awoke with her body sweating and her ceiling fan slowly curling around the room like an old cat about to take a nap. Her coffee skin was smooth and oily and wet and caught the sheets as she rolled from one position to another. Her skin smelled of tonic and perfume water. She finally gathered the strength to move toward the bath. She turned on the cold water only, slowly undressed, and with her hands pressed white on the side of the tub, her forehead cringed looking as if five black earthworms were crawling heavily across her brow. She lowered herself carefully into the water as goose bumps rose across her body; the water felt almost as if someone had sneaked in and filled it with ice and let it melt. She sighed when her belly was finally under the plane. The water continued to wiggle from the faucet and rose under her heavy breasts. Lilith lifted her breasts and floated them in the cool water.

It was under the mesmerizing cool of the water that she had her vision.

Eyes closed, she saw the entire community gathered around the courthouse. It was some sort of town festivity, she decided. She stayed in control of the vision and walked, concentrating on her hands. She knew prophet warriors were always able to focus on their hands, then survey the area and return to their hands as a point of focal force.

The grass was green and plush and she was not wearing shoes. There were bees feeding on the cherry blossoms just above her head and they were very busy, much too busy to be concerned with stinging her. She decided they were nice bees. Everybody was in their underwear and smiling and were gathered around someone in the center as if they were at the scene of some great crime nest. She moved closer. She was shocked when she realized who was in the center.

Len was alive and talking to the people. He was in his underwear, too, but his were red.

He was holding his hands out. Everyone was looking at him and then cupping their ears in their hands like some overdone ritual and then made three high pitched "hoots." Then, they would all politely pull out their underwear and look in to confirm something, then snap the elastic tightly back against their stomachs. It was almost like a square dance. Len was talking the entire time between snaps and looks, rather emotionless, until a pain so horrible overcame him, and without warning, his guts spilled out onto the ground and he held his head as if the sirens were calling him from the mast of a ship. His lips convulsed and moved, bouncing and stretching and twisting. Len's head beat with rising concern.

No one spoke or offered any assistance except for Crenshaw who would evanesce each time Len's head would swell. The others merely looked at Len in his red underwear and crazy lips and exploded entrails. The townspeople all studied his movements and read his each action like Tarot cards.

Lilith tried to move in her vision again. She was able, so she moved to Len and touched him. Len stopped talking like a machine abruptly turned off. Len's head grew larger and larger and the image of Crenshaw just below the tree flickered and finally popped out of sight.

The hot sun glared down on Lilith. She looked at all the faces who were turned to her now. The faces were empty and lost and looking to Lilith for guidance. They wanted her to tell them the secret, to offer them the apple of knowledge.

Suddenly, Len writhed back to life only long enough to let out a guttural shriek as his head exploded, and, like Zeus giving birth to Athena, Crenshaw popped through the cranium out onto the ground like a newborn child.

The striking of the cuckoo clock in the kitchen brought Lilith out of her trance. The little bird thrust in and out of the clock, standing at attention. The sun was rising in the morning sky. It was halfway to noon and seemed less tolerable. It raged yellow like an egg yolk across Lilith's white linoleum floor, painting the shiny white porcelain tub mustard. Lilith felt the cool of the bath and relaxed. Once clean, she patted her body dry, careful to get into every crease and roll.

She dressed and shuffled in her house shoes to the kitchen where she smashed red beans that she had cooked the day before in hot bacon lard with chili powder and seared the outside. On the back burner, she fried potatoes with onion and small squares of ham and scrambled eggs with green chilies and tomatoes. She squeezed lime over the beans and drank the rest of her ice cold tomato juice with pepper and Worcestershire and three fingers of vodka.

Her first few drinks in the morning were always her best. She could feel the liquor run through her veins and thin her sluggish blood and settle the gas in her stomach. The zing, when it hit her brain, was as pleasing as eating a fresh coca bean and feeling the push of the caffeine. She felt good now, clean and refreshed and ready to meet the day.

CHAPTER 17

▼

HOME

"There has to be order somewhere that allows us to sleep and wake with purpose, but with this comes undefined limitations: sorrow when things should be immaculate: laughter where tears and silence should prevail. Things have to be well somewhere at sometime. There will always be someone just behind us, friend or enemy. There will always be someone just behind them, mirrors facing each other reflecting nothing into infinity; it's the primary paradox. We must learn to find the simple yellow mornings and white bright afternoons and clean crisp evenings that let us sleep like twitching cats chasing some big fat imaginary mouse. We must not dwell on who stands behind us or why...." Dawn put the book down and sighed. She hated reading shit she couldn't understand. She just wanted to feel good and get through life without much thinking.

"Why don't they write in English, Mama," she yelled from the couch to Mary. Mary was in the kitchen cooking spaghetti.

"Who, honey?"

"Whoever this is I have to read for tomorrow." Dawn was in a special three week summer class that would get her extra credit so she could graduate.

Mary pointed her head toward the door and spoke louder. "You know I hated English when I was in school. I hated school when I was in school." Mary covered the boiling noodles and crushed the tomatoes between her fingers and one-smashed the garlic under the large blade of her knife.

Dawn got up and went into the kitchen and sat at the table.

The table was white Formica top and reflected a pale image of Dawn. Dawn watched herself talk in the faint image in the table.

"Are you making garlic bread, Mama?"

"I can." Mary immediately reached for the bread as if the question were actually a request.

"That's all right. I have a date tonight. I wanted you not to put so much garlic on mine." Dawn sucked on a piece of ice and spit it back into her glass of water.

"I ought to put on twice as much." Mary said it without laughing, but Dawn took it as a joke rather than a reprimand.

"You don't like Billie, do you Mama?" Dawn asked smiling.

"I just want you to stay home some nights is all."

"Mama, you're just saying that," Dawn revolted, but really deep inside she was not excited about the date. She and Billie would meet and talk about nothing and make out. That's what they always did and really she was a little tired of it; the excitement was gone. Actually it was Dawn who didn't like to talk about things; it was she that carried on the surface conversations, not Billie. Billie was very bright and thoughtful. Dawn was bright, too: She just didn't care to think, was all.

"Mama, I was going to the movies tonight."

"I'm not telling you that you can't go. I asking you to stay.'

"Stay and do what?" Dawn closed the book. Sometimes Mary kept little secrets up her sleeve that she pulled out slowly like a long golden string with diamonds in dropped sparkles.

"Go tell your brother to come down to supper," Mary said sassy.

"I didn't say I'd stay yet,' Dawn called over her shoulder to her mother as she climbed the stairs to Bip's room.

She passed a picture of Len in the hall. She started just to pass by it, but something grabbed her, not hard, but grabbed her, and it made her look at the picture. He was stanch and postured in his office with his hair all Dippidy-Dooed down with a half-smile like he was making a business deal. "That doesn't even look like him," she said as much for herself as for him.

Dawn turned around to Bip's door. "Now here's another story," she thought; she paused and rolled her eyes at Bip's door. She hated to knock, really, because she was afraid he might be up to some project that he'd have to explain to her before they went down to supper and take about a million hours.

She knocked.

"Enter," Bip called calmly from inside.

Dawn opened the door and peeked inside.

Bip's bunkbeds were in the corner squashed over as far as he could get them. Pictures covered the wall behind the beds. They were wax color, watercolor, tempera, and chalk. Some were discernible Greek mythological characters like the Minotaur and the Cyclops—more of an Ovid Cyclops than a Homer Cyclops with a kaleidoscopic eye and myriad of colors. Some of the other paintings were swirls and mixtures of colors that tried to blend with each other but seemed to fight even within the same canvas. His telescope was pointing out the open window. He had taught Dawn some of the constellations.

"Mama says to come down to supper." Dawn picked up a shirt and was going to take it to the dirty clothes and then threw it back down as if she were horrified at having any clue of a motherly instinct.

"What're we having."

"Spaghetti."

"Did she make garlic bread?" Mary's spaghetti was the best.

"I think she is now."

"Are you eating here?'

Dawn had not eaten at home with Bip and Mary in quite some time. There was always cheerleader practice or show choir or drama practice.

"Yeah, I think something's up."

"She's not crazy or anything is she." Mary at times could be reclusive and rather difficult. She had a dark, creative side that demanded attention once in a while. They understood it, but they didn't necessarily always enjoy it unless it was her crazy happy side.

"Happy, I think."

"Really." Bip was somewhat excited.

He put down his harmonica and stood up.

When Mary was happy she could be damn happy.

Dawn suddenly had a look come over her face and a smile spread. Bip had not seen her smile like a little girl in a long time. He smiled back honestly.

"What?" He knew something was up.

"Let's dress up for supper. It was almost ready a second ago and we could surprise Mama. It'd make sure her mood was good."

"And you'll stay even after supper."

"Yeah." Dawn moved over to Bip and bent down and looked him in the eyes. He was a handsome boy. She was a beautiful young woman.

"You're so good to me, Bip." She started crying without really knowing why and Bip joined her. They had been through so much.

"I'm so sorry about daddy," Dawn cried.

"Me too." He paused. "I'm worried about Paw Paw, too." Bip put in more concern.

They hugged very close and hard without talking, long enough for Mary to yell up the stairs. Her voice twisted and climbed each step until it found Bip's room and slipped through the door and found the two embraced.

"Three minutes," Dawn backed up and held up three fingers and smiled at Bip and wiped the tears from Bip's eyes and then from her own eyes.

"You've never been ready in three minutes in your life."

"Race you." She stuck her tongue out sassy.

"Close your eyes, Mama," Dawn stopped at the top of the stairs and held Bip behind her.

"If you're wearing that god awful red mini skirt I told you to throw away, you're not leaving this house." Mary looked up the stairs and saw no one. "Ya'll come on." Mary was starting to get a bit testy. She hated for a meal to get cold. Food is to be served hot. "The dinner's getting cold and the garlic's loosing its punch." She added the garlic part to test the waters.

"I'm not going, Mama." Dawn told her mother so that that could be out of the way. "Now, close your eyes."

Mary shuffled a few things on the stove, wiped the sweat from her face on her apron and then closed her eyes.

"O.K. My damn eyes are closed." Mary squinted her eyes closed hard. Mary was not the type to peek.

Bip and Dawn rounded the top steps and stood side-by-side.

"O.K. Mama. Here we are."

Mary opened her eyes. Mary had expected some joke or some broken vase or a white-underwear-washed-with-the-new-red-towel; instead, Mary's eyes lit bright and shiny as brown glass marbles.

Dawn's dress was black and short and the straps held the dress just square over her bare back. Her eyes were piercing green and her yellow hair crashed against her red lipstick. Dressing up to Dawn was elegance meeting desire. She was a knockout. Bip was in a simple little black suit with a white tux shirt with a red tie and cummerbund, the cummerbund was upside-down. Crenshaw had bought Bip the suit for the funeral, but also had in the back of his mind that Bip might need it for a quick wedding the way his Mary and Dawn were.

"You two look like honest to God angels."

"Mama, you're not mad at me are you," Bip was apprehensive.

"Why on earth would I be angry with you, baby boy?" She was taken aback tracing her mind for some clue to his question.

"It was the only really nice thing I had to wear," he indicated the suit.

Mary welled with tears for a second. "Oh no. Oh no, honey. No. You look absolutely heavenly. My little man."

The three ate at the kitchen table in the middle of the kitchen. Mary and Bip ate at the ends and Dawn was like a bridge between them. Mary had put spaghetti on each plate and covered it with the sauce of hand squeezed tomatoes and lots of garlic and marinated artichoke hearts and pepper, basil, and cilantro. She had started the sauce early so it could boil down to a thickness. She poured that over the spaghetti and sprinkled some Romano and Parmesan and put a few fingers full of capers on hers and Bip's. Dawn didn't like capers. Because of the celebration, whatever the celebration was, Mary had also topped each plate with a sprig of fresh parsley and a wedge of lemon. The garlic bread was pan fried in butter and sprinkled with oregano and black pepper and browned and sat in a plate in the middle of the table. Dawn was just starting to eat when Mary got up.

"Mama, don't get up. Just sit and eat with us." Dawn wanted everyone to be together. Sometimes Mary would get up and get to doing something right in the middle of a meal and actually forget to eat.

"I'm getting something special." She smiled impishly.

She got a backless chair; Bip had knocked the back off with his Bozo punching bag a year ago throwing it at Dawn who had eaten part of his brownie while he was in the restroom. She stood on the chair and reached way back in the cabinet and told Bip to come and get the glasses. She handed him three glasses he had never seen before. They were long stem crystal. Mary knew, but Bip didn't, that they were forty-eight dollars a stem. They were immaculate.

"Be careful with those, honey." She jumped down and dug into the back of the refrigerator and fished out a bottle of Champagne. Dawn raised her eyebrows.

"Come to mama!" Dawn loved champagne, as little as she even knew what champagne was. She liked the fizz and the bubbles. With her interest raised, she went and dug in the refrigerator and found the strawberries she had bought the day before at the fruit market. She dropped one in her glass and added a little sugar.

"Mama?" Mary shook her head 'yes' and pointed to Bip.

"I get to drink some?" Bip was kind of scared and excited.

"If you can open the bottle."

Bip had opened one bottle before and accidentally shot their cat, Rachel Ronteria, who had kittens in the fall. Bip, oddly, had always paralleled the two events.

Bip clutched the bottle between his legs and untwisted the wire and started to try to twist the cork in some direction away from his sister and his mother. For a second he couldn't get anything to move, then like a bullet out of a gun the cork fired and hit the light fixture on the ceiling and ricocheted into the sink and rolled under the cheese grater. The liquid boiled up out of the top and ran for a second onto the floor. He handed the bottle to Mary. She poured herself a full glass and a full glass for Dawn.

"You're not going out tonight? Right?" She was asking Dawn.

"Right."

She filled Bip's halfway.

"You're not going out tonight? Right?" She was telling Bip.

"Right."

Bip sniffed the glass.

"Take it real slow honey," She was talking to Bip. "A toast!"

"What are we toasting, Mama." Bip didn't see much to toast. His stepfather had been shot and buried. Crenshaw had been checked at the hospital, and they had kept him there running more tests.

"What did you expect life to be honey? There's not one human being in this world that hasn't been thrown a fast ball before they even had their bat up. We toast to your daddy, Dawn. He was a fine man. Both times around." They all drank. "And, Bip, to your daddy. He was one of a kind—thank God. And thank God you're just like the crazy loon." What Mary lacked in suave she made up for in brass honesty. She was right. She could sit and brood about how pitiful her life was and focus on the minor details, or she could pick up and go on. She wasn't negating her past. She was merely giving it recognition and putting it to a restful spot, like closing and shelving a book but not forgetting the plot and theme.

Bip smiled and lifted his glass and drank his first drink. It was infinitely better than the vanilla he had been used to drinking and he felt the immediate light-headedness. Dawn drank most of hers quickly and refilled her half-empty glass.

"Honey, at least try to make it look like champagne is new to you," Mary said to Dawn and Dawn poured a bit slower and filled her mother's glass, also.

Bip toasted each time someone made up a new toast but he was careful not to take too much. He didn't want to get sick or weird. Mary and Dawn, on the other hand, were downing each toast and following it with intermittent bites of garlic bread and bites of spaghetti.

After they had put most of their problems to rest by toasting them to death and eaten all the winding noodles they could, Mary got what was left of the champagne and they all gathered together and ascended to Bip's room.

Mary turned off each of the lights behind her and by the time they reached Bip's room, only his light was on. He quickly lit a candle and turned off his light. It took them several minutes to get used to the darkness. Mary and Dawn's hair and skin were satin under the soft glow of the light.

Mary and Dawn were drinking straight from the bottle now. They were drunk; they were not silly though, or even excitable. They were rather calm and complacent and thinking of nothing but hearing the crickets chirp outside of Bip's open second story window and feeling the cool night's air. The stars were piercing white like silver glitter spilled against the back of the night.

"Mama, did you ever wish daddy wouldn't of come back?' Dawn struck a whole note.

Mary didn't flinch. "Once."

"When?'

Dawn was trying to confirm thoughts.

"When he told me to get my own ketchup that time. That pissed me off. I'd been with you and Bip-baby all day long at the store shopping and studying for that Bible school crap, trying to learn my lines to be Mary Magdalene, and he had the audacity to say, when I asked him to get the ketchup, for him to say 'Get the ketchup yourself.'"

"I remember that," Dawn laughed and rolled back on the floor and took a quick sip of champagne, not like she was with her mother but rather with her friends. Her cheeks bubbled out like she had two cue balls in each cheek.

"I have the scope set up," Bip offered. He was really out of his element.

"Let's look at the damn stars." Mary stood up and meant it. She wanted to bury herself in the sky for a minute instead of hard soil and hot kitchens and cleaning damn house and gas for the car and stamps for the bills. "Let's look at the stars." She said it this time but pointed out the window and Bip knew she was serious.

"Can you see Orion, Mama?"

Bip was excited.

"Who can't see Orion, Baby? Show me a new one."

Bip rolled through his mind and rolled back and he couldn't think of one single constellation he hadn't tried to push on Dawn and Mary.

"Mama," he was embarrassed, "I can't think of one I've not already shown you."

"I got one." Dawn was emphatic and stood up like a teacher. "I found it the other night. It's a stick man with glasses behind a desk."

She showed the constellation to Mary and Bip at least six times and it included Orion's belt. Finally they saw it like watching clouds.

They named it "Len."

Bip fell asleep between Mary and Dawn on the floor and they all held each other, and the air conditioner clicked on; the hum lulled them to an easier sleep. Dawn and Mary were curled over Bip.

Mary woke after a bit. She was cold from the open window. Outside the crescent moon was like bleached bone in the sky; two horns plowing the sky together. She thought about closing the window, but instead she decided simply to cover them all with the black and white comforter from Bip's bed and go to sleep and dream. She knew she would never have this moment again.

CHAPTER 18

▼

THE HOSPITAL

The elevator was stuffed. The gurney with the female patient on the way to operation crowded the Martinez family into the corner. The patient was equally violated. She gazed at the ceiling as if her life had been lifted forward to this single moment of true honesty among anonymous humanity. The Martinez family had terse words with each other in short fricatives and glottal stops, and mother of the children told them to touch the gurney of the lady so they wouldn't give her the "Ojo." The lady merely continued to stare into space consumed with her destiny. Paul looked into the eyes of the lady. She didn't see Paul, but he saw her suffering.

Paul was anxious and uncomfortable about coming to see Crenshaw.

The elevator stopped with a slight rise followed by a fall and a jerk. The orderly wheeled out the woman into the hall and they grew smaller as shrinking walls framed them smaller and smaller and snapped shut.

"We need floor six, please. Seis." Tabot said to the little Mexican boy who had moved to the front of the elevator. He had squeezed between Walter and Paul on his way past.

The little boy pushed the six.

"I thought he's on floor five?" Walter asked.

"He's on six." Tabot knew. He had asked the candy stripe helper at the front desk.

"Is 'seis' six?" Walter asked.

"He pushed six, Walter."

"He's on five though."

"He's on six and he pushed six, Walter. Calm down."

The little Mexican boy asked Paul if he had any gum and Paul just stood there. Paul was chewing a piece of gum. He did that when he rode any elevator to keep his ears from stopping up. Even a rise of two or three stories made his ears pop. He attributed it to living all his life on the level plains of Texas where a lump in the soil was considered a mountain.

The boy pulled Paul's pants leg, and when Paul looked down, the boy asked again in Spanish. Paul tried to read his lips but could make nothing of it.

"That's rude." Walter took it upon himself to discipline the child. "He can't hear and you shouldn't ask for things unless they're offered," Walter continued. He spoke very slowly and succinctly in over-mouthed English.

The little boy was neither offended nor concerned with Walter's reprimand. In fact, he couldn't understand one word Walter had said.

The elevator stopped, lifted, jerked and sat back down and the doors opened in a spread to the sixth floor.

"I hate this place, Tabot." Walter was still uptight.

"Well, what do you want them to do, bring him out into the parking lot to the window of your car? Drive in patient visit?"

"There's a funeral home in California that puts the person in a display case and you just drive through and wave and be done with it."

"They're dead, Walter. They can't see you wave or care if you drive by anyway. Crenshaw isn't dead."

This was hard for all of them. Crenshaw was their friend. Crenshaw had been in the hospital for three weeks now. He had checked in for his head, which led to the stomach check, and he had never checked out.

Dr. Roy had found cancer.

"His room's down this way," Tabot pointed and led the way.

As they went by each room, Tabot and Walter made it a point not to look into the rooms. They had learned from experience that it was easier to ignore the pain and suffering of hospitals than to witness it and digest it. Pain is supposed to happen to someone else. It's the other person who is supposed to lose a limb in a car accident, or the other person who gets the chronic hepatitis from the one bad oyster, or the years of bacon and eggs that led to the heart condition that led to the attack that led to the horrible bland diet that led to death in life and fear and dread in living. The three men sensed that, to the patients, they represented a walking symbol of healthfulness, almost an animal of three separate parts: a trinity of living red flesh; the marked "it;" the left-handed guest at the dinner table.

Paul, on the other hand, looked curiously into each room and registered each individual as one who was simply in a struggle against the inevitable. Paul certainly recognized that all humanity must, at some exact second, face mortality—however inconvenient it might be. So he chose to wave and smile into each room. Some patients responded with a slight wave back or even a verbal 'Hello.' But a good part of the patients turned away in their winding sheets and gowns as if they were pitiful personifications of the diseases they harbored. One man even looked blankly at the ceiling almost as if he were waiting for it to drop on him and crush his body under the stark white nothingness. Paul stopped and looked at the man. The man continued his hollow glare; he looked like a pallid shell of flesh. Paul had the thought after a second that instead of dying, the man might just deflate. Paul even had a more horrible thought that if the ceiling did indeed fall on the hollow man, then instead of crushing the man it might actually pop him like a balloon.

Paul decided to quit looking into rooms and instead to simply walk down the hall, like Walter and Tabot.

When they reached Crenshaw's room the door was closed.

"This is it, Horace Erastisis Crenshaw," Tabot read the name on the door and pointed out the name to Walter. "I told you I knew where I was going."

"I still thought that Mary said he was on five," even in his defeat Walter was still unable to accept it totally.

"Is thiiis iiit." Paul had missed the formal announcement of "being there."

"We're here," Tabot pointed to the door identification again.

"What a middle name, 'Erastisis.' You'd swear you'd heard them all and you come to the hospital and find out Horace Crenshaw's middle name is 'Erastisis.'"

A muffled sound came from behind the closed door.

"And if you tell anybody my damn middle name I'm gonna put a IV full of rubbing alcohol in your arm." Horace was ready to see the three men.

"Well, this is the right room all right." Tabot said as he pushed open the door with anxiousness but excitement.

There was an immediate fall of face between the friends. They expected Crenshaw to be in his normal condition, only prone, perhaps in a smoking gown maybe even smoking a pipe reading the Journal. Crenshaw, however, was like a caged atrocity rather than a human being.

His eyes were sunken into his head and his mouth had curled into itself; he had taken his dentures out and they lay on the nightstand next to him in a plastic cup by his "nurses call" button. His cheeks were shadows and his arms and legs were pitiful. But the voice that came from the body was Crenshaw's.

Paul went over first and shook Crenshaw's hand. He was uncomfortable a bit. Even though cancer is not contagious, one still doesn't like to shake hands with it. Paul noticed the tube running over Crenshaw's shoulder and under the sheet to his chest.

"That's my chemotherapy. I won't feel too bad for a couple of days and then I'll feel like I'm gonna die and wish I would."

Tabot and Walter laughed uneasily. Paul noticed everyone laughing so he laughed, too.

There was a long silence.

"So what you been watching on the TV," Walter didn't know what to say but he knew he needed to say something to kill the electric silence.

"A lot of game shows and sometimes I turn that mute button on American Bandstand on Saturday and watch the girls. Some of those gals get dang near naked. Nurse told me I better quit getting excited without an outlet. It's nice having a remote."

They all just looked at him. How can a pitiful, dying man think about sex, they wondered.

There was a long silence again.

"When do you get out?" Tabot asked the next question.

"Tabot, do I look like I'm going anywhere soon." He was pumped full of tubes and hoses and tape and tags. "They opened me up and closed me back without so much as a appendectomy. Said I's full of the cancer."

"Did they say how the rock did all that, Crenshaw." Walter asked and was serious. He had tears in his eyes.

Crenshaw hooted and hollered at the top of his lungs and got so tickled that he almost passed out coughing.

"The rock caused the knot that caused the checkup that caused the questions that caused the other tests that found the cancer. Almost wish Buffalo would have throwed a bigger rock a little harder and knocked me in the grave with Len. Then, I wouldn't have to think about it. It would already be done and nobody'd have to come by. They'd could just look at me in the box and have a nice funeral and plop me in the ground and talk about how tragic it was that Horace Crenshaw got killed by that rock at that funeral. But as it is they'll talk about how pitiful if was that Horace got the cancer and suffered so long and how nobody deserves that." He paused. "Nobody does. But look up and down this hall. There's a bunch of nobody's in this hall that don't deserve it."

Crenshaw had changed. He hadn't changed his philosophy necessarily, but he obviously was playing a different ballgame than the three men in the room with him. Tabot remembered his father coming back from WWI without a leg and that he was different. He understood now. Once you smell death, you're not normal anymore. You're a standard deviation from the norm. Once you're pegged, you become part of the waiting room.

"I'm in purgatory now. I'm waiting. I know I'm waiting."

"What's the channel for the girls." Walter had the channel changer clipping through channels.

Crenshaw loved Walter's ignorance. He was trying to tell Walter a glimpse of the meaning of life, and all Walter wanted to do was to watch almost naked girls. Walter didn't have remote at home or all the channels like in Grandville. They found the channel and Tabot pulled up a chair and rested his feet on Crenshaw's bed and Walter sat on the end and Paul stayed in his chair. The channel was clear and clean and the screen was big and full of young full girls moving and gyring and twisting their thighs and hips at the camera in front of a whipped cream machine with smoke and bubbles.

Crenshaw realized he might be seeing a lot of Walter after this.

Paul tried to keep beat on his knee. He didn't know the sound was off.

They stayed until visiting hours were over.

CHAPTER 19

▼

SACKER'S GROCERY

Bip arrived at Sacker's Grocery just before two-thirty and was drinking a Big Red when he noticed how hot the air was. He had found a note in the mailbox that morning: "Meets me at Sacker's Grocery at 2:30." He sat down in front of the store window on the red-bricked ledge. He was small against the large window-pane. SACKER'S GROCERY curled above his head in a rainbow. Gram Sacker had founded the store after he moved to Flatland in thirty-three and tried to vote the county wet.

Bip crossed his legs like a woman and held his arms crossed over his knees. His head slumped gracefully over his Big Red that was tilted in his hand. The bottle was cock-eyed to the concrete, almost as if it were looking for something, but the red liquid logically moved in the bottle and stood parallel to the earth. He fully intended to wait for whoever had left the note until well after four. He wasn't sure if Lilith had left the note; it could have been from Billie for Dawn.

The sweat gathered in salty beads on Bip's forehead and grew together until Bip was finally a sitting, dripping, sweating machine; Mary had taught him how to sweat when they went to South Padre Island the summer after her divorce from Len.

The porter had told Mary and Bip at the Arroyo de Oro, "Mr. Bip,"—except he said 'Mr. Beep' because of his accent—"you take a lot of liquids and you sweat a lot. But to sweat, it is good. Sweating cools your body and you don't mind that you get wet." At first Bip had noticed that this kind of sweating had a sweet smell and was much cleaner than earned sweat like when Dawn returned from her dates with Billie. He thought she stunk most of the time anyway with her cosmetics and perfume. He liked people who smelled natural, not mountain-man natural, but not postured.

Bip perused his arms wondering if his skin was red because of sweating out the Big Red or from the burning eye of the sun. His mind wandered again. On his fifth birthday he remembered that Mary had made him a green birthday cake; Bip was born on Saint Patrick's Day. The cake had so much green coloring in the icing that all of his friends spit green for just a few hours afterward. Wendi Michael said it was "gross" and went home. It was that one event that Bip always pointed back to when summing up the mysterious separation between the feminine and the masculine. Wendi, he recalled, said she left because Bip burped too much, but he knew that somehow the green spit had made her evaluate him. Bip disliked being judged.

He looked at his arm and decided his sweat was somewhat of a light pink, and probably a combination of Big Red sweat and sun. He was wearing a white T-shirt, an undershirt of Dawn's. It was too long and the short sleeves were almost long sleeves, but the shirt was white and soft. It still smelled like Dawn. It smelled like Dawn and bleach. Mary bleached everything.

Just after Mary's divorce from Len, Robert, Bip's birth father, was killed in a strange accident. Bip didn't like to think about it but could not help himself at times. Robert was a distance runner and would disappear for hours at a time in the summers only to return like Moses from the top of Mt. Sinai, as if he had seen God and had some message to save humanity.

Robert always ran along the railroad track that was lifted beside the highway. Sometimes he ran on the ties of the railroad track, down the middle, which forced him to time his steps and pay very close attention to each one, jumping over cactus or a rusting spike sunning in the sand. The track was built up, higher than everything around it, so as he ran he always felt a bit otherworldly as if running in the clouds.

The run became ritual and Robert began running with cotton in his ears, thinking that if he heard the rhythm of his heart and feet and the depth of his breath that he could somehow reach some higher state of existence. He was killed just at the end of his run where the railroad splits the two main roads. He still had both of his ears plugged with cotton he'd picked from the field and a gentle smile on his face when the train hit him, pushing him roughly off the track like a stray cow. The engineer didn't even see him or slow down; he was eating a bacon and garden tomato sandwich.

Robert's death was not greatly mourned in the city because he seemed to have died happily. Mary, obviously, was very moved by Robert's death. She had loved him very much; she just could not live with him, which is why Robert ran so much. Bip remembered looking at the body in the funeral home and how it didn't even look like his father. Bip had thought Robert looked painted like a clown and his head was still swollen and looked like a watermelon replica stuck on a stickman.

Bip decided not to think about it anymore. He was even a little angry that he had let himself think that far.

He had practiced only to think about life as one second followed by another. So, he had a talk with himself and regrouped his thoughts and became himself within the moment again and felt the sun on his skin and the sweat.

Bip was taking a drink of Big Red when he saw Lilith turn the corner. Her body leaned right then left over each foot. Her house shoes sounded like sandpaper on the concrete. She saw him almost immediately.

"What you doing here, Little Boy?"

"I found your message." He opened a second Big Red. Lilith continued toward Bip until she was standing directly in front of him.

"Does you believe in secrets, Little Boy?"

"It said for me to be here at the grocery. And I'm here. I'm not scared. I'm a Scout." Bip was trying to convince Lilith that he knew that it was her who had left the message.

"Lordy, it's as hot as an exhaust pipe on a motorcycle."

At one time Lilith had owned a Honda Ninety that she rode around town on. But because of her tendency to drink too much, she had too many spills and burns and near death incidents. The Methodist Women gathered a pool of money and brought the motorcycle from her at twice what she had paid Tabot for it and gave it to "Thanny" the dumpyard's gatekeeper who turned it into a very nice sculpture.

"Little Boy, gives me a drink of your soda-pop." Bip gave Lilith the bottle and she rubbed the bottle on her forehead then took a big swallow. Her body shook like she had just taken medicine. She smacked her lips.

"Lilith ain't had no Big Red without rum in a long time. It's better with the rum."

She gave Little Boy a few quarters.

"Go inside and get your Lilly a Big Red."

Bip took the quarters. "But what about the message?"

"Lilith done gonna forget her message if'n she don't has a drink soon." She sat down heavily on the windowsill. Mary drove by just as Bip went into the door and out of sight. Lilith raised her black hand and waved, "Afternoon, Miss Mary."

She was used to seeing Lilith on the corner.

Sometimes Lilith would get too drunk and Buffalo and Fox would have to come to pick her up and carry her back to the house. There were even rumors that once they had to put her in a wheelbarrow because she was too heavy and they were both drunk. Either way, she was often a test on the city's sense of moral decency. But she never cursed or got loud or ran off business. In fact, if anything, she attracted people to the store just to visit, which helped Sacker's business and that was fine with him. He offered to get her a lawn chair but she refused it saying she didn't want to make herself a habit, even though her presence already was a habit.

Bip came out of the store just as Mary passed from the other direction obviously double-checking the situation. Bip saw the tail lights light up like two red-candy suckers. Mary started to stop but then she went on.

"There goes my Mama," Bip said as he took several tries to open the can. "Sacker was out of bottles." He finally bent back his fingernail before he popped open the can. He took a drink and then handed the can to Lilith.

"You better go on and get you another swallow before I fix the can."

Bip did as he was told and took another drink.

As Lilith took her bottle from beneath her dress, she looked at Bip who was anxious.

"You sweat good Little Boy."

"Mama taught me how to sweat good."

"That's good. You gots a good Mama, Little Boy. When she ain't being a bitch, you gots you a good Mama. Does you Mama drink, Little Boy?" Lilith poured the dark brown rum into the small hole of the can, not spilling a drop, then put her thumb over the hole and turned the can upside down then right side up. When she took the thumb off of the can it spewed just a bit in a little cough. A drop landed next to Bip's mouth so he licked it and tasted the dark liquor.

"She only drinks on special occasions," he said.

"What, pray tell, is special to that woman?"

"The other night Mama drank a whole bottle of pop wine with a cork in it. But she doesn't drink as much as you."

"Nobody drink as much as Lilith, Little Boy. I gots to drink to keep the bad prophet away."

"When you see things?"

"That's right, Little Boy. But I's having trouble keeping the dark away just lately." Her mood changed drastically, seriously. "I ain't loosing my power," she said defensively. "Pray tell, it's just that …" She paused. "Little Boy, does you dream?"

"Everybody dreams, my teacher says."

"Don't you tease Lilith with 'teacher-say.' I ask you, does *you* dream?"

"Yes, Ma'am."

"What kind of dream?"

"I dream strange dreams mostly. I walk in my sleep, too." Bip closed his eyes and pretended to walk like a zombie.

"Hallelujah!" Lilith threw up her hands so quickly that she threw Big Red on her own face. She just wiped it off and licked her fingers. "You's one of the chosen."

"I dream about Wendy naked sometimes."

"Lilly ain't interested in no naked women dreams, Little Boy. They's important, but they's your business." She took a long drink. The liquor was starting to work on her like a screw tightening. She was excited. "Does you ever dream about the town?"

Bip suddenly became a little scared. He had dreamed about the town just the night before. It was not a pleasant dream. "Yes, Ma'am," he said reluctantly.

"What does you dream about our town?"

"It was about the town, but more about the fire and Pawpaw." Bip's eyes got big and white and the sweat on his arms seemed to dry and leave salt like scales on his skin.

"Little Boy, is you all right?"

"Yes Ma'am," Bip answered positively, even though he was feeling a little sick to his stomach now.

"Take's just a little drink."

Bip took the big Red can and sipped the red liquor. He didn't cringe and even took a little more. He felt the heat of the red liquid flow down his stomach and he started to sweat again and his body began to cool.

"Those people who burned were awake when they burned, Miss Lilly. The girl was pulling at the door but the old man was holding her back because he didn't want to get out. He wanted to burn Lilith." Bip was crying now.

"How you know that? Just cause you dream it, you think it have to be true?"

"I heard Mr. Watts say that the girl and the old man were burned together and had to be pried apart."

"Why you telling Lilly this."

"I think Willie burned down the Rose and the King's Inn 'cause he was smoking."

"Lilly always say smoking is a terrible thing. Buffalo smoke sometimes, and when he do I just tell him to sleep outside. Mix smoke with Thunderbird and you gots a powerful smell."

"And my Pawpaw's face kept flashing over the face of the burned man and his skin was pulling back from his mouth and his teeth were showing and his eyes were wide like he's seeing something terrible coming fast, Miss Lilith."

"What you think he see? Little Boy? Tell Lilly what you think he see."

"Can I have another drink?"

"Hell no, you can't have another drink. You done had plenty. I tell you something right now, young man. Your muse is good. Mine mess with me day and night like a sick baby-child riding my skirt with hands that clutch and cling and won't let go. My prophet cry on my hip like a starving baby that never get any better but never die neither. This tough world about to gnaw Lilly's stomach through. Look straight in my eyes Little Boy."

He looked into her coffee eyes.

"Watts said James flooded the room with gasoline and set the fire himself. He knew he would be convicted. He so drunk though that he didn't know that Willie May and Benzel were in there, too. He was crazy with fear. It weren't you fault. You hear me."

Bip shook crying. He felt relief but still could not shake the picture of any human being having to embrace another in the mouth of a fire. He remembered a story Crenshaw had told him one time of this wine god who was born when some Greek god showed up at this princess's room and got in her bed and burned her up; the wine baby was born from them and he lived in the sky until he was a teenager. Bip had always wanted to be the wine-baby and live in the sky until he was big. He had seen too much death. He was tired of loss.

"We got to take the cancer out of you Pawpaw. We gots to go at night." Lilith got up and began shuffling down the street, unaware of her movement. She was going back to her house.

"Wait?! What did you say?" Bip wiped the tears from his eyes on the back of his hands.

"We gots to go at night." Lilith got up and began shuffling down the street, unaware of her movement. She was going back to her house.

"Where do I meet you?" Bip called after her.

"Come and get me at the house, but don't go through the bar. I'll put the liquor for the men's in the other house tonight and Buffalo can run the shop. You come to the house at night, late."

"Yes, Ma'am. Yes, Ma'am." Bip was smiling.

Lilith turned around dramatically and pointed at Bip. "Your Mama ain't gonna like this worth a shit."

"My Mama ain't gonna know."

Lilith turned and started to shuffle down the sidewalk. Bip heard her burp and break wind and mumble 'scuse me', more for herself than for Bip. She fanned her dress.

"Miss Lilly?" Bip asked to her back.

"You don't want to know, Little Boy. You just remember what Lilly tell Little Boy," Lilith said without even turning around and without even slowing down. She added, "Little Boy, you brings everything lucky you own in this world and the other. Go by the hospital, now, and see how your Pawpaw is doing. We ain't got much more time."

CHAPTER 20

▼

BIP AND MARY AND CRENSHAW

"Hold my hand, Bip. Children under twelve aren't allowed in the Cancer wing." Mary held out her hand.

Bip didn't take her hand; instead, he walked forward as if he were in control.

"Doctor's can't do anything Bip. You heard Dr. Roy say that Daddy has the cancer and that treatment is over and that only time will tell. Take my hand even if you don't want." She grabbed his hand.

His fear and anger and confusion melted into sweat in her palm.

The hall was white; the nurses pushing carts wore dresses of white. The lights forced their long bodies into the hall like a vanity mirror and they were white. Even the clock on the wall was white.

"Seems like they'd let him go home, Mama," Bip said softly. She let go of Bip's hand.

Mary went to the end of the hall, outside of Crenshaw's room. She looked like hell. Bip had gone back home after his meeting with Lilith and then called Mary at the hospital to come to pick him up. Mary had been at the hospital all day. Crenshaw's condition was pitiful.

"Daddy's getting worse, Bip." Mary felt she always needed to be honest with Bip. Bip didn't need things euphemized at this point. "I can't believe some disease found him so tasty." Mary walked back to Bip and took on a different mood for Bip's sake.

He chipped up until his mother's hand ran through his hair and he melted again. He felt like a small roller coaster rising and falling; but worse, as if under the coaster a boiling tub of hot pitch-tar or some curse was waiting below: under the skin of the air in the hall; under the skin of the conversation, under the metronomic mechanism of the clicking white clock, and under the looks and the tears that everyone held back.

"Bip. Look at me, Bip." Mary tried to prepare Bip. "Daddy doesn't look so good right now ..." She started and stopped again.

Bip had had enough preparation.

He knew his grandfather was sick. This was something he had to do, not some suit he didn't want to wear, or red beets he didn't want to eat.

Bip put his hand in his pocket and felt a Cicada shell he had pulled off the Elm tree just outside the hospital; the crackling shell had crumbled in his pocket. He pulled his pocket inside out and brushed the brown flakes onto the white-tiled floor. Immediately he wished he would have waited until he would have gotten over dirt or grass to drop the broken bits. Here they sat precariously on the white tiled floor like brown flakes, waiting to be mopped and washed out and down the drain with everything else in the system, only eventually back into the earth. Mary was standing, sweating. She smelled more familiar than the antiseptic of the hospital. Mary's perfume mixed in a combative but sweetening way with the Lysol and Clorox and alcohol, and the two smells wrestled to the floor and mixed in the shell of the broken Cicada.

Mary had tears in her eyes and Bip moved to her; she could feel Bip's tears wet the stomach of her dress. Mary always had a way about her that took candy and icing and truncated them like a sickle through a stout green weed to reveal what must be seen.

Bip wanted Crenshaw back to his milk-white self instead of mustard yellow because his entire insides were slowly stopping working. Bip cried harder.

Why did he have to know all this school science stuff that talked about insides of bodies and how they worked? He wanted to be stupid for a second, to know nothing. He wanted Crenshaw suddenly out in the country, out of the city. He wanted Crenshaw sick because the god's were angry or he had ridden over some sacred burial ground of that other tribe, or that the Jubo spirit had cursed him for not riding backwards over territorial boundaries when he entered the Tiwanee camp with a black ceremonial spear. He wanted an solid reason.

But, Bip knew, really, that Crenshaw had done nothing to deserve this. But that's what we're taught: no one dies of natural causes anymore. He probably carried his milk wrong, or was schooled in some asbestos riddled one-room schoolhouse, or ate lead paint when he was a crawling infant.

"Mama, what did Pawpaw do?"

Mary just held him closer. She knew his mind was traveling down every crossroad he could find.

"Pardon?" She said 'Pardon' from a play she'd been in, but everyone, including Bip, always liked it because she only said it when she really wanted you to repeat what you said, otherwise it was pretty much with Mary, "Beg your goddamn pardon," which obviously thrust something else into the conversation.

"What did …" he stopped and backed away a bit. "What did Pawpaw do?"

"What do you mean, 'Do?'" Mary was trying to understand and be patient.

Bip's eyes welled up again with tears. He was empty and thought about once when Crenshaw had taken him fishing and how excited he was to catch a fish and after hours of fishing for Bass and Bip whining about catching nothing, Bip insisted that they catch something. Crenshaw, after cussing about tangled lines and disaster and noise in the bottom of the boat, boated over to the docks and seeded the water with a knuckle full of corn and baited Bip's line. In a matter of seconds, Bip had hooked a large Carp. The fish, while extremely large, fought very little and hung on the line like a tire rather than a fabulous fight to the finish. After a lame netting and the dragging the fish from the water, Bip remembered Crenshaw thumping the fish on the side. It made a sickening hollow sound, like a flesh and blood thumped watermelon. He told Bip that Carp, while big, were riddled with bones the size of needles and had no meat to speak of. Bip remembered his catch growing heavier and heavier in his hands as Crenshaw waited for Bip to say whether to keep the fish or not. Bip knew that Crenshaw had been trying to get across to Bip that sometimes in life when you try to make something happen instead of being patient then you end up with a big hollow nothing.

He needed to see Crenshaw alone.

"I don't want to see him."

"What baby?" Mary was waiting, as if in a trance.

"I don't want to see him"

Mary looked Bip hard in the eyes.

"He may not get better, Bip. Really."

"He won't …" and Bip stopped. "Not like this. When do you go to supper, Mama?"

After, Crenshaw was alone in his room. He had just tried to lift himself enough to move from the sheets that were sticking to his bare skin; the robe had shifted and shifted. Crenshaw figured they made them open in the back just to further humiliate and inconvenience the patient. He suffered pain with no relief now; even the pain killers were not working; they had hooked him to machine that dispensed morphine now every so often.

He turned on the television and then turned it immediately back off and rolled his head to the side and looked blankly at the wall. He wanted to scream but realized there was really no reason to.

"This is what it comes to. What a bunch of shit," Crenshaw told the ceiling.

He knew he was merely waiting now to die. Nothing could be done.

The tiny knock on the door at first was an image. He waited and nothing. He looked back at the wall. It was about supper time.

"Pawpaw?" Bip's voice crawled under the door.

Crenshaw's eyes welled up with tears.

His grandbaby-boy had come to see him.

"Get your ass in here," Crenshaw took every bit of oxygen he had to call Bip in.

Bip cracked the door as if he were a spy.

"Well, come on in you lunatic." Crenshaw motioned and Bip slid across the floor on his belly to the bed.

"Well, for God's sake, this ain't no prison. Get up off the floor. You might get a disease." Then Crenshaw rolled his eyes to himself. 'A disease like cancer,' he thought.

"Pawpaw, I snuck in." Bip was truly scared. He had come back after Mary left.

"Come here. Really? There's no reason to be scared at all."

"Pawpaw, they told me I couldn't come in without an adult. But I had to bring this present." Bip plopped on the bed and buried his face in Crenshaw's chest and hugged him as hard as he could; Crenshaw's pain was a phantom now.

Bip fished and fished in his backpack and finally produced a can of Vienna Sausages and a blueberry Pop Tart.

Crenshaw hated Vienna Sausages. Mary used the little weenies in everything: sandwiches, slaw, sometimes even in oatmeal. Still, Crenshaw realized that Bip was trying to bring some of the outside world to Crenshaw however small it may be. "Well, bring it over here and crank that baby open." He rolled over on his side and coughed.

"We don't have to eat it Pawpaw. I just figured we get it out of the kitchen so Mama wouldn't cook it." He looked at his grandfather. "Why don't we just leave it for the nurse and kill her. Then, we could bust you outa here. We can eat the Pop Tarts." He knew Crenshaw liked Pop Tarts.

Crenshaw's laugh started deep in his congested lungs and shook until Bip hugged Crenshaw's emaciated body.

"Ain't they feeding you nothing, Pawpaw."

"Nothing but shit potatoes and green beans and god horrible Jello. What I need is a belt of Wild Turkey and a chili dog."

"Do you really, Pawpaw?"

Bip wanted to please his grandfather.

"I can get a chili dog at the Seven Eleven and Lilith could give me the Wild Turkey."

"You need to stay away from that witch."

Bip was uneasy, but he wanted to tell Crenshaw why he had come.

"Pawpaw, Miss Lilly says she might can help you." Bip looked at his grandfather and raised his eyebrows.

"Bip, honey, come here." Bip sat on the bed beside his grandfather. "I got the cancer, honey. It's something that ain't got a heal to it."

"She says that if she has the heal, then she can make the disease leave your body. She says she healed Spooky of the cancer."

"What is she gonna do? Slap the hell out of me." He remembered when she had tried to heal Paul in the bar that night. He cringed remembering the blow. "I don't think that I want her to slap the sickness out of me."

Bip didn't say a word. He simply looked at Crenshaw and didn't blink.

"If you're gonna die Pawpaw, then why would it bother you if she tries." Bip was starting to cry.

"She'd never get past the nurses."

"I got past the nurses."

"You don't weigh three-hundred pounds."

"She says she can be invisible if she needs to be."

"Anyone who drinks as much as that woman is invisible."

"Pawpaw," Bip's eyes continued to swell. The room closed in. "We got to do something for you. You look pitiful."

"I am pitiful." Crenshaw's body was a road map of cancer cells reading and constructing and moving healthy cells and tunneling through his insides. His body had become a host.

"Tell her to bring enough liquor for me, too. And if she slaps me, you're getting a spanking." Crenshaw laughed and ended coughing. "What's it gonna do? Kill me." He laughed at the joke again. "Go ahead and bring her."

Bip fell on his grandfather's chest and cried. Crenshaw held him for a while.

"I didn't sleep a wink last night, Pawpaw." Bip yawned and after a bit Crenshaw noticed that Bip was asleep on his chest.

"You poor baby boy, you've had such a hard time," Crenshaw held Bip gently and waited uncomfortably for the next dose of pain medicine to flow through his veins like a fix.

When the nurse came in an hour later, she found Bip wrapped solid in Crenshaw's arms. They were both asleep. The nurse woke Crenshaw and told Crenshaw that Bip was not in compliance with the rules. Crenshaw vaguely apologized, and called her a 'bitch' under his breath, and sent Bip on his way.

After Bip left, Crenshaw picked up the phone and dialed Mary's number.

"Hello," Mary was vacuuming.

"Honey," Crenshaw started.

"I'm sorry, I can't hear you." She turned off the vacuum and took the scarf she was wearing and wiped her face. She had been cleaning during her supper break. She thought of housework as therapy.

"Mary."

"Oh, God! It's you, Daddy. Is anything wrong? I was just finishing up the housework and was coming up to keep you company." Mary had kept a vigil pace during Crenshaw's illness. He appreciated her attention and that her concern was genuine. Right now his concern was genuine, too.

"Baby doll, listen, so I don't have to talk too much. Bip came by to see me."

"Bip's at the store for me, daddy." She was confused.

"No, he came by to see me. He brought me a blueberry Pop Tart."

"Bless his little heart. Did you eat it?"

"What I could, I did. But listen. Bip is brainwashed by that Lilith. He thinks she can heal me and is planning to break in here sometime and fix me with the heal."

"Well, Daddy maybe ..."

"I'm dying! Ya'll need to get that through your heads, honey, and you don't need to let him be encouraged or he'll just be disappointed and feel cheated and lied to."

"Daddy don't say you're dying." She knew it was true, but she'd be damned if she'd say it.

"Listen, I want you to take care of that situation. He'll get hopes and expectations."

"Someone's coming in, Daddy, it might be …"

"OK. I'm off. Take care of my grandbaby boy, you hear?"

"I always do."

"I know that. I'll see you in a bit. I've got to wait for the …" He stopped in mid-sentence. She could tell he was in pain.

"Go to sleep, Daddy. You don't even have to say goodbye. I love you." She heard the phone rattle around for a second, then it clicked and a dial tone that sounded like it could purr its mechanical dial-tone-I'm-waiting-for-eternity frozen in time.

CHAPTER 21

▼

THE INTERVENTION

The town had all pitched in to help to clear the burned site of the Modern Barbershop and to build a makeshift building until the contractor could come in the next week to start on the new shop. After Mary had talked to Crenshaw, she fed Bip his macaroni and cheese and drove straight to the haphazard shop. All the men were gathered there. She thought they might be working, but instead, as always, they were simply talking.

She slammed the door to show the men she was there and that she meant business; it popped back open.

"Easy, we just got that hung yesterday. I'm not sure how much abuse it can take," Selmer was a bit stern. She was entering a sacred place in transition.

Mary didn't say a word.

The tension was syrupy and thick, as if Len were being shot all over again on the front steps. Paul even looked up at the door, almost hearing "that noise" again. Mary was overly dramatic at first, acting as if she might even leave, so Walter leaned over from his chair, pulling it on its front two legs by leaning his fat belly forward, and he pushed the door closed, just enough so Mary was somewhat committed to staying in. She fished her hair around until she was convinced it was stylishly wind-blown and waited for Walter and Tabot's sympathetic eyes to turn back to information-seeking eyes. It was when Tabot turned the paper page and immediately after the dropping of section C of the Grandville Daily that Mary felt appropriate in revealing her need.

She assumed her "stoic dignity," stance. This was an old acting ploy. She would establish a vulnerable side, then, BAM, be a rock hard bitch. The pull off was to look as if the world made her tough as nails, even though her heart wanted to be sweet and kind and giving.

"Boys, we got trouble," Mary said with her hands on her hips in a perfectly postured pose.

"Right here in River City," Tabot finished the next phrase from the shine stand they had made from two of Paul's kitchen chairs and a step-aerobic bench they found in Walter's attic.

"I suppose I deserve that. Tabot, that boy of mine is done in deep."

"With Billie?" Tabot wasn't sure what the conversation was just yet.

"Hell, no. That's my daughter." She said flippantly. "I gave up on her coming around months ago. That's something she has to decide. I'm talking about Bip and Lilith."

"Then, why in tarnation didn't you go to Watts," Tabot was concerned.

"What? And tell him to arrest Miss Lilly for talking to my baby-boy."

"Then, that's your problem, Mary, but if we …"

"Her problem between painting her fingernails and brushing her hair," Selmer finished under his breath. Selmer had never cared for Mary's vanity. Selmer's daughter had not even worn make-up until she was in her first year of college, where she also got pregnant.

"Do I talk about Cindy like that, Selmer?' He didn't think she had heard. "Bip's smart. Disciplined. He's a hell of a fine boy with good sense," Mary said. Then she mumbled, "Least I thought he had good sense."

"What's that mean?" Tabot was interested.

"They's planning something."

"How do you know that?" he prodded Mary on.

"Daddy called me and said Lilith was gonna put the heal on him with Bip."

"Pardon?" Tabot sat forward in the shine stand. He really was taken back.

"So, you think they're up to something good, or no good." Selmer went around the front of his barber chair and sat in it and pumped himself up three pumps. All the chairs had mostly survived the fire and the men had recovered them temporarily with old Levi's.

"How you gonna find out?" Walter said.

Paul was following the conversation the best he could. He sat in his chair, too. No one was getting his hair cut.

"Can't find out 'cept to follow 'em around," she hesitated and added, "They're planning some exorcism. Tabot, is that legal to follow someone around?"

"It's acceptable as long as you don't touch 'em or injure their person or threaten 'em or kill 'em or nothing like that."

"Well, hell, I ain't gonna go around touchin' on her or threaten' her person. I'm just gonna watch her and make sure she doesn't lead Bip down some stream he can't swim back up." Mary needed to calm down. She was pacing and grinding her hands. She wanted anyone to do whatever he or she could for Crenshaw, no matter what. But she didn't want Bip to be lured into something dangerous.

"It's gonna be hard to follow her without her noticing. She's a witch, you know." Walter said dead serious.

"She's not a witch. She's just a fat Black woman who drinks way the hell too much," Mary sighed.

"She healed that baby black boy that had the Polio. Doctors said to let it alone so's it could die."

"Well, that's just hearsay. No truth in it. I think she made up the whole story just to prove she had the heal." Mary was getting more and more confused. What if Lilith had the ability to heal? She had heard of healers before over at the Assembly of God.

"She slapped Paul up side his head trying to heal his hearing problem," Walter remembered and blurted out.

Paul rolled his eyes in his head remembering.

Mary looked at Paul, "Paul, are you still deaf?"

Paul answered, "What?"

"Well, then she didn't fix it," Tabot answered.

"She doesn't have a car," Walter offered.

"What's that matter?"

"Why do you want to follow some woman who drinks too much who doesn't even have a car? How dangerous can she be?" Walter's logic was always a bit simple.

"She's gonna poison his mind, Walter. Cain't you see that? I ain't worried about her driving' 'em off no goddern cliff. I'm worried about her making him think Daddy's gonna …!" Mary finally broke and Tabot held her. He knew what she was going through. Practicing law, he knew that sometimes you just had to keep faith in a miracle.

"You think she's gonna kill him?" Walter jumped back into the conversation unannounced.

"Cancer's gonna kill him, Walter! The cancer! And Bip is gonna lose if he believes that some miracle is gonna occur. She's gonna poison his mind, Walter, stupid. Not his body."

"Mind's part of the body," Walter retaliated, but not with much force.

"She's gonna goddamn push a child where children shouldn't have to go! I don't even know why I put up with how stupid you are, Walter!"

"Well, if you're gonna just yell at me, then maybe I don't feel like following no walking witch 'round town for a good part of the night."

"You do what you want! But she's brainwashing your grandbaby boy too, Walter!" Mary jumped at Walter.

"My grandbaby, Clinton? She ain't better to be talking to Clinton." Walter's tone changed.

"She's down at the Grocery every day, Walter. I seen her talk to Clinton before," Mary lied.

"Well, that's a different story. Your Bip's always leaned to the mysterious side. But Clinton is a solid, good boy."

"If you weren't right, I'd knock you clean out of your chair, Walter. But Bip is a little strange and that's why I worry. He's got an overdeveloped imagination, and the last thing he needs to develop is a friendship with a lady who thinks she's a witch who drinks to keep her spells in check."

"Is that why she drinks so much?"

"My grandmother drank a lot. She said it was to help her hemorrhoids," Selmer said as he spun around in his chair.

"My grandmother dipped snuff," Walter entered the competition.

"Powder or Skoal?" Selmer asked.

"Both at the same time."

"That is kinda strange."

"Can we meet here after Bip leaves the house, Selmer?" Mary attempted to get the conversation back to the matter at hand.

"I'll open the shop for you, if you need a headquarters, but I got Lion's club tonight."

"Well, the Lions can damn sure make it one week without you, Selmer."

"They's electing officers tonight. If you're not there when they elect officers, you usually end up president for the year."

"We'll lock it behind us."

"I'll come by after meeting, if I don't get hit with a gravy biscuit. Last week Dr. Bill ruined my shirt. Just ruined it."

CHAPTER 22

▼

THE PREPARATION

The sun burned and grew larger and larger as it reached the horizon until all that was seen were stretching poles of light that rose and backed up in the sky until darkness melted and poured over like molten steel into some hidden die cast. The night was set.

Bip put on his Sunday shoes that Crenshaw had given him that he had put lucky pennies in. He grabbed his lucky green rabbit's foot. He knew his cap was on his bullhorns he had bought in Mexico. Mary had told Bip the horns were fake because they were red on the tips, and if they weren't fake then they were gross, which was all the encouragement Bip needed to buy them. They had been very awkward to carry on the plane. Bip had even poked one man just above the eye. The lucky hat was his Mutant Slugger's minor league hat. Mary had coached the team last summer and insisted on the name, and the Mutant Slugger's, much to the dismay of the Red Sox, and Yankees, and traditional others, had even won one game.

Bip put on the Mutant Slugger hat and bellowed like a bull and looked in the mirror. He was taller tonight, he thought.

He was nervous. Even though he was nervous, Bip wasn't scared. Bob the Cat and Rachael Ronteria, Bip's two cats had heard him getting ready and had climbed the tree and jumped through the window. He gave each of them some hard cat food. Bip left the house just before nine. Mary had put him to bed at eight and checked on him at eight forty-five. He was convinced that she thought he was asleep. He slid out the window, dropping just under the Magnolia, landing on the crackling polished leaves. He checked his flashlight and accidentally shined it in his eyes so that he blinded himself for a few moments, enough that he didn't see Paul across the street slink from his car and crouch behind it.

Paul had been elected to follow Bip. The men figured since he was deaf, he could be the quietest, which was wrong. Perhaps, more correctly, they all knew that Paul was the only one of them who was not afraid of Lilith.

Lilith had switched from beer to rum to vodka by seven and now was working to get the clearest, cleanest high-octane buzz she could attain. The world sounded like a hum to her, a quiet pleasant hum. Her skin tingled and she thought she seemed a bit more agile and strong.

"Lilly gonna have to be strong for Little Boy," Lilith said outloud to herself as she moved from her chair at the kitchen table across the black and white checkerboard floor. She rubbed her toe on some of the tile squares that had faint magic marker numbers on them from the neighborhood children playing hopscotch in the kitchen during the Juneteenth celebration. She had chosen to clap time while the children hopscotched. She stopped at the cabinet and grabbed the vodka bottle by the throat and squeezed out another count.

Lilith usually counted to five when making a drink, but tonight she was counting to seven. She poured the vodka. She got a block of ice from the freezer and the ice pick and broke off three clear chunks and dropped them into the glass and topped off the glass with orange juice, straining the pulp. She always made vodka drinks in tall crystal. She felt that made for a cleaner hallucinatory state.

"Where that Little boy? I'm starting to feel a stir," Lilith lifted the drink to her thick lips. Little Boy was just turning down the alley leading to Lilith's house. He had decided to take the alley rather than the dirt road because he felt more comfortable there. Paul was still following and now Mary and Tabot and Walter were informed of the situation because Paul had squeezed the Walkie Talkie.

Something was "Going Down" as Watts would say.

Paul was to continue to follow Bip while the others held down grand central at the barbershop. So Paul followed Bip crouching behind trash cans, sliding along fences, jumping from telephone pole to pole looking left and right and holding his hands out for balance like a Broadway tap dancer, all while Bip walked a calm, straight line to Lilith's.

They passed Barton's gas station, Alton's Corner Cafe, turned left after the railroad tracks, crossed at the light, and finally turned down Lilith's dirt road.

Bip paused a minute before climbing the three steps of Lilith's porch. They cracked slightly under his little weight. Bip hesitated before he knocked on the door. Then, he knocked confidently, calling out, "Miss Lilly, you home?"

Lilith opened the door as Bip stepped back to allow the screen to pass in front of his nose.

"Where you been, Little Boy? Lilly startin' to worry."

Lilith stuffed her big body into the doorway, blocking the light behind her so that her face was just a shadow. Paul dove into a bed of giant marigolds and tried to be still. He hadn't known they were being watered; still, he lay almost rigid in the mud and fragrance like a body preserved for a funeral. Paul saw the lights dim as Bip entered the house. Lilith was tense, but she softened and she hugged Little Boy. Her big round shadow covered Little Boy.

Paul lay still for a minute, then ran serpentine to the house, tripping over the push-mower next to the front stoop which sent him head first into the sunflower bed. He paused in the sunflower bed, careful not to spill any colors from any petals, then plowed through the mint and cilantro stirring a small tornado of fumes that rose and sat on the roof of the house which were finally dragged like witnesses into the kitchen.

"They's someone in the bed," Lilith rushed towards the door. Bip walked like a chess piece over the checkered floor.

"I'm sorry, were you having company?" Bip turned his eyes to the bedroom.

"Lord, child they ain't been nobody in that bed since Cletus, 'cept Buffalo, but that 'cause Buffalo need Lilly sometimes. He need me bad sometimes, child. I does that for mens whose wives leaves them." She paused and started again, "Little Boy?"

"Yes, Ma'am."

"They's someone in the *flower* bed," she emphasized 'flower.' "You can see him from here." Lilith lifted Bip up so that he could see out the window. Paul waved from the flowerbed.

"Oh. That's just Paul. He's been following me since I left the house." Lilith lowered Bip and sat him on the cabinet next to the gold sugar bowl. Lilith relaxed and leaned against the metal trash can and laughed. "You better tell him to get himself in here before the spirits start a-walking. He ain't gonna wanna be in that there flower bed, and that's a fact."

Paul stayed in the flowerbed, confused as to how Lilith and Bip had sensed his presence.

Lilith left the trashcan and got her drink from the table and took a deep, thirsty drink from the vodka and orange juice.

Bip wiggled on the counter.

Paul was now standing in full view, his head in the window without trying to disguise himself. Bip even looked straight at him. He was reading Bip's lips.

Lilith reached up and back, deep in her cabinet. LICKER was painted on the door in white in big letters as if she had to be reminded where the bottles were. She pulled two bottles from the back: one was Pernod, a liquor like eating one million black jelly beans shoved across one palate; and Frangelico, a smooth hazelnut.

"Bip, you got to shoot the liquid brownie." Lilith thought Frangelico tasted like a liquid brownie. She was insistent. He didn't even hesitate. He poured a finger in the bottom of an old jelly glass with Yogi Bear and Fred Flintstone dancing while Barney and BoBo were making peanut butter and jelly sandwiches, and he lifted the glass and poured the liquor into his mouth. He started to swallow.

"Hold it there and close your eyes," Lilith closed her eyes too, but the room started to reel like a circus ride. She added, "But Lilly gonna keeps her eyes open 'cause the room tend to move on Lilly when she close her eyes."

Bip held the liquor in his mouth. At first it burned around his teeth just at the gums. Then, it seemed to help melt his fear.

"Swallow." And he swallowed and he felt the liquid rush down his tunnel to the cave of his belly and spread and reach out until he got chilly bumps and "Yipped" an uncontrolled yip. Then he began to speak without hesitation.

"What are we gonna do to Pawpaw, Miss Lilly."

She rubbed his head. "You just leave that to Lilly. You needs to go into Lilly's room and gets her Voodoo bag."

He started into her room even before her sentence was over. "What does it look like?"

"You won't miss it."

"Miss Lilly, you said you's a witch when I first met you."

"I is a witch."

"What's the difference in being a witch and Voodoo."

"What's the difference in a skillet and a frying pan."

Paul shifted his weight. He wasn't sure if he had read the last part right. He wasn't sure if they were talking about sorcery or supper.

Suddenly, awkwardly, Paul fell through the screen of the door he was leaning on and splayed on the kitchen floor.

"I been meaning to get that screen fixed. Paul, gets you some liquor if'n you's gonna help." She turned to Bip, "I'm sure your mama sent him to keep an eye on us." Paul couldn't see her lips. "But he be OK. Maybe he can help."

"Do yooooou have annnyyy beeeer?" Paul committed himself. He figured he might need a belt of something to get through this ordeal.

"They's quarts of Cobra Malt in the ice box. But Paul boy, beer not the best elixir for this. You just like Buffalo. Likes that beer."

Paul simply wanted to stay alert.

Paul had already turned around and had his head buried in the cold box. He opened a bottle and took a drink and belched inside his closed mouth. He tried to give Lilith a couple of dollars.

"Everyone gets a drink. We gots to get going for my sister go to sleep." Lilith's sister worked at the hospital.

Lilith grabbed the vodka. Paul got a quart and Lilith poured a tablespoon of Frangelico into the jelly jar. "You can have one more drink, Little Boy. This might be hard and this ease the edge a little."

"Wee caan taaake my c-c-caar." Paul was loosening up. "Buuut we'll h-have to waalk to iit."

"Lilly don't mind no little walk."

Bip got the Voodoo bag and followed Paul and Lilith out the door to the road and they started their walk to the car under the bright, full moon that lit the night, a soft light like a night light in the room of a child too young to dream. Bip held Lilith's hand as she waddled slowly down the road. Paul on the other side, belched again and put his hand out offering to carry the Voodoo bag. Bip held it for a few steps and then surrendered it to Paul.

Bip squeezed Lilith's hand and Lilith squeezed back.

'They were going to heal Pawpaw,' Bip thought to himself and smiled.

CHAPTER 23

▼

THE EXORCISM

When Paul did not return to the command central, the others began to worry about him and decided the time was ripe to find him. Mary was about to drive the entire group insane. Mary trusted Paul, however, and knew as long as Paul was with Bip that Bip was relatively safe, as long as nothing happened that required that Paul be able to hear.

Mary was sitting in Paul's chair. She was unconsciously pumping herself up with the rod on the side of the chair then letting herself down with a hydraulic hiss.

"They left all right. But who in the hell knows if they're going straight to the hospital."

"We can put a stop to it when you say Mary," Tabot said.

Mary stared somberly and dead-eyed ahead. "I want them to go. It's the last chance. It's the last chance."

"Paul's there. He won't let anyone harm Crenshaw."

"Buzz Paul's Walkie-Talkie," Walter suggested.

"Who in the hell gave Paul a Walkie-Talkie?" Mary was appalled.

"It wasn't me. Don't look at me. I hate Walkie-Talkies. Even as a little kid at Christmas I hated 'em." Tabot defended himself.

"I gave it to him," Walter admitted. He didn't see any harm in the gift.

"What in the hell is a deaf man gonna do with a Walkie-Talkie?"

"He can talk, Mary," Walter stood up. He was tired of Mary's abuse.

"He can talk, I'll give you that, but he can't respond if we call him." Mary backed off a bit, but she made sure her point was firm.

"Maybe we should monitor the channel."

"Maybe we should get off our asses and go," Tabot said. He kept rethinking the situation. "He really may be in danger." His tone was serious. "Lilith's father was Branch Jones."

"Who the hell is Branch Jones," Walter asked. He really swore he never heard the story.

"Spider Monkey," Tabot said as if that were enough.

"You mean the man who murdered that family with the TV!" Walter was excited. This was almost star status. "Hell yes, I remember him." He had never even slimly connected Lilith with Spider Monkey.

"Walter, Branch killed the father with the portable up side his head and then let loose with that nineteen inch on Brenda and the girls."

"That's horrible."

"Hell, yes, it's horrible, when they found Spider Monkey, he's eating a frozen superdog out of the refrigerator that weren't even cooked, and drinking a glass of Enfamil," Tabot said.

"Baby drink?" Walter was confused. "He was drinking baby drink?" Mary was even a bit taken in.

"That's what I'm tellin' you. This is no ordinary man."

"If his corndog was frozen, then of course it wasn't cooked," Walter had found his logical brain.

"Of course a frozen corndog isn't cooked," Tabot said demeaningly.

"You said he's eating a frozen superdog that wasn't cooked."

Across town, Paul threw his empty quart of Cobra Malt liquor in the weeds. The pollen rose and attacked Bip and made him sneeze several times, and his nose began to run enough that he held his head back.

"Are you sick, Biiiip? Heere," Paul lifted Bip up and carried him on his shoulders. Lilith carried the Voodoo bag. Bip held Paul's forehead and crouched forward, putting his stomach on the back of Paul's head.

"Don't you be sleeping, Little Boy. They's too much to do," Lilith shuffled forward like she was carrying two halves of the town in each shoe.

"They's Orion right up there," Bip pointed to the eastern sky. He was tired. Everyone was tired. "See his big belt. Those bright stars shining like big silver studs. Then you just make a stick figure out of him, his head and his legs." He pointed out each star with patience as they walked.

"What's he holding?" Lilith decided to see the constellation and not think for a minute. Bip was awake now with his head thrown back, his throat was long and glowed under the dim moon. Paul was even looking now because he had felt Bip's weight shift.

"That's his shield. Some say he has a sword, too. He's protecting the twins from the Bull. See that horn?"

"Yes."

Bip doubted she really did, so he tested her. "Where is it?"

"The Bull is over the man."

"Orion."

"What that bright star?"

"That's his dog, Sirius."

Paul almost fell in a pothole but regained his balance. He was trying his best to see the stars.

"The twins are right behind him. Lying on their side. They have the same head."

The sky had become a dot-to-dot movie show with great battles taking place on the black cyclorama of the sky. Lilith relaxed and took her bottle and regained her composure.

Mary had not thought much about how she was dressed. In fact, she just noticed she was wearing her yellow nightie stuffed in her jeans; she looked like a wild buttercup, her hair grabbed at the roof like petals opening under a bright incandescent bulb.

"I swear I feel like beating the hell out of someone with the strop on that chair." Mary grabbed the strop on the chair. Walter sunk in his chair. "Lordy, what should I do?"

Everyone turned the question over and over in his or her mind a few times looking at if from all angles, front and back and side-to-side like a child inspecting an ant in a jar.

Finally Tabot spoke up. "I think Bip is doing something he needs to do."

Mary ran her fingernails through her hair. For once she was not being dramatic. She was just starting to cry. "What am I gonna do? What am I gonna do with that child? Papa told me not to take that cold medicine when I was pregnant. But, no, I wouldn't listen. I just had to keep on taking it, and now I've got a child that's crazy. Ten years old and the child is a lunatic." She ended by sitting back down in Paul's chair, her sandals up on the footrest. Only her left toenails were painted flame red. Her right toenails were yellow and natural. No one said a word for several minutes. Then Mary jumped out of the chair and snatched the Walkie-Talkie out of Walter's hand.

Walter checked his hand for injuries.

"How do you work this sonofabitch!" The chair was spinning like a sick drunk.

"Are you sure you think you need to be using that?" Walter offered.

"Walter, you have the IQ of a retarded sheep."

Walter's feelings were hurt. His son had raised a sheep in 4-H, and he remembered having to bring the sheep out of the snow into the barn because they were too stupid to seek shelter on their own.

Mary punched the button.

"Paul, you's beeping, honey," Lilith said to Paul as they neared Paul's car. Paul could see his car and he pointed at it. "Paul Boy," she touched Paul. "Paul, honey, your britches is beeping." She pointed to his waist.

Paul pulled out the Walkie-Talkie and spoke into it just like he and Walter had practiced.

"Coome in Cooomaand Ceeentral." He let go of the button after counting to two.

"Paul, is that you? Where in the hell are you?" Mary's fingers were white.

"Did theeey answeer?" Paul asked Bip and Lilith.

"They says to ask you where you is?" Lilith frankly was unconcerned with anyone stopping them.

"Roooger Wiilcoo and ooooover. Weee are preseeently in rouute to the hospital. Over." He counted to two and let go of the button.

"Well, you can just turn around and bring that child back with you." Mary's lips were curled over the box like elastic putty melting on the word "you."

"Diiiid theeey saay anythiiing?"

"They told you to turn that thing off, 'fore you runs down the battery," Lilith responded. She was trying to keep Bip's mind clear as possible.

Bip knocked on Paul's head and bent his mouth over so Paul could see his lips. Paul had to read Bip's lips upside down. He had never done that except when he had talked to his granddaughter once after she had taken up doing Penny-Drops on the monkey bars at the school's playground.

"Let me see it, Paul." Paul handed the Walkie-Talkie up to Bip. He was glad to get rid of the responsibility. "Mama?"

Mary about fell down. "Oh, it's my baby doll!" She punched the button. "Honey, are you all right? You need to forget this nonsense and get back here."

Bip was stern, to the point, and unmoving.

"Mother, you know Pawpaw has the cancer. The doctor's said he can't operate. Keep your Walkie-Talkie on. I'm going to turn ours off, but I'll call." Bip tried to be tough, but he started crying. Lilith ripped the Walkie-Talkie out of Bip's hand.

"Dammit woman, you got to get a hold of yourself and let this boy help me or we ain't gonna do one bit of good. Do you understand me?"

Silence.

"I said "Do you understand me?!"

Mary turned the Walkie-Talkie off without responding. It made a signed-off signal on Lilith's.

"That means it's off, Miss Lilly," Bip said through his tears.

Lilly slung the Walkie-Talkie against the light pole at the corner and the black plastic ripped apart and tick-tanked on the concrete; the battery shot out like a bullet and slid like shattering teeth across the gravel street.

Paul drove Lilith and Bip to the Hospital in his long green car. Bip sat between Lilith and Paul in the front seat. They looked like a poorly made sandwich with Bip being the insides. Bip was tired and spent and running on simple concern and love for his grandfather.

"Did Little Boy puts the bag in the trunk?" Lilith was making sure she had all her Voodoo equipment. Bip had placed the Alligator suitcase into the dark trunk of the car. Paul had helped him lift the case. The case was coarse and worn, but it had no visible marks in the tough Alligator hide. The word 'Voodoo' was white painted on the leather handle.

"What exactly are we gonna do, Miss Lilly?" Bip was scared. He had never been to any kind of exorcism before.

"We gonna get that beast outa your granddaddy. That what the Cancer is, a beast. My Pappy die of the Cancer. I was too young to spell him then. Mama did what she could, but she was a shitty witch. She never get her fix right. She would drink too much and say the wrong things and eat too much sweets. A witch got to always be on the edge where suffering and indulgence collide."

Paul looked at Lilith. All he could make out was 'collide.' So he looked back to the road quickly for the impending accident. His was the only car out, though.

It was almost midnight and the streets were sticky, and the heavy dew smacked against the tires as the car rolled silently under the heavy night.

"Mmmight r-rain toniiight." Paul tried to enter the conversation. He had noticed some clouds building in the west.

"Hope it don't, Barber Man. Rains is good for usual days, but when you's witchin' or trying to get homemade jelly to set up, you better off without the rain."

Bip was squirming in the seat between Lilith and Paul.

"Little Boy, you better gets all your wigglin' over and done with, 'cause when we gets into the ceremony you gonna have to be extra still and do what Lilith say."

Bip tried to stay still but couldn't.

"Miss Lilly, are you gonna be callin' on the devil or anything ugly to get into my pawpaw?"

Lilith laughed. Bip was glad she laughed.

"Lilly don't have nothing to do with the Devil. Devil can sit on a tack, far as Lilly concerned. Evil ain't what make people sick. Disease make people sick—and age. You Granddaddy ain't old enough to die yet, though. We just got to trick the disease with life, not by scaring it with evil. You scare it with evil and you just asking to make some deal with the devil, and Lilly don't want to have nothing to do with the Devil. Devil can go down to Georgia, far as Lilly concerned."

Lilith opened her bottle and Bip could smell the liquor. It smelled very strong and the odor was pungent but in a strange way enticing. She took a drink and cringed and wiggled and let out a "Woo!"

"Lilly ain't done no exorcism in a while, not since I cured Buffalo's shingles."

Bip pictured Lilith on top of Buffalo's house dancing and doing Voodoo with her suitcase in one hand and a bottle of liquor in the other.

"You voodooed his house?" Bip was confused.

"His disease, boy. A rash." She didn't explain any more. "This particular liquor only come outta the cabinet when Lilly got to do the heal. That probably why Lilly didn't have the heal on Paul boy that night she try to heal his ears up."

"How we gonna get into the hospital?" Bip began to be concerned, first, not that they heal Crenshaw, but at least get the opportunity to do so.

"That where Lilly's connections come in. Lilly know someone everywhere in this town. Cheetah's wife work nights for the hospital. That my sister. She gonna let us in the Cafeteria door. We supposed to do a secret knock." Lilith lifted up and adjusted her dress and opened the bottle but screwed the lid back on without taking a drink.

"What's the secret knock?" Bip asked.

"We supposed to knock loud enough to wake her lazy ass up, is the secret. And she owe Lilly the favor 'cause I let her sleep over when Cheetah had that cough that kept him sick for a week. Said she couldn't get a lick of sleep during the day cause he's coughing all over the house like a cat stuck on a fur ball." Lilith made a face like a choking cat. Bip laughed. Lilith rubbed his head and looked out the front window and didn't talk for a while. Paul leaned forward and looked at the two and saw they were silent. He started to yawn, but decided if he did, then he might set off a chain reaction and set the whole car off on a yawning frenzy. So he yawned with his mouth shut and Bip looked up at him during the yawn and wondered why Paul was making such a strange face. Bip yawned.

"Stay alert Little Boy. You gonna have to be strong for Lilly and for your Grandpappy. Lilith gonna ask you to help and you gonna have to do some gimmes for Lilly, gimme this and gimme that, like a surgeon helper."

"You ain't gonna cut pawpaw are you!?"

"Lilly don't even cut her own steak, Little boy. Calm down. You can read can't you?"

"Yes, Mam."

"Then you just have to read and hand me what I ask for. You ain't scared of snakes is you, Little Boy?"

"No Mam." Little Boy lied.

"Well good, 'cause they things in that bag that'll scare a snake outa it's skin."

Bip didn't answer but immediately started trying to guess as to what might actually be horrible enough to scare a snake. When he was loading it, he didn't remember hearing anything that sounded alive. He pictured himself being brave for his grandfather and lifting gorilla heads and tarantulas and leeches and …

"Turn in here Paul boy," Lilith bumped Paul's arm and pointed to the parking lot behind the hospital. "Parks by that brown van." She poked him again and pointed. "Those are sure pretty hubcaps on that car." One of the doctor's cars had gold hubcaps. "No sir, Lilly ain't never seen hubcaps pretty as that."

Paul stopped the car and turned off the lights. The headlights folded back inside the car as if the beast were being put to sleep for a bit. The car was silent. That night was silent except for a mild rumble in the deep corners of the clouds over by Sunset, the small oil town just west of Flatland.

"Those damn rain showers better stay over west or Lilly might have to throw a fit."

Paul got out of the car and popped the trunk open and waited for Bip to crawl between the steering wheel and the vinyl seat. He popped out on the asphalt stepping on a weed that was just coming out of a small crack and walked back to Paul who was looking at the Alligator bag. Bip was not nearly as anxious to carry the bag now after Lilith had asked him about snakes. Before, he had thought of himself like carrying in Jimi Hendrix's guitar to a concert and everyone seeing. Now, he stood a minute until Paul looked at him to encourage Bip to get the bag. Paul had not heard the conversation.

Bip reached into the trunk and grabbed the handle hard like a bull rider. He had to either commit or run away. Paul helped him lift the bag and set it on the ground. Bip listened for animal sounds or clinks of glass or metal ringing against itself, anything that might give indication as to the contents of the Voodoo bag. Nothing.

Lilith went to the door of the Cafeteria behind the hospital and took her fist back and banged the door.

"She better have her ears on, or Lilly'll be all over her like gravy on Thanksgiving."

Bip was surprised that the thud was as loud as it was. 'So much for being discrete,' he thought. Bip picked up the suitcase and held it away from his leg even though it was heavy.

"Little Boy, you be ready when Janus open the door." He felt the same feeling of wearing a mask at Halloween and the tension of being himself and the mask, too; he was Crenshaw's grandson, his blood line, but he was, also now, some Voodoo child helping Lilith. Lilith looked at Bip and saw his confusion in what his role exactly was.

"He your Pawpaw, Little Boy, but that don't mean that you can't put that aside for a minute and be his helper. I need all of you, boy. You got the power, too. That why I brung you along with me."

Bip felt uncomfortable about Lilith saying he had the gift. He didn't have any gift the best he could see. The only gift he had at the moment was his ability to hold a suitcase that had, God only knew, what was in it. He was following some Voodoo woman breaking into the hospital with a deaf man, who now was standing at the back of the car looking at the stars pretending to be whistling.

"Come on Paul," Bip grabbed Paul's hand and pulled him toward the door.

All three had just settled in and Lilith was about to hit the door again when it opened and a black face peeped out with silted eyes.

"Lord Jesus, I tell you to knock, not to bang with a baseball bat. Lord Jesus, God Almighty. My ears is ringing. Make me spill my buttermilk."

"I told you tonight was the night."

"Don't tell me 'I don't know.' 'I know' what night it is. You think 'I don't know' what night it is?" Janus was one of Lilith's older sisters and she didn't have quite the reverence that some of the community outside of the family might have for Lilith's talents, just as Jesus was probably just the "favorite child" to his brothers and sisters. "Get your Voodoo ass in here."

The door opened just wide enough for Lilith and Bip and Paul to slip in.

"Lord, girl. Why you got all the lights off in here." Lilith's tone and mystery was entirely gone when she talked to her sister.

"I figure if you gonna beat the door down, then someone gonna come to check. Well, girl, all they gonna see is dark 'cause the light switch is here by the stove, and I'm black." Someone kicked something. "That better not be my Buttermilk which just done got kicked over."

Suddenly everyone felt a presence outside the door of the kitchen and froze. Bip clutched Paul's hand. Paul knew something was up. The door cracked open and a plane of light spilled across the kitchen and reflected off the aluminum pans and silver knives and clear glass bowls and dishes, flashing quick postcards of the room. Bip saw an orange carrot end, then a chrome refrigerator handle, then a knife twist with bright-blast of light then disappear in opaque black.

"Janus are you in here? Was that you?" The voice was Becky Fancher, the incredibly fat nurse.

"I's in here Mrs. Fancher. I's just after that mouse again."

They had placed glow-in-the-dark particles in the trap food. That was supposed to help to track the mouse by the droppings. Janus had come up with the idea so she could sleep more. Besides being incredible fat, Becky Fancher was also fairly dense. She thought the idea was novel. Also, that kept the two women from having too much to do with one another which was fine with both.

"I'm just about to give up on this mouse and go check on Mr. Crenshaw."

"Okie Dookie. I'll be in the Break Room." The door closed.

"Yeah, where you always is eatin' your Ding Dongs and drinking god awful whole milk. That woman gross me out. Eat all day and night. Maybe you could voodoo some of the fat off of her ass."

Janus turned the light on and the white clearness broke the room like a picture flash and blinded everyone.

"Damn girl. Why didn't you say, 'I'm gonna blind you now,' or something. I feel like I just watched Buffalo fire up his cuttin' torch while the Lord Jesus took a snapshot of me with a God camera."

"You didn't tell me you was bringing no big man with you." She was referring to Paul.

"He's insurance for the child to make sure I don't kill nobody."

"Well, I hope he fit in the food cart." She pulled back the cart curtain and motioned for Bip and Paul to get in. Paul pointed to the cart and Lilith held up her fingers in a 'little bit' gesture. Paul crawled in and Bip crawled in and sat on his lap. The curtain closed. Lilith carried the suitcase and walked beside Janus. The staff was use to seeing her with her sister; they weren't necessarily happy about seeing Lilith, but they were used to seeing her.

Bip held Paul's hand tightly. In all the preparation, Bip had not thought exactly what condition Crenshaw might actually be in. Janus opened the door to Crenshaw's room, which was in a corner of sorts, out of the way as if they were placing him somewhere he could pass away without having to be the center of attention.

"You on your own, Lilly. And, if Fat Fancher find you in here, I don't know nothing about it."

Lilith didn't even respond. She looked around to make sure no one saw them come in and picked up the triangular wooden doorstop, and once inside, she wedged the door locked from the inside. Bip and Paul tumbled out of the cart and found their legs.

Crenshaw was yellow; his eyes were slits, but through the slits his whites were yellow; his fingernails were yellow. His mouth was agape and each breath rattled and crawled out of his lungs and the new air somehow found its way shallow into his lungs. He had tubes in every hole of his body and the room smelled of urine and medication and of stale food and bleach and death.

A single tear rolled down Lilith's face. "Oh, my dear sweet child. My dear sweet mother of Jesus. I believe we too late." Lilith ran her fingers over Crenshaw's bald head. His eyes closed. He was unconscious. He had just finished his last round of chemotherapy and radiation. The morphine machine clicked and Crenshaw's face seemed to untie.

"What do you mean, 'We're too late,'" Bip said.

Paul was simply standing looking at Crenshaw's broken body with a blank distant stare. Paul was very concerned for Crensahaw. They had always had an unspoken bond that went beyond Paul's condition. They were human; and humans aren't the same and humans are the same. Paul was graphically reminded that he was mortal.

Bip grabbed Lilith's hand. "Come on Lilly. We got to get a move on." She looked down at Bip and realized he had not prepared himself and was still denying Crenshaw's condition.

"Little Boy, slow down. Paul, see if he still breathing on his on." Paul read her lips and went to Crenshaw and examined. There was oxygen in his nose, but it was merely to offer him the purest chance with each breath; still, he was not 'hooked up.'

Paul looked at Lilith.

"If you have any power, beyond liquor and luck and prayer and passion, you owe it to this boy," he said purely and succinctly and without stuttering.

Lilith stood and looked Paul in the eyes. She finally responded, "Lazy don't come from Lazarus," she said. Then, she shook her head, "Yes," to confirm to Paul that she realized the seriousness of Bip's conviction.

Bip was not even paying attention. He was trying to get brave enough to open the Alligator case.

He lay the case down and popped the left side and began to pop the right side in order to open the case.

"Wait!," Lilith's urgency almost pushed Bip back on his backside. His heart rushed. There *was* something alive in the case, then, he thought.

"You got's it up side down. Lilly know one thing. What you got in that box you don't want all over."

Bip remembered a story Dawn told him once. He couldn't sleep, so she told him a story about Pandora. The story was inappropriate at the time; it was a bit scary, but Dawn felt it had an attentive quality. He suddenly wondered if he weren't supposed to open the 'Voodoo' case, to dabble with this other side.

Bip was confused as to whether he really believed Lilith was a witch, or some Voodoo queen, or someone who simply believed she could alter seeming fate. Conversely, Bip knew when he bounced a basketball three times, he almost always made the shot.

"Shall I open it, Miss Lilly?"

"Slowly. And Paul Boy you gets on the other side of the bed. Don't no man need to be squatted down in this bed like this with his lungs spittin' up." She was being more of a nursemaid than a witch, Bip thought.

Bip squared off against the Voodoo case and turned it over and popped the right side. The case popped to a moment of repose that was slightly open as if it had to breathe or a Genie was going to smoke out and ask his desire.

Bip backed up and left the lid down to listen for animal sounds. He heard a stir. 'Oh God,' he thought. 'What on heaven and earth have I opened.' He heard scratching, or kind of like scratching, a moving. It was a sound that Bip knew was larger than a mouse or a gerbil. Whatever was inside was trying to get out.

"Miss Lilly, there's something in the box."

"They better be something in that box or we in trouble."

Bip finally got the courage up to open the box.

Nothing jumped out. Nothing crawled out or slithered out or roared out. The box was riddled with labeled mason jars of various sizes: 'rabbit's foot', 'seeds', water labeled 'Port-au-Prince/Jordan', and he stopped with "Snake God Zombi." A snake was in a jar and it was alive. Maybe that was what Bip had heard. He had never seen a snake like this one before. Bip looked on the other side and a shock ran down his body. He saw the stick figure Lilith had made of him out of the popsicle sticks, and the eyes had faded and the mouth was faint. She had dressed the stick figure in a pair of Ken pants and shirt and it looked sporty, but like new clothes on a deflated man. Just beside the stick figure all dressed up was a still-born baby that had been put in alcohol and vinegar in a jar. Bip got sick to his stomach. He didn't throw up, but he was on the edge of the earth. Also, there was wine in a jar and a very old looking and beautiful golden Goblet.

"Little Boy, we ain't got much time. Hands me the baby in the jar and the snake. Paul Boy, you needs to hang this up." She grabbed the stick boy of Bip and Paul hung it above Crenshaw's bed.

Bip pulled down his Mutant Slugger hat. He had certainly hoped that the baby in the jar and the snake would, absolutely and positively, be the absolute and positively last things to come out of the case. Still, he looked at Crenshaw who had moved a bit but was still unconscious.

"We calling on things that give life, Little Boy, not the things that take it away. The baby, give Lilly the baby. Don't be scared." Bip handed her the jar almost mechanically. "This baby was stillborn, bless its little heart and it has all kinds of live that was in it that got locked up and didn't get to get spent." She started to open the jar.

"Holy Cow, Miss Lilly, do you have to take it out of the jar."

"Don't talk!!" Lilith had changed and she was like Bip had seen her only once before. Paul wished now that they had brought Buffalo.

Lilith paused and got her vodka and raised her bottle of vodka to her mouth and drank a last bit as if to fix the moment.

She unscrewed the lid of the jar that held the embryo and thumb and fingered the embryo out of the mixture. The smell was beyond any description. She held the child just over Crenshaw's body and moved it all around like some mechanical ritual or radiology machine. When she got by Crenshaw's face, a slight wince covered his brow as if smelling salts were being given an unconscious boxer.

She was mumbling the entire time with heights and valleys, and Bip tried to make out the words but only caught scratches and small blurbs. He felt like he was in church, but in some secret Sunday school class that only the preacher and Jesus knew about. He felt that Lilith was doing things that were on the edge of sacrament and sacrilege. He made out "In the name of" and "Children" and "Faith."

"Water." She was working like a surgeon, now. She put the Baby back into the jar, but she didn't close the lid. Bip wished she would have closed the lid. He wanted that to be over.

She asked for the water, again.

He handed her the water that was labeled Port-au-Prince/Jordan. The mixture was of saltwater from the Port-au-Prince in Haiti and water from the River Jordan. The sand and mud wrestled with each other in the bottom of the jar. Lilith said words in some cryptic language before she opened the jar and even did the Catholic crucifix cross across her chest. Paul saw her, and being Catholic he recognized that at least, and without thinking he responded the same. Bip did the same just because he had seen Paul do it.

Lilith opened the jar and stuck her finger way down in the water to the mixed mud and sand and rubbed some on the forehead of Crenshaw. Crenshaw lay unmoving. She handed the jar back to Bip who closed the lid and placed it back in the case.

"It has to go back in the place it came out of, Little Boy."

Little Boy was going to say 'OK.' But he remembered that Lilith didn't like to be taken 'outa no trance.' So, he merely made sure he did as she asked.

"Gives me the snake." The Label read Zombi. The snake was running circles in the jar like a caged tornado.

Bip held the jar by just the lid.

"Don't you drop that damn jar, Little Boy! Hold it right!"

Bip wrapped both hands around the jar. He was much more frightened of Lilith than of Zombi the Tornado Snake God.

Lilith took the snake and bowed to it three times and crossed herself again and started to unscrew the lid. When she did the snake stopped swirling in the jar and became still as if it might strike.

Lilith lifted the stillborn embryo out of the other jar with her left hand. Bip's face screwed up with marked concern.

"Please, Lilith don't …"

Her look at Bip at that moment could have set a spewing volcano to rest.

She lowered the embryo into the jar and set it in the jar with the snake. And like a child spinning on a playground, the embryo slowly and gradually gyrated. The snake increased and increased in speed and abandonment, circling and circling, and touching his scales against the skin of the stillborn child until exhausted. Finally the snake lay in rest at the bottom of the jar, and Lilith reached in gingerly, seemingly concerned about being bitten. Her face was dripping sweat, and all of her body was shaking except for her two fingers that were trying to lift the child. She finally got a touch on 'it' and lifted the body out and in one fluid motion screwed the top on Zombi and handed him back to Bip who gladly, even almost smiling, put the snake back in the case.

Lilith cradled the embryo in her palms as if she held a new born child.

"The wine, now, Little boy."

There was a knock at the door.

"The wine, Little Boy!"

"Should we ..."

Paul got the wine out of Bip's hands and gave it to Lilith. Lilith opened the wine.

"Lilly?" The voice outside the door was her sister's. "Fat Fancher's on her way for rounds." Her whisper was louder than most people's regular voice.

Lilith didn't even flinch. Bip was sweating now.

"Take. Drink. Do this ..." and she drank of the wine. And handed it to Paul and he drank and he handed it to Bip and he drank twice and handed the rest to Lilith. There was still a good bit of wine left and Lilith turned it up and drank it as if she didn't want it, but as if she had to complete the jar before she could go on. She handed back the jar to Bip and he thought that he saw her eyes reel just to the left.

"Lilly, she's coming ..." Bip heard footsteps.

"She'll be coming round the mountain when she comes. She'll be coming round the mountain when she comes." Lilith's sister broke off the song. "Miss Fancher, why does you figure that lady in the song rides six white horses when she comes?"

"I haven't the slightest idea. Why would you be singing in the middle of the night in a hospital?"

Lilith handed the wine jar back to Bip. He put it up.

"I likes singing. It keeps me awake."

"Then, maybe you need to sing all the time."

"I always wanted to make a record but Diana Ross done beat me to it."

Lilith put the child back in the alcohol and vinegar and Bip placed the jar back into the case; he wasn't afraid of it now.

"OK. Let's have a look at Mr. Crenshaw. Is he looking better?"

"Now that he through with that Chemo?"

Paul opened the window and just outside was the tee box of the seventh hole of the country club. Bip had never got to go to the country club and had always wanted to. Paul lifted Bip out and handed him the case, and then, head first, he shoved himself through the window. Bip had no idea how Lilith was going to squeeze herself through the window, but her hands popped through first and then her head and then her waist just snuggled in the window.

Paul and Bip pulled and shortly Lilith popped out of the window like Pooh Bear out of the honey tree and plopped onto the tee box. Paul closed the window just as Mrs. Fancher pushed the door with her heavy weight and unwedged the doorstop on the other side of the door.

"How on earth did that get there?' Lilith's sister was looking at the stick figure swinging above Crenshaw and she began singing. "She'll be ridin' six white horses …"

"This room is a mess. When's the last time Mr. Crenshaw was bathed. For God's sake, he has dirt on his head. Land's sake alive. What am I gonna have to do to find good help around here?"

"Oh, looks at this cute baby doll." Janus tried to cover for Lilith. "I'm gonna go and looks for those mice, Mrs. Fancher."

"OK. I'll be in here with Mr. Crenshaw." She cleaned the room, and, after a bit, she sat in the chair for a second and looked at the swinging figure above Crenshaw. Ken's pants fell off the stick figure onto Crenshaw's forehead.

CHAPTER 24

▼

THE RELEASE OF CORNDOG

No one knew what to do with Corndog.

The philosophical question was obvious: could Flatland "off" Corndog merely because he was wild. What the townspeople did not realize was that Corndog was not going out of his way to anger anyone. He was simply being Corndog. He had an innate quality of honesty. He didn't run in circles and simply snip at humanity's heels for any other reason than that, according to Tabot, "In his insides, Corndog was truly an existential dog." He was not nearly as contrived or concocted as the city might think: he was neither connected to any master nor "doggily" to any other dog. Corndog was "Corndog," a loner searching for his place in the wild. That was his purpose.

Corndog had yearned to live in the wilderness since he was just a puppy, and with every master he had had, he had dug holes under their redwood fences or jumped from his doghouse desperately over the pickets, firmly committed to return his body like a precious Christmas gift to the wild. However, there was an elastic paradox stretching, pulling Corndog to and from his community, "Of Corndog's need to return to the wild," and that, "Of the city's commitment to domesticate or to destroy 'the animal.'" Thus, ever since the jailhouse episode, Corndog had remained in the jail cell. He was very sad and unhappy.

Walter and Paul and Tabot and Watts and Selmer and Clifford and Crenshaw were at the donut shop having morning donuts and coffee. Crenshaw's recovery had been slow but he was in miraculous remission now and his old personality was crawling back out from the fear and detachment of having seen death's face.

"They leave that thing in your chest. They leave it inside your chest." Clifford was gathering as much information as he could for when the barber shop opened back up in two weeks; they were closed down totally now while the finishing touches were being put on the shop.

"Yep, they leave it in like a sprinkler system and hook you up and fill you up with that damn poison." He took a drink of coffee. Clifford almost expected it to squirt out of his chest.

"Like I was saying," Watts tried to get the conversation back to Corndog, "That dog needs to be put to sleep. He's dangerous for one thing, and no one wants him. The people that have tried to keep him in their backyard always end up calling Flora's boy in just a matter of days. He needs to be put to sleep and I'm sick of smelling his mess."

No one responded. The problem was not really a problem to anyone but Watts, really. Watts was the one who had him caged at the jail and had to feed him everyday and listen to his barking and carrying on. Crenshaw, strangely, had a suggestion.

"I'll take him with the Scouts and we'll free him in the wilderness. They can get a badge and I can make sure Corndog gets what he deserves."

"You're gonna 'off' the dog in front of the Scouts," Tabot was taken back by Crenshaw.

"Hell, no." Crenshaw was angry. He had no intention to kill the dog. He wanted to return it to its "natural" habitat. He had been the one on the bed in the hospital. He had been the one who felt his own will slide out of his body every time a drug or medicine or treatment had taken place. He cherished moments now, but he would never tell the others that.

"He deserves to be put out where he can live and have a normal life and die when it's time."

Corndog listened to the muffled voices through the towsack; he was lying on Paul's driveway, on the concrete wrapped in the dark towsack seeing only small pins of light and once in a while a red lip or blue eye of the men that moved. The burlap smelled rough and sandy like potato peelings grated then pressed through coarse hemp. Corndog was looking at Crenshaw's lips when Tabot asked the question.

"Are you sure we shouldn't off him?" Tabot's concern was legal.

"Why the hell would we kill him?"

"He's a danger, Crenshaw."

Crenshaw grabbed the bag by the puckered top and put it into the trunk of the car and slammed the trunk.

Corndog lay still at first in the pitch black trunk with his eyes open; then he closed them to check to see if the darkness was the same.

It was.

He decided to leave his eyes closed and just to pretend that he was blind.

His first pre-immediate death vow was to free himself from the burlap bag. So Corndog lay himself down in a comfortable position, eyes closed, and he began to chew the bag. In his chewing he felt the spare tire, and it was then that Corndog decided that if he were truly the dog he thought himself, he would chew through the tire as well as the burlap.

Committed and determined, he snarled up the side of his lip, and in Elvis fashion he began to chew.

Crenshaw picked up the Scout troop at Flora's; she had agreed that the Scouts be part of the "Corndog Release Program." She felt that the Scouts would learn a valuable lesson from returning a wild animal like Corndog to his natural habitat. The Scouts loaded into the back seat of the car and sat in the skinny lap of Tabot and the soft lap of Walter. Walter held two. Bip sat up front and even tried to help Paul drive, but Paul politely pinched Bip and pushed him over between himself and Crenshaw.

The ride to the dump was really rather short. The dump was just past the sewer that stood in a stinking lake just south of town behind the graveyard. When the southern wind blew, which seldom happened in West Texas, the smell of the city folded back on itself like an unwanted blanket in summer. But now the winds were moving slowly southerly and the smell was the cottonseed oil mill and irrigated water on dry soil.

The city dump also housed the city pound. Corndog had calculated by the turns and the speed of the car that the dump was where he was headed.

Soon out of the bag, Corndog committed himself to the worn tire. He rolled over and used his strong neck to twist and pull at the rubber catching his teeth in the valleys of the rubber treads.

The car slowed as it pulled up to the gatekeeper's shack.

The gatekeeper had lived in the shack that guarded the dump ever since Crenshaw could remember.

"We're at Thanny's house. You boys need to shut up for a second and let me get us by the gatekeeper." Crenshaw hated this part of going to the dump, but his heart was really on letting the dog have a chance out in the country. The gatekeeper would allow dogs that showed marked potential as needing to live to be allowed to stay out at the dump facility rather than being put to sleep; he also made sure that each animal had food and got his shots.

"I think I've seen this guy in town one time is all," Tabot said. "When the high school choir did that revisionist, all-bodysuit-Oklahoma-deconstructionalist show." Tabot had been to New York once and considered himself quite the authority on theater terms.

"They looked like a bunch of fags up there being farmers and cowmen. Looked more like fairies and elves," Crenshaw added. Then, he started off on poor rendition of 'O the fairies and elves should be friends. One fairy likes to hold his wand: the elves all think that they're James Bond.' "How could someone do that to 'Oklahoma'?"

The gatekeeper's position at the dump was to keep anything unfit from entering the pit, and once allowed in, he was to keep it from ever exiting.

Paul stopped the car by the hand painted "HALT" sign.

"Do you honk? Or do you just sit here?"

Paul sat still and seemed to know what to do. He had brought a mattress out recently.

Paul thought he just touched the horn, but it went on and on until Crenshaw reached over and pulled Paul's hand off the horn.

"Soooooorreey," Paul slurred.

Bip looked up and was almost frightened to see the gatekeeper's shack. It sagged under the weight of the sky. The heavy shingles curled to the center of the roof and sat there in repose, gathered like flat stones in the center of a mountain stream. The rest of the house billowed out as if a reckless giant had stepped on a marshmallow and graham cracker house, forcing the center down and the sweet white mallow from the crust.

The sun was starting to set.

The TV antenna twisted into the air like the legs of a fly on its back crawling against the sky. The glass in the window frames was painted red and they glowed. Small glitches of light shone like laser beams where holes had been scratched in the paint to see out. Bip saw the large head of the midget floating around in the house in dyed red silhouette. It peeked out and stopped, and Thanny's voice rose and seemed to be coming from the inside of a large tin can.

"We're clothed!" Thanny lisped in a yelling voice from the inside of the house.

"Well, you better be decent. I have children with me," Crenshaw pulled uncomfortably at his pants.

"We're not open. We're clothed."

"Lord, I forgot how that man talks. It gives me the Willie's."

Willie, one of the Scouts in the back seat laughed because Crenshaw had used his name like that. Crenshaw reached under the seat and grabbed a box of chocolate covered cherries he had brought. Word had it that Thanny would bargain for candy.

"Ith that your car, Paul?" The hunchback's tone changed; he wasn't sure he was talking to a safe party. At one time when Bruce lived with the hunchback, they had cut their hair after hours with Paul. They liked blocked cuts so they would look the same.

Thanny moved ever so slightly in the window, cocking his head. Bip saw a glimpse of a shirt and figured Thanny was dressing. Thank God, Bip thought. He pictured the hunchback coming out of the house naked and it scared him.

The door opened. He decided to make a dramatic entrance by slamming the door open to stand in the white light like a tiny but important god. He jutted out his jowls, firm in a silhouetted profile, his hunch sitting like a special little mountain on his shoulder. He knew his duty was to own as much of the moment as he could.

"It's a midget!" one of the Scouts screamed.

The small man stopped and raised his head from his feet, which wasn't very far, and looked to the car. He had been eating and still had a large piece of carrot on his chin. He fumbled in his pocket until he pulled a pocketknife from his pants and broke the blade out.

Deep inside the dark trunk, Corndog chewed heavily on the tire, switching sides, turning his head and using different teeth each time; his wiry fur stood on end and seemed to work as a plane of non-friction support that allowed him to slide and turn as if on ice.

Thanny lifted the knife to his mouth to dislodge some meat from between his two front teeth. After the piece of meat was on the knife blade, he wiped the blade on his pants. He had obviously made the pants himself from cotton flour sacks. Thanny was heavy, so as he started to move again toward the car the Scouts saw his thighs move like Goo clutched to his bone under the thin cloth.

"Prentice says he's gay," Tabot said.

"Well, better luck to him," Walter said.

"Well, we're not here to have sex with him. I just want to tell him about the dog."

Thanny neared the car, much to the wide-eyed chagrin of the Scouts.

Seeing Paul reminded Thanny of Bruce. His mind raced forward as if he were looking at a jigsaw puzzle that was feverishly building itself. He remembered Bruce'th, 'his loverth', decision to pursue a career in refrigeration repair. Thanny paid for all of the classes at the local community college. That's where Bruce fell in love with his instructor, Thanny said, and left the hunchback for Richard, only to be dumped by Richard, the instructor, who returned to his wife, whom Bruce had never seen until he had seen Richard in the grocery store kiss her right on the mouth. He briefly made remembrance of the "Theet Potato" incident that had haunted his and Bruce's separation, but he quickly shoved those thoughts out; they were too freshly open and tender to the touch to think about.

Thanny's head just cleared the opening of the window and looked like a head of cabbage floating in the frame.

"How might I help you gentleman." His head rose into the frame of the window and rubbed his flat nose.

"We have a dog for the pound."

He lifted his two hands and almost pulled himself up to look in the car.

"I don't believe I thee a dog."

"He's in the trunk," Crenshaw spoke across Paul.

"Ith he to be terminated?"

Crenshaw didn't feel like carrying on. He held up the box of candy.

"No. We want you to accept him. He is wild, very wild"

"Well, I don't know about a wild dog ...," Thanny stopped for a second. Corndog quit chewing on the tire and rested and Crenshaw rolled his eyes. The midget was being too dramatic. The little man didn't get to practice his authority very often. Crenshaw sighed to add tension to the moment and Walter shifted in his seat, so that the little man would feel as if he had pressed the men enough to hold the upper hand.

"Listen, Sugar Britches, you want this or not."

"Mr. Crenshaw," suddenly Thanny was almost cryptic. "You can take anything in, but nothing cometh out." His face was dead sober as he opened the box and popped a cherry into his mouth. "You hear me?"

Angered, Crenshaw, reached over and pulled the gearshift into gear and the car started to move forward. Paul reacted by taking the wheel and assumed the driving position.

Thanny yelled after the car, "If that dog'th really crathy, he ought to be put to thleep."

"Do you really think he's gay," Walter asked as he looked back in the road at the little man who now was holding his head dramatically in his hands as if he were betrayed.

"If you mean happy, I don't see any reason he should be; he's fat and ugly and he's a midget," Crenshaw answered even though he wasn't sure to whom the question was directed.

"And he's rude," Tabot offered.

"He had a nice smile," one of the Scouts in the back seat offered. None of the men said a word. Tabot even rolled his eyes.

The car was tense. No one really knew what to say or how to react as Paul slowed to a stop in front of the big stacks of garbage.

The Scouts unloaded, some plopping down on a mattress just in front of the car, and then Bip settled on a red velvet couch that was missing the two back legs. When he leaned back the couch tumbled over backward, puffing dust from under in a small cloud that finally settled in a little dust storm by Crenshaw's feet.

"Get off that mattress. You don't know what's happened on that thing."

"It's allllrieeeght," Paul slurred. "It's miiine." He looked at it with almost tearful eyes. Then, he winked at Walter. "That was a good beeeed."

"Everyone, the moment has arrived!"

When Crensaw put the key in the trunk, everyone became silent. Even the wind seemed to settle for a moment. And the sun seemed to tread water for a moment before it drowned into dusk.

"He's gonna want out of there," Tabot said.

Tabot had scooted just behind Crenshaw. "Scoot your ass back and quit scaring me," Crenshaw said and turned close enough to kiss Tabot. "I know that!" Crenshaw looked right at Tabot as if to say 'you think I'm some kinda goddern idiot?'

"Everyone gather 'round the trunk. And when I pop the trunk, we'll grab the sack, commence to throwin' it to the ground, thus so." Crenshaw always adopted a strange-explanation-vocabulary whenever he wanted things to go just so. "And I'll get the gun just in case." Crenshaw knew the dog was dangerous.

"Why don't you get the gun *now,* just in case something's wrong?" Carl, one of the Scouts asked.

Crenshaw mumbled, "It's in the trunk with Corndog."

"Great! That's just great, Crenshaw. That dog's so evil, he's probably figured out how to shoot us and when we open the trunk he'll hold us for ransom at the fag midget's sex shack."

"Get around and shut up. He's just one dadburned dog!"

Crenshaw was beginning to be a bit put out with the sissy attitude of his party. Everyone stiffened up and gathered around the back of the trunk and Crenshaw inserted the key.

Just as the key popped the trunk to repose.

Just as the setting sun flooded red into the darkness of the trunk.

Just as they realized Corndog was not still in his sack.

Corndog chewed the trigger of the shotgun which shot the tire and through the back seat of Paul's car. The explosion sent every one but Paul down to his knees. They were convinced that Corndog had learned the secret of the shotgun and was now going to murder them all. They all were trying to figure out if the dog could possibly reload the gun. Paul, now sensing some kind of danger, fell to the ground.

Corndog shook his head a few times, opening and closing his mouth trying to get his hearing back. His eyes adjusted quickly to the light. He jumped from the car trunk to freedom, biting Crenshaw's ankle as he passed.

He ran directly to the largest heap of trash and climbed directly up and sat proudly on top beating his large tail against the trash of the city.

Crenshaw bumped his head on the bumper hard enough to knock himself down and restanding found the shotgun just as Tabot took it away from him and without aiming pumped all four shells into the air roughly in the direction of Corndog. But Corndog stood rigidly, his chin proudly in the air, his paws a bit pointed out and at attention. He almost cowered a little on the third shot when Tabot demolished a creamed corn can just below Corndog. The corn still in the can splatted towards the orange-black sky. One blotch landed dangerously close to Corndog's mouth, and in defiance, he lopped out his long tongue and took the corn into his mouth like a prize.

Just as Tabot reached for more shells, the trash heap started to move and it seemed to be crumbling underneath Corndog, growing smaller. Crenshaw was trying to wrestle the gun away from Tabot.

A nutria is a rat that lives near water and is about the size of a small dog. The nutrias had infested the sewer water ever since Branson, the ex-mayor's son's son, had visited Baton Rouge in the thirties, and at the advice of a salesman with a beard, he had brought back a pair to breed to raise for their pelts. They escaped almost immediately, chewing through his wire fence, and had ruled rampantly in the dump ever since. They had even been considered for the town mascot—the Flatland Nutrias—during the great prairie dog debate.

Corndog was not sure why they protected him. Maybe they thought he was one of them. Moonpie Boogie Dew even came up and sat beside Corndog. Maybe this was just the way of the wild. But within seconds the herd of nutria had the Men and boys in the car head first, butt first, stuffed like olives in a jar, and the car was started and the dust rose from tires.

In the fading dust of the tires, the nutria turned and walked back to the garbage mountain and stuffed their bodies back under the refuse and firmed Corndog's perch.

Corndog smiled. He already liked the rules of the wild, so he let out a long, happy but sort of mellow "Ahhhhoooooooooow," with his lip curled in the best Elvis snarl he could make.

CHAPTER 25

▼

THE WAITING ROOM

Imagine winter coming, dropping like an uninvited guffaw on your summer doorstep, snow and ice and unpleasantness. Or imagine the once strong arms of the oak sagging under the insatiable hunger of the mistletoe.

Cancer twists through the body like a rancor through the mighty shark. It leaves the carcass numb, dumb, and surprised. It crowds the organs, pushes the intestines; it is a flower that grows and blossoms and reproduces; it is nature at its best, reproducing with unmatched speed. In those enlarged photos it looks like a horrible insect with creepy legs, and its Achilles' heel, ironically, is that it is designed to kill the very host that feeds it.

Breathe. Feel the air go in and out with ease, the warmth in your throat. Move. Imagine what must happen in your brain and muscles and nerves to twitch and the tendons that must start up and flex and read their maps and construct their moments.

Crenshaw's cancer had not only returned, it had catapulted and landed squarely in the pit of his stomach. He even swore that his belly button was some absurd focal point for the disease.

He couldn't digest any more. He waited for the double dose of morphine, Crenshaw tried to talk to Bip and Mary and Dawn who were in the room with him.

"Pawpaw, can we get you anything?" Dawn was trying to help.

Crenshaw was just on the verge of becoming unconscious and probably would not come around again.

"This is horrible," he muttered. The look in his eyes was distant now. In spite of the family being there in the room with him, he was alone. He was alone with the inevitable. He knew he was going to die. He knew it was coming. His last breath. His last smack of his lips. His last wiggle of his fingers. His last.

"Can't the medicine ... let me click this." Bip messed with the morphine dispenser.

"I wish you could break into that sonofabitch. Why can't they give me more. What's it gonna do kill me!" he yelled. "Oh God!" The pain grew unbearable again. He started coughing. His lungs sounded wet and shallow.

Mary pulled Bip back. Censhaw had been fairly stable for two days and now all his organs were shutting down and his skin was yellowing and his life was being buried under the medicine and pain along with his personality. Now he went in and out of a comatose state. He cringed at the pain even when he was completely knocked out. His body pulled and tugged at the disease, trying to wrench it out.

Bip wiggled away from Mary's arms back to Crenshaw. His touch opened Crenshaw's eyes.

Bip said, "I love you, Pawpaw."

Crenshaw's eyes looked into Bip's soul. The look was desperate and brief and a lifetime. "I love you, too." Crenshaw's hand squeezed Bip's.

The machine clicked and the next dose was given.

"Thank Jesus." His eyes melted and closed and the pain was eased for a second.

"Dawn why don't you go to the Burger Barn and get us some cheeseburgers."

Mary and Bip and Dawn hadn't eaten in almost a day. She gave Dawn a twenty-dollar bill.

"What do you want, Mama."

"Diet Coke and a Burger Barn with bacon and cheese."

"Bip?" Dawn was writing things down like a secretary.

"Jr. Burger Barn ... No, a superdog. And get a lot of mustard. And a Big Red."

"Fries?"

They both wanted fries and both had forgotten to tell her.

"Bip, do you want to go with me?"

"Why don't you go with her, Bip?"

"No." He turned on the TV and turned the volume down to almost nothing. The Cowboys were playing Philadelphia.

Outside the door sat most of Crenshaw's friends, even his brother and older sister were there. They looked like him and Bip and Dawn had never met any of them until now. They saw mannerisms and strange resemblance's in their faces or in their walk or the way they said "Chinese checkers" and things like that. His sister looked like Crenshaw with a wig on.

Dawn came out of the door. Everyone looked to her for a report.

He's sleeping and I'm going to the Burger Barn. Several others gave her money and placed orders. Dawn didn't mind. She figured she'd make about forty or fifty bucks just going for burgers. Her cousin decided to go with her and they drove his pickup. Lilith was just entering the hospital when Dawn was leaving the parking lot. She was coming to see how Crenshaw was doing and to eat lunch with her sister, Janus.

"Mama, look who's on."

Mary looked at the screen and Bob Hayes was holding his knee.

"Hallelujah, thank God for the Cowboys even though they can't play worth a shit." Mary and Bip loved the Cowboys. They loved yelling for them and yelling at them when they played badly.

Mary sat down and took her shoes off. Bip relaxed some.

"Turn it up just a little." The sound let them drift away from the cold hospital for a minute and slide into the warm armchairs of the living room and ice in glasses and popcorn and sometimes nachos. Bip was even trying to learn to eat Jalapeno peppers some.

Bip looked to see if Crenshaw was out again. He was. Bip figured he had about ten minutes before Crenshaw would start to writhe for more pain medicine. Bip sat Indian sit in the chair.

Philly marched the ball down the field and got to the nine yard line and Dallas stopped them over and over and over and they kicked a field goal and the commercial came on and GI Joe was driving a car and went to pick up Barbie at the dream house and she escaped the Barbie Dream house and slid down and Ken didn't see her until she and GI Joe were driving off almost hitting the dog. Then, Eddie the Mattress King, yelled for thirty seconds, then made his arm go around and around out of socket while he pounded mattresses while prices fell and fell to rock bottom.

Outside the window Bip saw Olin Martin squash his beer can and burp and tee up his ball and he "knocked the shit" out of it. The cart ran over the already squashed can and flattened it even more.

Crenshaw quit breathing.

Mary noticed first. She waited.

The game was just back on and Bip looked over at Mary. Her eyes were so full of tears. She was motionless. Bip looked at Crenshaw. He body was still, nothing moved. His mouth was gapped open.

"Mama? He's not ..." Bip got up and was just about to run to the hall to call the nurse when Mary grabbed him as hard as she had ever grabbed him and held him tightly. He squirmed and tried to get away. He started to scream for the nurse and she put her hand over his mouth and held him rigid. She said the Lord's Prayer because she knew it lasted almost thirty seconds. "Our father who art in heaven, hallowed be thy name. Thy kingdom come, thy will be done on earth as it is in heaven. Give us this day our daily bread and forgive us our trespasses as we forgive those who trespass against us. Lead us not into temptation, but deliver us from evil. In the name of the Father, the Son, and the Holy Ghost." She held her breath ten seconds. "Amen." She wasn't sure if she did it all right and even wondered if she might have mixed in some of the Apostle's Creed. But she didn't care. She just wanted it to be over for Crenshaw.

She wanted no chance of Crenshaw being revived by a nurse or doctor. He had suffered enough, and as difficult as it was, she wanted her father to have peace now from all that suffering.

Her grip loosened on Bip who was in a frenzy. Bip hit the morphine machine and punched the button and yelled for Mrs. Fancher, and doors started opening and covers flew back. Mary grabbed Mrs. Fancher's hand hard.

"He's dead. He hasn't breathed in two minutes."

"How do you know?"

"Because I Goddamn timed it." Nothing more was said between the two.

Bip looked at Mary. Betrayal and confusion and emptiness riddled his fear. Mary looked back at him with unconditional love and open arms.

Bip refused her arms and ran from the room and relatives and friends and even Paul couldn't hold him long enough to get a both hands on him and he slipped through everyone's hands until he saw Lilith standing just in front of him. No one said a word.

Bip looked at Lilith. "You ain't no worth a shit witch!" he yelled.

He wanted to bury his head in her belly and cry until night cloaked everything; instead he spit on her left shoe and ran out the back door of the hospital.

CHAPTER 26

▼

GRAND OPENING

GRAND OPENING was written in big words on the hard, polished window of the ULTRA MODERN BARBERSHOP. Selmer and Clifford and Paul had all agreed to rename the shop to try to update things. The three chairs were the same, recovered in leather, but everything else was new. The porcelain sinks were squeaky white. They had new stops on the bottoms of their chairs. The floor was white tile and was laid very square and correct and level. The walls were white and the waiting chairs were vinyl and comfortable. The shades over the window were lined up and the air conditioner was refrigerated and almost too cold for some of the customers who were used to only evaporative cooling.

No one talked too readily. Everyone liked the new shop and they were glad to have a permanent place to go again, but Crenshaw's death had silenced their voices. He would be missed.

"I thought the reverend Lee did just a marvelous job with the service, just marvelous." Selmer finally said something. He was cutting Watt's hair.

"I meant to get my hair cut before the funeral," Watts said.

"Now, you know we worked as hard as we could to get open ..."

Watts cut over him. "You know what I meant."

Paul was cutting Tabot.

"Who was that did the Eulogy?" Tabot Asked.

Walter piped up.

"That was his brother from Wisconsin."

"Well, he didn't know shit about Crenshaw is all I can say. I don't even think that they had seen each other since they were little boys. I hadn't even heard Crenshaw talk about him." Tabot was airing a gripe that all the men had shared. Of all the people chosen to tell about the highs and low of a man's life, a brother whose last memory was of Crenshaw dropping him on his head out of a pickup window in the Piggly Wiggly parking lot was not the logical choice. But, he was chosen by the family. In fact, Mary had been disappointed that she and Dawn and Bip had all been pushed aside by the bickering of these brothers and sisters that came out of the woodwork for the funeral, and who then disappeared like fallen leaves in a windstorm two hours after the service. One sister had even sung at the funeral. A cat slammed in a car door under the scream of a blaring car horn would have sounded better, Tabot had observed.

The door opened. Walter was trying to get in the door with a large box. It was very awkward.

"Don't worry about the air getting out. We got refrigerated now. Doesn't take that long to cool back down." Selmer snapped his fingers on 'that long' and the scissors flew out of his hands into Watt's lap.

"Goddern! Be careful, Selmer"

"Well, it's here." Walter put down the box and went and got another small box and came back in.

"Well, get in the middle so's everyone can see."

"What is this?" Tabot was interested. Everyone stopped cutting hair. Paul was smiling. It had been his idea for the shop. He thought it would finish everything off nicely.

"Dad-a-dad-a." Walter sang a fanfare with Dad a Dad. "Is everybody look-ing?"

"Everybody's ready," Tabot looked around and confirmed.

Walter got out a pocketknife and cut carefully along the box top and flipped back the lid and lifted out a chair that had been varnished and recovered and the screws had been replaced with golden screws. He placed the chair in the corner and went back to the little box and opened it and took out the brass plate.

He read the plate aloud as he placed the plate over the chair where the plate would eventually hang.

"In memory of Horace Crenshaw who's always next in line."

He polished the seat off with his sleeve of his shirt.

"That's nice. That's just really nice." Tabot was honestly moved. "Who thought of that?"

Selmer pointed his scissors at Paul.

"That's nice, Paul. Really nice."

Paul smiled and pretended to whistle.

Lilith opened the door to her porch and the door started to close before she could grab the corn she was going to shuck and the extra sack, so she had to start and stop several times before she got everything the way she wanted it. Finally, she sat down on the porch in her rocker and opened the sack in front of her and peeled back the green shucks like cellophane. She saved the shucks for later when she made tamales; she wrapped the masa and meat in the shucks and steamed them. She had learned the recipe from Rosa Gonzales the Mexican bootlegger. They sometimes exchanged recipes in jail after raids.

Lilith had been shucking corn for a while and had about three sacks full and the worms cut out and all the shucks she wanted to keep before she noticed a feeling of something in the road.

Bip was standing in the hot sand in front of her house. His hands were behind his back.

She stopped rocking.

Bip looked bigger now, standing alone on the dirt road. His glasses were clean; his forehead was shiny; his eyes were crystal clear brown. He looked straight into Lilith's eyes.

Lilith started to rock and shucked a corn.

"Go on and get outa here. Go on. 'Go on,' I said." She continued to look at him.

Bip wiped his nose but stood rigid.

"Go on!" She spoke louder.

He spoke loudly from the road.

"I got some Popsicles. Some red."

"I eats little boys, you know?" She rocked and shucked still not looking away.

"I know."

"But I don't eats mens."

Bip didn't say a word. He just kept staring at her.

"Those Popsicles gonna melt out there under the sky." The wooden floor beneath her chair creaked and moaned.

"I'm sorry I spit on you."

"That's OK. Lilly needed a bath anyway and lord knows them shoes is done outa style. You just helping Lilly stay current in fashion." She was still wearing the shoes. "Come on ups here and gives me a Popsicle."

Bip took his first step to the porch when Mary drove up and stopped the car. She put her head on the steering wheel. Bip stopped. Lilith stopped rocking. Mary was exhausted.

She got out of the car and looked at Bip. He could be strong and big with Lilith, but when he saw his mother he melted back into a little boy.

She said very slowly and with concern and love, "I've been looking everywhere for you, honey. Everywhere."

Ever since Crenshaw's funeral, Bip had hidden or been aloof or had not spoken when spoken to. He hadn't done much of anything.

"Are you OK?" Mary needed Bip to respond. "Do you want to go home?"

He shook his head 'no.' "Not yet."

In just a matter of minutes, Bip and Mary were on the porch with Lilith and Lilith brought iced tea out for Bip. Lilith gave Mary a strong rum and coke with picked ice in a tall crystal glass. At first Mary pushed it away, but then she looked at her boy and the sun and the corn and took the glass and grabbed a piece of corn to shuck.

"On Friday, if you comes back to Lilly, we'll make us some tamales. Takes all day."

Across town Dawn scooted closer to Billie in the station wagon as it climbed Rabbit Hill. They were going into Grandville for supper and a movie. Billie had saved an extra twenty from his paycheck and Dawn had some leftover money from going to get the milk at the store. The dirt rose after the tires passed over and swirled and settled back down as if each grain had a particular position on earth. Billie turned onto the paved road and the hum of the station wagon disappeared into the stillness of the day.

978-0-595-47612-1
0-595-47612-0

p 45 - he face
p 56 he had see
p 59 I didn't NOW
p 108 I asking
p 120 wasn't Bip a product of
the second marriage, afte
mary & dan divorced?
p 163 only mention of SPC

Printed in the United States
207015BV00001B/277/P